NAT STARED AT THE GUN. "I HATE TO SPOUT CLICHÉS, BUT YOU COULD HURT SOMEONE WITH THAT."

"Yes, I could," Freddie agreed.

Her blue eyes blazed with determination. Nat thought she would be even prettier if her chin weren't quite so stubborn. "Listen, I just played Good Samaritan. Rescued you, treated your wounds—even fed you. Threatening me with my own gun isn't a very nice thank you."

"Mr. Steele, you're no kindhearted hillbilly who lives in these mountains. I know what's growing in this field, but I don't care. I just want my glider to stay right where it is so a rescue party can see it from the air and get me out of here."

Nat wondered why, when everything was going so smoothly, this beautiful, dangerous woman had to crash-land her glider in this particular field and threaten everything.

CANDLELIGHT SUPREMES

133 SUSPICION AND DESIRE, *JoAnna Brandon*
134 UNDER THE SIGN OF SCORPIO, *Pat West*
135 SURRENDER TO A STRANGER, *Dallas Hamlin*
136 TENDER BETRAYER, *Terri Herrington*
137 THE FIRE IN HER EYES, *Sabrina Ryan*
138 SPLENDOR AT DAWN, *Linda Randall Wisdom*
139 FOOTPRINTS IN THE SAND, *Erin Dana*
140 RECKLESS ABANDON, *Megan Lane*
141 WINDS OF A SECRET DESIRE, *Deborah Sherwood*
142 MYSTERY IN THE MOONLIGHT, *Lynn Patrick*
143 ENDLESS OBSESSION, *Hayton Monteith*
144 MY DARLING PRETENDER, *Linda Vail*
145 UNDERCOVER AFFAIR, *Sydney Ann Clary*
146 THE WANDERER'S PROMISE, *Paula Hamilton*
147 LAYING DOWN THE LAW, *Donna Kimel Vitek*
148 ROMAN FANTASY, *Betty Henrichs*

QUANTITY SALES

Most Dell Books are available at special quantity discounts when purchased in bulk by corporations, organizations, and special-interest groups. Custom imprinting or excerpting can also be done to fit special needs. For details write: Dell Publishing Co., Inc., 1 Dag Hammarskjold Plaza, New York, NY 10017, Attn.: Special Sales Dept., or phone: (212) 605-3319.

INDIVIDUAL SALES

Are there any Dell Books you want but cannot find in your local stores? If so, you can order them directly from us. You can get any Dell book in print. Simply include the book's title, author, and ISBN number, if you have it, along with a check or money order (no cash can be accepted) for the full retail price plus 75¢ per copy to cover shipping and handling. Mail to: Dell Readers Service, Dept. FM, P.O. Box 1000, Pine Brook, NJ 07058.

IN THE HEAT OF THE SUN

Anne Silverlock

A CANDLELIGHT SUPREME

Published by
Dell Publishing Co., Inc.
1 Dag Hammarskjold Plaza
New York, New York 10017

Copyright © 1986 by Louise Titchener

All rights reserved. No part of this book may be reproduced or transmitted in any form or by any means, electronic or mechanical, including photocopying, recording, or by any information storage and retrieval system, without the written permission of the Publisher, except where permitted by law.

Dell ® TM 681510, Dell Publishing Co., Inc.

Candlelight Supreme is a trademark
of Dell Publishing Co., Inc.

Candlelight Ecstasy Romance®, 1,203,540, is a registered trademark of Dell Publishing Co., Inc., New York, New York.

ISBN: 0-440-14134-6

Printed in the United States of America

December 1986

10 9 8 7 6 5 4 3 2 1

WFH

To Our Readers:

We are pleased and excited by your overwhelmingly positive response to our Candlelight Supremes. Unlike all the other series, the Supremes are filled with more passion, adventure, and intrigue, and are obviously the stories you like best.

In months to come we will continue to publish books by many of your favorite authors as well as the very finest work from new authors of romantic fiction. As always, we are striving to present unique, absorbing love stories —the very best love has to offer.

Breathtaking and unforgettable, Supremes follow in the great romantic tradition you've come to expect *only* from Candlelight Romances.

Your suggestions and comments are always welcome. Please let us hear from you.

Sincerely,

The Editors
Candlelight Romances
1 Dag Hammarskjold Plaza
New York, New York 10017

CHAPTER ONE

"What you doin' down here, Freddie?"

Hank watched as Frederica Davenport strapped herself into a five-point harness. Her slim, neat body reclined in the cockpit of her brother Bert's Schweizer 1–26, a medium-performance sailplane.

As Freddie jammed the last snap into place, she grinned up at the older man, her small white teeth flashing. "Oh, I needed a rest, so I took time off from the radio station and told Bert I'd house-sit for him while he and Gracie went on vacation."

"Well, that's something new." Hank scratched his grizzled chin. "Since when did a bundle of energy like you ever need a rest? And it looks to me like it's Bert's plane you're sitting in, not his house."

Freddie winked. "What he doesn't know won't hurt him."

They were both well aware that Bert wouldn't mind if his kid sister used the Schweizer. The Davenports were a flying family, and sailplanes were their passion. Freddie had soloed in her first glider at the age of fourteen. Now, at twenty-six, she was an accomplished pilot who'd successfully completed a dozen cross-country trips.

"I'm all set for my tug," she pointed out.

"You are, huh? You never was the patient type. Always in a hurry." Affectionately, Hank ruffled her short brown curls and then started to lower the clear shield to seal her into the Schweizer's bubblelike cockpit. "Where you goin' today, if I might be so bold as to ask?" he said just before closing the shield tight.

"I don't know," Freddie responded with a cheeky grin. "But don't look for me anytime soon." She glanced around meaningfully. It was a perfect September day in Georgia; fluffy cumulus clouds dotted the blue sky like cotton balls. "In weather like this I could stay up there forever, and that's exactly what I feel like doing."

Hank merely chuckled. "Just don't fly too close to the sun and get your pretty little self all melted, that's all." Stepping back, he signaled to the teen-age boy who was holding one of the sailplane's wings steady and then ambled to the towplane.

When the towrope was secure, he got inside and revved his workhorse engine. A few minutes later, attached to the tug by a two-hundred-foot length of braided polypropylene cord, the Schweizer rocketed along the ground at bone-jarring speed.

Inside, Freddie watched the rough terrain whiz past and hoped her craft would be airborne in time to avoid the bump just ahead on the grassy runway. Hank Pritchard's gliderport amounted to ten acres of untended field and a few makeshift buildings. He was chronically casual about everything—including FAA rules—but even he would admit that the runway was less than perfect.

Firmly tethered to his tow plane, the Schweizer lifted in time, and Freddie heaved a sigh of relief when Hank began to circle the field, dragging her behind him. Higher and higher they ascended until the altimeter read two thousand feet. Then he flashed his lights, and she pulled the yellow knob that released the tow rope. When the umbilical cord snapped loose, Hank sheared off to the left and she to the right.

For several minutes she just floated, enjoying the space and silence. Then she started looking around for a thermal, one that would carry her even further from the bonds of earth.

Free, she thought as she found an updraft that lifted her toward the morning sun. Free! And oh, how she needed to be free. Freddie hadn't been kidding when she'd told Hank that she needed a rest. Lately the pressures of her job—she was continuity director at a prominent Nashville, Tennessee, radio station—had been getting to her.

It seemed as if she were constantly under strain, running around making sure there was no dead air space, lining up commercial messages, coddling the whims and idiosyncrasies of the various deejays. But it wasn't just her job that was making her tense. Ever since her breakup with Carter, Freddie had been in a rut. It was time for her to put her life back on course.

Well, that was what she'd come back home to do. She needed to be alone so she could relax and think. But for Freddie the ultimate release from tension wasn't going to be watching television in her brother's big empty house or lying around next to his sinfully luxurious pool. It was going to be escaping the bonds of earth altogether and flying as the hawk and eagle flew. During her vacation week, she intended to spend as much time as possible soaring.

As the sun climbed higher in the sky and she with it, Freddie discovered that the weather was even more perfect than she had thought. Thermals rose from the earth's heated surface like coils on an innerspring mattress. She was lifted by one, and using the clouds as markers, she flew to the next and then the next. Inside her womblike cockpit, there was little sound. Aside from the soothing swish of air over the wings, total meditative silence prevailed. The effect was refreshing, and as her first hour aloft passed, she could feel herself unwinding. Far below, the cares of her day-to-day world began to seem unimportant, and gradually they slipped from her consciousness altogether.

On a day like this, she could go anywhere and do anything, she thought. She was truly as free as a bird. Gazing around, she saw the line of the Blue Ridge Mountains in the distance. A smile tugged at the corners of her mouth, and her big, long-lashed eyes lit with a daring thought. She could go slope-soaring.

The mountains were a long way from the gliderport, and no one knew where she was headed, but the perfect weather and her euphoric sense of release made anything seem possible. So what if she had only the wind and her own skill to keep her aloft?

Two hours later, Freddie was riding the currents along a high ridge, floating like a bit of thistledown in the wind. When the air was deflected against the side of a mountain, it rose upward for thousands of feet. Lured by these ideal conditions, she was deep in the mountains, beyond any place she'd ever flown before in this area.

If she got onto the downwind side of these slopes,

she'd be in trouble. But Freddie had no intention of doing anything so foolhardy. As long as she stayed on the upwind part of the slope, her plane could glide for hours on the narrow band of rising air. She only had to remind herself to check the altimeter from time to time to make sure she didn't go so high that she ran out of oxygen. Usually that happened at around twenty thousand feet, but glider pilots had been known to lose consciousness at fifteen thousand. Right now she was at fourteen thousand. She should probably start down, she thought. But somehow Freddie couldn't bring herself to do it—not quite yet.

Forgetting the altimeter, she watched as a hawk far below her soared effortlessly, its wings outspread. He was doing the same thing she was, working the mountain, using waves of wind to float into the sun's eye. Her own eyes misted as she was overcome by a strong feeling of kinship with the beautiful creature.

"Hello, my friend," she whispered softly. "Isn't it wonderful?" She looked up toward the sun, which seemed to be getting closer and closer, and blinked, then blinked again. Slowly, her eyelids slid closed.

A number of minutes later they popped open, and Freddie gazed around fuzzily. Instinct warned her that something was terribly wrong, but for several seconds she was too disoriented to take her situation in. Then her eyes flew wide open in horror as she realized what had happened. She was no longer on the upwind side of the ridge. Somehow, her craft had gone over the top, and it was now caught in the downflow. There was no time to wonder how it had happened. Freddie's pilot survival training took over as she concentrated on making the best of the dangerous situation.

Was there any possibility of pulling up into the wind again? But no, she was too far into the downflow for that. Sometimes, when the wind was strong enough over the top of a ridge, it created a wave effect that one could ride. But that wasn't the case today. Once she fell into the bottom of this trough, she wouldn't be carried up again. Her plane was sinking at the rate of two hundred feet a minute, and there was no way to make it climb. That meant she was going to have to find a spot to land.

But where? As she floated downward, all she could see in the wild mountain valley below were trees and a steep gorge through which a narrow strand of water flowed. She knew someone who'd landed in a river once and floated downstream for miles. But the rock-strewn thread of water below wouldn't accommodate such a joyride. Of course, if worse came to worst, she could land in the tops of the trees. She might survive; but would the Schweizer? The thought of tearing Bert's beloved sailplane to pieces horrified her.

Her eyes strained as she scanned the forbidding terrain that was now getting ominously close. Then her brows lifted slightly as she picked out what looked like a break in the foliage. It seemed to be an irregularly shaped field. Although some type of green shrubbery grew there, it wasn't as tall as the surrounding trees. Freddie pushed her stick to the right. Obediently, the sailplane banked sharply. Then, righting her sleek craft, she headed for the field.

It was an unpleasant landing. The limited size of the cleared area didn't allow for anything more than an abrupt touchdown. And the bushes growing in it were tall and sturdy. They made horrible scratching and grinding noises against the Schweizer's Fiberglas body.

When the sailplane finally came to a shuddering halt at the far end of the field, Freddie sat motionless for several minutes trying to compose herself. Her harness had kept her from rattling around too badly inside the cockpit, but she was still shaken up. The palms of her hands, still clenched on the stick, were sickeningly damp. Her stomach was doing a tarantella, and there was a horrible tightness in her chest.

What happened? she wondered. How had she suddenly found her plane on the downwind side of the mountain? She swallowed and faced the fact that it was her own fault. She'd been riding too high, and she must have blanked out for several minutes from the thin air. That was the only explanation.

Shaking her head to clear it, she unclamped her rigid fingers from the stick and looked down at her harness. Since sailplanes had no engines, when they crash-landed there was no danger of an explosion. On the other hand, without a tug there was no way of getting back up into the wind. The sun, shining down full force, was making the inside of the small compartment uncomfortably hot. Her hands fumbled with her harness straps.

When she was free, she undid the latch on the cockpit shield and pushed the bubblelike structure up. The rush of fresh air that fanned her cheek and lifted some of her damp curls from her forehead was a big relief.

When it wasn't supported by wind, the Schweizer was as unstable as a canoe. Now its nose was propped up by a partially uprooted bush, and its broad wings were resting on other bushes. Climbing out was a shaky operation, but at last Freddie managed to jump down to the ground.

When she landed, her legs felt rubbery, and she came close to collapsing. But she drew a breath to steady herself. Then she made her way around the Schweizer to take stock of the damage. Its smooth coat was badly scratched and abraded, but much to her relief, it did not seem to have suffered much damage structurally. Sailplanes were sturdily built.

Drawing another deep breath, she raked both her hands through her short curls and looked around. It was time to consider how she was going to deal with this situation. She guessed she was somewhere deep in the Blue Ridge Mountains, very possibly in one of the national forests. When she was young, she and her family had gone camping in the Chattahoochee National Forest several times. It was a gorgeous place, abounding in waterfalls and fantastic natural scenery like that gorge she'd flown over.

But if this was government land, what in the world was a field of bushes doing in the middle of it? Turning away from the Schweizer, she walked down a row of the tall shrubs, staring at them curiously. Maybe the field was some sort of government-sponsored agricultural experiment. Freddie paused to peer at one of the extremely healthy-looking specimens. They weren't anything she recognized—not that she knew much about horticulture. She was certain, however, that they weren't tomatoes or any of the other plants that her mother had grown in the family garden.

Curiously, she reached out and broke off a long thin leaf. After running her finger along its serrated edge, she lifted it to her nose and sniffed. It had a distinctive aroma.

All at once, a distressing notion struck her. In many ways she was a fairly conservative person, but at the radio station where she worked a few of the deejays smoked pot on a regular basis. There had been a lot of drug busts in Nashville lately, and she remembered seeing news clips showing narcotics agents destroying growing plants. Tall with spiky leaves, they'd looked like the greenery that she was now surrounded by. She stared down at the leaf in her hand. Oh, God, had she landed her plane in a field of marijuana?

Freddie's eyes widened, and a quiver of alarm shot up her back. If so, whose field was it? And what would the proprietors do when they found her strolling around examining their illegal crop? Minutes earlier, when she'd awakened to find herself falling out of the sky, she hadn't panicked, but terror coursed through her now.

Something told Nat to approach the next field with more caution than he had the others. His instinct was soon confirmed by Pinky. All morning, the old dog had been lollygagging at his side, chasing squirrels and rabbits like a pup without a care in the world. But now he froze on the path, and a low growl rumbled at the back of his massive throat.

Signaling for silence, Nat took the rifle from his shoulder and glided silently but purposefully through the trees. Cautiously, he approached the field. His ears picked up rustling noises. Someone or something was definitely moving around out there. Pushing a branch to one side, he peered past it. What he saw made his thick blond eyebrows rise sharply. He hadn't known exactly what to expect, but a downed glider nesting on uprooted hemp plants hadn't been part of the picture.

Carefully keeping behind the trees for cover, Nat edged toward the downed plane. If they'd come, he preferred not to be seen. At this stage it would be foolish to provoke a confrontation. There was a shortwave radio hidden near his campsite, and he wanted to be able to use it to summon help when the time came.

A movement drew his attention from the plane. A young woman was standing under one of the bushes. Nat's eyes narrowed when he saw her pluck a leaf and sniff it. Surely she wasn't one of *them*. From the back he couldn't tell much about her, only that her shapely legs were slim and tan and that the khaki shorts she wore molded a nicely rounded bottom and nipped in to a trim waist. Then she turned slightly, and he got a view of her profile.

Despite the tenseness of the situation, he immediately liked the way her blouse was filled out. His gaze moved upward. Below dark tousled curls, her brows were level over eyes that he couldn't see from this distance. But something told him that they were pretty enough to match the rest of her. *Surely* this wasn't the enemy, he told himself again. But what the hell was she doing here?

She was standing almost motionless, giving the scene a tableaulike quality. Suddenly, that changed. Dropping the leaf, she swiveled and began to walk quickly toward the end of the field. Nat knew all about the booby traps here. There was a deadfall in the direction toward which she was going, a dead tree rigged to crash down on whoever trespassed on the field at that point.

He stepped out into the open. "Stop!" he called to warn her.

She looked over her shoulder. Her eyes widened when she saw him, and then she began to run. Abandoning all caution, Nat dropped his rifle and took out after her. He'd been a hurdler in college and had won a few medals for the hundred-yard dash. Even so, she had a good head start, and she was fast and scared.

"Stop!" he called again. But the command had no effect, so he decided to save his breath and put all his energy into running her down before she reached that deadfall. It was a massive tree, and if it hit her squarely, it would break her back.

A few feet away from the thing he thought he had her, but she swerved to one side and then dodged under his arm.

"Damn!" he exclaimed as a piece of her cotton shirt tore in his hand. Then her flying feet tripped the wire, and he heard the sickening preliminary sounds of the crash he'd hoped to prevent. In desperation, he lunged at her legs, caught her pumping knees, and threw her roughly to one side.

Her arms flailing, she screamed as she went down and hit the ground full force. There was a loud crack, and then all hell broke loose. The dead tree fell with an echoing thud. The brittle ends of its branches tore through Nat's shirt, but he was hardly aware of the pain. What had happened to the woman?

As soon as the tree stopped moving, he extricated his upper body from it and pushed himself to his knees. Then he looked around and saw her. The branches that had lacerated the skin on his back and shoulders had done a worse job on her. She'd been closer to the trunk, and so she had caught blows from thicker branches. One appeared to have clipped her on the neck, and from the way she was lying, he guessed that she'd been knocked out.

Pinky was dancing around and barking as if it were the end of the world. "Quiet!" he told the dog sternly.

Turning back to the girl, Nat moved some of the debris away. He gently rolled her over so that she was no longer lying face down in the dirt. Then he put his ear to her breast. The heartbeat behind the mound of warm, soft flesh that grazed his cheek was strong and regular. Relieved, he drew back and examined her legs and arms. Although they were scratched, nothing appeared to be broken. The sturdy shorts she wore had protected a sizable portion of her lower body, but nothing had protected her chest and shoulders. Her light cotton blouse had been torn and was stained in spots with blood.

He studied her face. Was she really unconscious, or was she faking it? Under his scrutiny, the silky black lashes that swept her cheeks didn't move. He decided that she really was out. So what now? he asked himself. He could stay with her here until she came to. But that could be dangerous. There was no telling what Pinky's infernal barking might have attracted, or when the harvesters intended to show up. And Nat had to do something about that damned plane of hers, too. He decided it would be better to get her to a safe place before he took any further action.

"All right, pretty mystery lady," he muttered, "I'm going to take you home with me."

Pinky had been sniffing curiously at her knees. Nat ordered him back and got to his feet. He hoisted the woman into a dead man's carry, so that she was draped over one of his shoulders with her admirably shaped bottom in the air next to his cheek. It was not a very dignified posture, and if she came to while he was carrying her like this, she probably wouldn't be pleased. But, he told himself as he walked back to retrieve his gun, it was a fair hike back to his camp, and he wasn't Superman.

When Nat finally reached the sheltered glade where he'd set up temporary housekeeping, she was still unconscious. Carefully depositing her beneath the shelter of a spreading oak, he stared down at her worriedly, wondering if she were hurt more seriously than he'd originally thought. That blow might have given her a concussion. If it had, what could he do about it? For that matter, what should he do if she woke up feeling bright and chipper? Damn, but this was awkward!

Taking a towel off the line strung between two trees, he dampened it in the stream next to his tent. He squatted and laid the cool, wet terry cloth onto her forehead; then he rocked back on his heels and studied her face. She really was pretty. Her red-brown curls framed a face that was strongly carved, with level brows, a small, straight nose, a full, tempting mouth, and a square, rather challenging jaw. His gaze drifted up to her long lashes, and he wondered about the color of her eyes. Were they big and brown, or green like emeralds, or blue like wet pansies?

Annoyed with himself, he pushed the silly speculation aside. What was she doing here, anyway? Nat's mind returned to the scene in the field. There was no way to tell whether she'd come on purpose or if her presence was some sort of mishap. She obviously hadn't known about that deadfall, so the evidence pointed toward the latter. Either way, he couldn't afford to take any chances. If she wasn't seriously hurt, he'd just have to keep her quiet for the next few days so she couldn't interfere with his mission.

Nat turned his attention to some of her other injuries. Luckily, he had packed a decent medical kit in with him. Her scrapes and cuts would need to be cleaned and treated, and judging from the blood-stained condition of her blouse, some of the worst ones were concealed by the flimsy material.

His eyes were drawn to the full thrust of her breasts. Quite the Florence Nightingale, huh, Steele? he thought as his fingers went to the button just below the warm hollow of her throat. He undid it, and then his hand moved down toward the next fastening, which was nestled invitingly in the valley between her breasts. He tried to ignore the sudden heat below his belt; he frowned and did his best to concentrate on the job at hand. But his noble efforts were suddenly interrupted by a cool voice.

"Why are you unbuttoning my blouse?"

His hand froze and his gaze jerked upward. Surrounded by spiky black lashes, her eyes were very big and very blue. And for what seemed like forever, all Nat could do was stare into them as if he'd been poleaxed.

CHAPTER TWO

Actually, Freddie had been conscious for some time. She had started to come to while she was being carried. It had been no pleasant thing to wake up to find herself dangling headfirst over an unfamiliar male back. If her awakening hadn't been gradual, she would have yelled. But since it had been a slow process, during which she'd had to cope with a throbbing headache as well, she'd had time to gather her wits.

As she'd stared down at the lean, jean-clad hips swiveling beneath her with each of her captor's long-legged strides, she'd realized with growing horror that the man had to be the same one who'd chased her. Her first instinct had been to struggle. But that, she immediately realized, would be stupid. For one thing, he was carrying a rifle. For another, he was big. Although she could see from her very excellent view that his buttocks were narrow and tight, his shoulders were extremely broad. From where she dangled, it looked like a long way down to the ground.

What's more, he was probably dangerous. Certainly he had no regard for the law if he was cultivating his own private marijuana crop on government property. Freddie controlled the shudder that threatened to run through her. She didn't want him to know that she was conscious. She needed time to think her situation through.

It wasn't a very uplifting process. Only a short while before, she'd been windborne, as free as a bird and very content. Now she was lost in what appeared to be an uninhabited wilderness and was the prisoner of a man who carried a gun and who might at this very minute be plotting to murder her. Where was he taking her? she wondered. And what was he planning to do with her when they arrived?

Then she focused on the dog. She'd been so preoccupied before that she hadn't noticed the creature that trotted a few paces behind the man's heels. The dog—if that's what it could be called—was without a doubt the ugliest animal she'd ever seen in her life. And if the sight of it hadn't frozen her with horror, she would have screamed.

Massively built, it had the squat, short-legged body of some type of bulldog. But its spade-shaped head was like nothing Freddie had ever encountered. Its huge jaws were actually square—more like those of a rhinoceros than a canine's. It had tiny lashless eyes, surrounded by rings of pink flesh. Through the short, coarse white hair that grew over the rest of its body, the pink flesh beneath showed through clearly.

Just then, it looked up, and its black slits of eyes caught Freddie's. A shudder that she was unable to suppress passed through her. The dog looked just as mean as it was ugly. What kind of man would own a hideous animal like that? Her captor walked into a glade where a small tent was pitched, and Freddie realized with a cold feeling in the pit of her stomach that she would soon be finding out. Still at a loss as to how to cope with the situation, she closed her eyes and waited to see what would happen next.

A moment later she felt herself being lowered to the ground. It was a relief not to be hanging over his shoulder any longer. Her whole body ached and throbbed, and her head felt as if it were about to shatter into small pieces. She was tempted to open her eyes and look around, but the surface of her skin prickled, and instinctively she knew that he was standing somewhere very close scrutinizing her. Freddie kept her eyes tightly closed and did her best to look unconscious.

All the while, her thoughts raced furiously. What should she do? Make a break for it? But that was ridiculous. He'd already demonstrated that he could run her down. And then there was that horrible, vicious-looking dog to consider. Maybe this man didn't intend to murder her, she thought. Maybe he'd carried her here because he had other things in mind. Like what? Her brain reeled, and she experienced a moment of pure, unadulterated panic.

A few seconds later, she was astonished to feel something wet and cool being placed on her forehead. It felt soothing, and under any other circumstances she would have been grateful. Apparently, she was the prisoner of a considerate outlaw. Freddie was sorely tempted to steal a peek. But then she had the sense that she was being studied again. It was a physical sensation. Her skin tingled, and she could literally feel his inspecting gaze skimming over her body. She was aware that he'd changed his position and had dropped down onto the ground beside her.

Then his fingers were on her chest. His warm masculine hand was moving between her breasts—to do what? Undress her? And then? This was too much! Freddie's eyes snapped open, and she focused on the top of the man's sun-streaked, ash blond head.

"Why are you unbuttoning my blouse?"

His head jerked up, and Freddie stared into her captor's face. It was a shock. For some reason, she'd expected him to resemble his evil-looking dog, but he did not. If she was about to be assaulted, she mused distractedly, she certainly couldn't complain about her attacker's appearance. His ash blond hair framed a strongly molded, masculine face that, despite a longish-blond moustache, was close to being downright handsome. In fact—why quibble?—it *was* downright handsome, moustache and all. Under thick blond brows, the eyes that met hers were gray and watchful. They were so compelling that suddenly she was aware of nothing else. As if she were in the grip of some powerful force, she stared into them and held her breath while she waited to hear what he would say.

Straightening slightly, he rocked back on his heels. His gaze never left her face.

"There's blood on your shirt," he said politely. "I was just going to take a look to make sure it was nothing serious."

She looked down at her blouse and saw that he was right. She started to push herself up on her elbows, but then she sank back down again with a groan, her head whirling. "Oh!"

"Feeling woozy? I'm not surprised. You fell pretty hard." He moved one long forefinger back and forth in front of her eyes, watching her pupils closely. "You don't appear to have a concussion, though."

No thanks to him, she thought. She'd fallen hard because he'd thrown her to the ground. Electing not to comment, she lay still while he finished unbuttoning her blouse. He wasn't acting like an attacker, she thought hopefully. Maybe it would be okay.

"You have a nasty cut there," he remarked in his pleasant baritone drawl. "I'd better put something on it."

Rising to his feet, he disappeared into his tent. While he was gone, Freddie took a desperate look around. She was lying under a tree in a clearing. Twenty feet to the left, there was a stream. She glanced to the right and froze. The dog was there, sitting back on its thick haunches, regarding her with its malevolent, unblinking stare. She was almost glad when her handsome jailor reappeared.

As he strode toward her, she got a better look at him. He really was tall—tall, lean, and broad-shouldered. A stray finger of light that glinted through the leaves bathed the top of his head, and suddenly his longish silky hair was the color of buttercups. What, she wondered a bit giddily, was he doing growing marijuana in these forsaken mountains? The man could probably make a fortune on Madison Avenue posing for all types of advertisements.

"What's your name?" he asked as he squatted down beside her once more.

She watched him warily and considered refusing to answer. But what would be the point? "My name's Frederica Davenport, but I'm called Freddie."

He cocked a golden eyebrow. "I can see why. Would you like a couple of aspirin? You can wash them down with this." He proffered a canteen.

Gratefully, she accepted. But then she had to allow

him to prop her up so he could hold the canteen to her lips. The feel of his strong, warm palm supporting her neck was disturbing, and when she finally lay back down she felt more rattled than ever—not to mention sore. Her entire body seemed to be a mass of scratches and cuts.

Methodically, he cleaned the wound on her shoulder and then applied antiseptic. "Well, Ms. Davenport," he said as he rebuttoned her blouse, "tell me about yourself. What are you and your plane doing in the middle of a field in the Cohutta Wilderness?"

Freddie blinked. "The Cohutta Wilderness? That's where we are? I thought this was the national forest."

"The Wilderness is a thirty-five-thousand-acre area inside the national forest." He took her arm and began to wash the scrapes on it. "Tell me what you're doing here."

Refreshed by the cool cloth on her forehead, Freddie was beginning to feel a little less helpless. "Tell me what *you're* doing here," she retorted.

"I'm a resident."

"On government property?"

His gray eyes regarded her levelly. "A lot of acreage within the national forest is still privately owned. I'm on my own ground. You're the one who's in trouble, Ms. Davenport, not me."

Although his remark had been made in a quiet tone, it sent a chill through Freddie's blood. Silently, she watched as he applied disinfectant to one of her scratches, and she tried not to wince when it stung. He might be handsome, but now that she studied him closely, she saw that he also looked strong and determined. There was nothing weak about his jaw, and those gray eyes of his could probably be colder than an iceberg in February. On the other hand, he was not a ruffian, and he certainly didn't behave like a crazed drug addict. What sort of man *was* he? she wondered. What was he up to? And what were his intentions toward her?

"You haven't told me your name."

"It's Nat. Nathaniel Steele, at your service."

As Nat tended to each of her arms and then her legs, Freddie told him about the glider and gave him an edited account of her accident.

He listened silently, then he packed up his medical kit and sat back on his heels. "If you're such a hotshot glider pilot, why did you come down in the middle of a mountain range?" he asked bluntly.

Freddie tried to look nonchalant. "I miscalculated. It can happen to anybody." She saw no reason to explain her stupid error in judgment.

"Why did you pick that particular spot to land?" He continued to study her.

She shrugged. "It was a field—the only one I could see." Freddie wasn't going to admit that she knew what was growing in his garden. Maybe if he thought she hadn't identified his marijuana, he'd let her go. It was a faint hope, but right now she was ready to cling to anything.

"And that's the only reason?" His scrutiny was painfully sharp.

"What other reason could there be?" She did her best to look ingenuous. "How far is the nearest telephone?" she asked. "I have to call the gliderport and let them know where they can find me."

For the first time he looked amused, and he even went so far as to smile, revealing even, white teeth. "You're in the middle of a wilderness, Ms. Davenport. There are no phones—or even roads, for that matter. Only a few footpaths for the bears and wild boars."

"Bears and wild boars?" Freddie repeated suspiciously. Surely he couldn't be serious.

"Yes." He stood up and looked down at her from what seemed like a great height. "How are you feeling?"

"Better. A little light-headed, but that might be because I haven't eaten since breakfast." She'd brought a bag of sandwiches in the Schweizer's cockpit, but then she'd been so enthralled with her joyride on the slopes that she hadn't gotten around to opening it.

"You haven't had lunch?" Frowning, he glanced at his watch. Then he walked over to a tree near the tent where his food bag had been rigged up. He lowered it from an overhanging branch and pulled out two thick pieces of smoked ham and an apple.

"Thanks," Freddie said as he set the food down next to her on a paper napkin. Mustering her courage, she added, "If there are no roads or telephones, how am I going to get out of here?"

"Well, that's a problem."

She peered up at him through her lashes. "I have to do something about my plane."

"Don't worry about your aircraft."

"But I have to—" Once more she struggled to sit up. Just as she managed to prop herself on her elbows, Nat bent. Gently but firmly, his large hand came down and pushed her back flat.

"I said don't worry. I'll take care of your plane. In fact, I'm going to go do that right now."

"You are?" A bubble of panic rose in Freddie's chest. "But it's mine! I want to go with you!"

He shook his head. "You aren't going anywhere. You're going to stay right here and rest."

Freddie looked around wildly. "You intend to leave me alone here? But I thought you said there were bears!"

Once more, white teeth flashed in Nat's bronze face, but his voice was dry when he answered. "Don't worry. You won't be alone. My dog here will watch over you." Turning his head, he gave a curt order. "Pinky, guard!" Then he picked up his rifle and strode out of the clearing.

Nat heard her call after him, but he steeled himself to ignore the frightened sound. She'd be all right as long as she stayed there, and Pinky would see to it that she didn't go anywhere. Nat regarded his dog as a lovable old guy, but he was well aware that the bull terrier looked about as appealing as an imp from hell. Once the dog had bared his teeth at Ms. Frederica Davenport, she wouldn't try to make trouble. And trouble was one thing Nat had enough of right now. He had to do something about her damned plane before it attracted attention. The last thing he wanted was a search party to spot it from the air and come zeroing in on the field.

What a situation, he thought irritably. He'd spent a month setting this trap up. Now, just when he thought he had the whole thing under control, some lady drops out of the sky to mess up everything. Of course, he had to admit that from what he'd seen so far, she was a beautiful woman. A vivid image of plump young breasts straining at a functional white cotton bra rose to his mind. After he'd opened her blouse, it had taken just about all his willpower to dress the wound she'd had low on her shoulder without embarrassing himself.

Shaking his head, Nat forced the enticing image of Freddie's breasts from his thoughts and concentrated on the task at hand. Once more, he approached the field on silent feet. He pushed some foliage aside and stared out. Everything looked just as bizarre as it had when he'd left it. Like some sort of demented overgrown cagle, the glider was still nesting atop the hemp plants. Damn, and there was his hat lying in the dust, where it must have fallen when he took out after Freddie the Flyer. What a piece of carelessness!

Scooping it up, Nat strode through the rows of tall plants toward the aircraft. He tested its weight and walked around it, then stood scratching his head. The thing was probably about six or seven hundred pounds—certainly too heavy and ungainly for him to carry out. But he couldn't very well wheel it out, either, not without knocking even more plants down, which might well alert his quarry and spoil his carefully laid out plans.

Of course, he could always take an axe to the thing —and right now he was tempted to do exactly that. But surely there was a better way. He cocked his head and considered. Glider pilots must go down in out-of-the-way spots all the time. They must have a simple method of dismantling their planes so they could be conveniently transported.

Lifting the cockpit shield, he glanced around inside and then searched the compartments. Eureka! he thought when he found the tool kit and instructions.

* * *

Pinky squatted on his haunches a few feet away and watched Freddie with tiny, flat black eyes.

"Nice doggie."

He made no response to that, but a few minutes later, when Freddie sat up shakily and tried to get to her feet, he bared a row of sharklike teeth and growled low in his thick throat.

Freddie sank back down, a jolt of fear running down her spine. "Killer" would have been a more appropriate name for him, she thought. Clearly, Nathaniel Steele's animal wasn't just guarding against wild beasts; he was guarding against her as well, and he appeared to be very well trained and loyal. For several minutes she lay motionless, staring at him warily. What would the hideous beast do if she tried to leave? Tear out her throat? He certainly looked capable of it. Freddie shivered. But she couldn't lie there like a statue for what might be hours.

Slowly, she placed her hands flat on the ground and propped herself up into a sitting position. The dog watched closely, but he made no sound. She moved so that her back was against the tree. Again, Pinky was mute, and for several more minutes they eyed each other.

She had to get out of there. For one thing, she had to find out what that man was doing to her plane. It constituted her only chance for escape. Knowing Hank and his easygoing ways, it would be another twenty-four hours before he really started to worry. And even then he would have no idea where she'd gone. As long as the Schweizer was in that field, it was like a marker. If a search plane were sent out sometime tomorrow, and if it flew over these mountains, the glider would be seen. But if it weren't there, it could be weeks—if ever—before she'd be found.

Freddie eyed Pinky. Somehow she had to make friends with the dog. But how?

"Nice dog. You know what? If you got to know me, I bet you'd like me a lot better than that criminally inclined master of yours. How about coming over here so I can pet you?" she murmured in her most seductive tones.

A slight flattening of the ears was Pinky's only response.

Freddie glanced down at the food next to her. She'd grown up with dogs, beautiful collies and handsome German shepherds, and she knew something about how a well-trained canine's mind worked. She was well aware, for instance, that if she offered those ham slices to Pinky, it would only make him distrust her more. But dogs weren't as intelligent as humans, she reminded herself. And this one looked particularly thickheaded. Surely there was a way to outsmart him.

Freddie picked up a piece of ham and looked at it, turning it this way and that as if it were a work of art.

Pinky lifted his head.

"Doesn't this look good?" she said, infusing as much enthusiasm as she could muster into her voice. "I bet it's going to be delicious!"

Pinky's nostrils flared.

Freddie took a delicate bite and then licked her lips in an elaborate ceremony. "Umm! It's absolutely scrumptious!"

The dog's tiny opaque eyes followed her movements minutely.

Freddie let the ham slice dangle from her hand,

and then with a flick of her wrist, she sent it skipping along the grass in Pinky's direction.

He staunchly refused to be tempted and gave her a suspicious look. An ominous growl began to rumble in his barrel chest. But the growl was cut off by Freddie's sharp command.

"Pinky, stay! Don't touch the food!"

Confused, the animal looked from Freddie to the meat and back. He hadn't been going to touch it, but if he didn't, that meant he was obeying an order from the woman that his master had told him to guard.

"That's a good boy," she praised with a brilliant smile.

He whined faintly, even more bewildered.

Satisfied, Freddie picked up the second piece of ham and started the process all over again. This time the results were better. When Pinky left the meat alone and she praised him, he thumped his stump of a tail and started to pant.

"That's a good boy," she told him again. "You've been a very good boy, and now you may have your reward." She pointed at the ham.

He looked at her doubtfully.

"It's all right now," she assured him. Gingerly getting to her knees, she crept forward. Picking up the slice of smoked meat, she offered him the tempting morsel and hoped that he wouldn't decide to take her hand off along with it. "You've been a good boy, so now you can have a treat."

Whining again, he glanced from her to the meat. It was obvious he knew that something wasn't quite right here, but he couldn't remember what it was. And he was starting to salivate. He accepted the meat from her hand and ate it with relish.

Triumphantly, Freddie delivered the rest of the ham to Pinky and watched him devour it. Not bad for a mere slip of a woman, she told herself. Of course, she wasn't out of the clearing yet, but she was almost certain that she was on the right track.

When he finished his meal, she patted him and told him what a fine dog she thought he was. That was a lie; she still thought he was a monstrosity. But Pinky accepted the compliment and, to her astonishment, when he was through eating, he rolled over and offered her his almost hairless pink belly. Patting it lightly, Freddie laughed and decided that maybe he wasn't quite as hideous as she'd originally thought.

Then she stood up and looked down at her scratched and smarting limbs. She still felt shaky, and she hurt like hell, but she figured she was in better shape than she'd been in earlier.

Ten minutes later she polished the apple, which was all that remained of her lunch, took a bite, and strolled away from her former prison with her former canine jailer at her side. "We're going to find your master," she told Pinky. Removing a small compass from her pocket, she peered up through the leaves to take her bearings from the sun.

"Damned nuisance!" Nat muttered as he carted one of the sailplane's wings into the woods. Maneuvering the ungainly thing through the trees and undergrowth wasn't easy, but he decided he had to get it far enough away from the field that nobody was going to stumble over the thing by accident. A couple of hundred yards from the site, he looked around for a place to hide the wing.

Since the only cutting tool he had with him was his

hunting knife, it took him a good half hour to hack off enough pine branches to cover the wing adequately. And of course, he was going to have to go through the whole process two more times with the sailplane's cockpit and remaining wing.

Taking a deep breath, he surveyed his work and then turned to head back toward the field. The shadows were already lengthening. It was going to be near nightfall before he finished this job properly. That made him think about Freddie and how she was doing. Pinky was a good and loyal dog, so Nat knew she was all right. But he supposed she was probably worried.

All the time he'd been working, he'd thought of her off and on. She'd shown up at a particularly bad time, but if he had to have a problem, he couldn't have asked for a much cuter one, he admitted to himself. Her big blue eyes and sweet little body intrigued him, and she was bright and sassy, too. They hadn't exchanged many words, but he could tell there was a brain behind her pretty face.

He was wondering what kind of woman she really was when he stepped through the line of trees and back into the field. Then he froze. "What the hell!"

Pinky was sitting by the partially dismantled plane. His tongue was lolling out of one side of his mouth at a ridiculous angle. When he spied his master, he waddled toward him.

"What are you doing here?" Nat demanded sharply. He looked around, but the field appeared to be deserted. Scowling, he began to stride toward the aircraft. "What happened to Amelia Earhart?" he snapped. "You were supposed to guard her." Then he stopped short once again. The rifle that he'd had to leave behind in order to carry the wing was no longer propped inside the open cockpit.

"Amelia Earhart is right here," a woman's voice announced. Freddie, who'd been crouched behind the other wing, stood up and stepped around in front of the disabled Schweizer. She was pointing Nat's gun at his chest, and she looked very much as if she knew how to use it.

CHAPTER THREE

Nat cleared his throat as he stared at the gun. "I hate to spout clichés, but you could hurt someone with that, you know."

"Yes, I could," Freddie agreed. "My daddy belonged to a gun club. I got in a lot of target practice early in life, and I know how to use this." The rifle barrel, which was still pointed firmly at his chest, didn't waver.

Nat's gaze shifted to Freddie's face. Beneath her level brows her blue eyes blazed with determination. Her full lower lip stuck out as if her teeth were clenched behind it, and he found himself thinking that she'd be prettier if her chin weren't quite so stubborn. "What's this all about?" he asked quietly.

"Let's stop the games, shall we?" Freddie gritted.

"Sounds fine to me. I just played Good Samaritan. I rescued you, treated your wounds—even fed you. Why are you threatening me with my own gun? It's not a very nice thank you." Nat took a step forward, but when she stiffened and raised the rifle a notch, he froze.

"You're no kindhearted hillbilly who just happened to be passing by when I had the misfortune to land here. I know what's growing in this field. These are marijuana plants."

He regarded her thoughtfully. "How do you know?"

"Come on! Listen, I really don't care about your garden. All that matters to me is my plane." She shot a pointed glance at the lame glider. "I want it to stay in one piece right here where a rescue party can see it from the air and get me out. So turn yourself around and take me to where you've hidden the wing."

Nat hesitated, wondering whether or not he should try to explain the situation to her. But would she believe him? Even if she did, that wouldn't change the fact that her priorities were in conflict with his. What's more, other lives might be at risk here. He had very good reason to know that giving sensitive information away to an outsider at a critical moment could be disastrous and should be resorted to only when there were no options left.

"Go on, turn around and march!"

Freddie's voice rose shrilly, and for the time being Nat elected to play along. Pivoting on his heel, he caught sight of Pinky. The old dog squatted a few yards away. A faint growl curled at the back of his throat as he stared worriedly from his master to his supposed new friend and then back again. Obviously, he was disturbed that Freddie was pointing a gun. It occurred to Nat that whatever witchery she'd used to win the animal over could now be negated by a curt order. If he told Pinky to jump her, the animal would obey.

Freddie, who was more frightened than she'd ever been in her life, had the same thought. "Don't even think it," she hissed into Nat's ear, jamming the rifle barrel firmly against his backbone. "If you tell that dog to attack me, I'll shoot him between the eyes, and at this range I won't miss."

"I wasn't going to," Nat said truthfully. He'd dismissed the idea instantly because once Pinky was put into attack mode, his jaws were about as easy to pull apart as a sprung bear trap. It was very possible that the animal might do her some real harm before he could be pulled off. Putting up his hands in a gesture of submission, Nat began to walk back toward the trees. Freddie followed behind, and Pinky, still growling deep in his throat, trotted alongside.

Once they were out of the late afternoon glare and the cool shadows from the pines had closed around them, Freddie asked, "How far?"

"Not more than a couple of hundred yards. I didn't feel like dragging that wing any farther than I had to."

"Take me there now, and no tricks!"

Nat threw a glance over his shoulder. Gripping his rifle as if her life depended on it, Freddie scowled at him fiercely. Her whole body was rigid. She was scared out of her mind, he thought. But that only made the situation extraticklish. In his experience, nothing was more dangerous than a terrified person —male or female—brandishing a gun.

"Would you really shoot me?" he asked, injecting a touch of playfulness into his voice as they plodded along.

"Yes. Don't imagine for a minute that because I'm a woman I wouldn't have the nerve to pull this trigger," Freddie retorted belligerently.

"A real tough cookie."

"You better believe it!" Actually, she wasn't sure

what she'd do if he challenged her. It would be easier for her to imagine herself using the gun against him in self-defense if he'd behaved toward her like the criminal she was sure he was. But he hadn't. And he was so damned good-looking. A sudden image of Nat Steele lying at her feet covered with blood because she'd pulled the trigger assaulted her imagination, and she was so shaken by it that she stumbled and almost dropped the gun.

Pinky's low growl grew ominous, and Nat issued a sharp command: "Quiet, boy. It's all right." Once again, he glanced back at Freddie. "I wouldn't want you to shoot my dog. He and I have been together a long time."

"Then you did the right thing to quiet him down." But as she spoke the words, Freddie realized that despite her tough talk she really didn't think she could use the rifle on Pinky, either. In their short walk back to the plane together, she'd grown almost fond of the ugly brute.

"This is it," Nat said shortly.

She stopped and glanced around. He'd done a good job of hiding the wing. If she hadn't been told it was here, she would have passed it right by. But now she could make out an area where branches had been cut and artfully arranged. "Very clever," she said. "But I'm afraid you're going to have to undo all this work."

"Just what is it you expect to accomplish by this?" Nat turned to face her, and she glimpsed irritation behind the cool manner he'd assumed.

"I've told you several times. I want you to put that wing back on my glider."

"Then what? We're alone together in thirty-five

thousand acres of wilderness. It could be days before a search plane happens this way. Do you plan to hold a gun on me all that time? Or will you shoot me in the back after I've restored your damned wing?"

Freddie's face turned red, and she retreated a step. "Hank Pritchard, the man who owns the gliderport I fly out of, is a personal friend of mine. I'm sure he'll be around by tomorrow. Now just clear away that brush and do as I've told you."

"Yes, ma'am." With a grim expression, Nat set to work.

As Freddie silently looked on, she chewed on her lower lip and thought through the questions he'd posed. She was sure Hank would eventually spot her plane in this field—although not necessarily by tomorrow. How *was* she going to spend that time? When she'd decided to turn Nat Steele's rifle on him, she hadn't thought beyond stopping him from taking the Schweizer apart. Now she realized that she'd created a whole new set of problems for herself.

With a grunt, Nat removed the last of the branches so that the wing was revealed—a stark white shape that seemed utterly alien in the mountain setting.

"Now what?" he asked.

Freddie came to attention. "Now you pick it up and carry it back."

"Simple as that?"

"You did it once. You can do it again."

"Anything you say, boss lady." From beneath the lock of fair hair that had slid over his forehead, Nat shot her a brief, cynical look and then squatted down next to the wing. His cotton shirt was damp with sweat, and Freddie studied the way it clung to his broad back. "Get off, Pinky," he said to the dog, who was sniffing around the Fiberglas wing.

Freddie knew that besides being large and unwieldy, the wing wasn't all that light. As Nat grasped it and strained upward, she watched in fascination. Beneath his clinging shirt, his muscles tensed. Although the man was obviously strong, he seemed to be having a lot of trouble. She frowned. If he was having such a hard time lifting it now, how had he ever managed to get it this far into the woods by himself?

He grunted and then lurched to one side, half stumbling. Automatically, Freddie ran forward to put a steadying hand under the teetering wing. Then everything happened very quickly. As she leaned over, slightly off balance, Nat straightened effortlessly. Swinging the long, narrow wing with ease that belied his former struggling act, he knocked Freddie's legs out from under her. The rifle flew out of her hand and she went sprawling.

"Oof!" she grunted as she went down on her back. Although the wind had been knocked out of her, she wasn't knocked unconscious, as she had been in the last fall she'd taken. She knew that she had to retrieve the rifle. Desperately she tried to scramble back onto her feet. But Nat was too fast. He dropped the wing and threw himself down on top of her, flattening her body beneath his. But even then, Freddie wasn't ready to give up. Frightened to the bone and cursing her own stupidity in letting down her guard with this dangerous man, she thrashed with every bit of her might. For all she knew she was fighting for her life.

For several minutes the woodland serenity was broken by the gasping breaths and muffled blows of a silent but determined struggle and by Pinky's excited barking as he danced nervously around the two combatants. Beneath Nat, Freddie bit, scratched, and wriggled, inflicting enough damage to enrage a saint. Her pumping knees, jabbing elbows, and raking fingernails bruised him and drew blood. Many of the wounds Nat had received earlier in the morning while rescuing her from the deadfall were now painfully reopened.

Fear and adrenaline gave her more strength than Nat would have believed possible, and he was humiliated to find that it took all his effort to subdue her. He finally pinned her beneath him so firmly that she couldn't so much as twitch, but even then she didn't yell uncle. Instead she glared up into his set features and abused him verbally, calling him every name, in a long and quite inventive string.

It made him crazy with fury. "My God, you need your mouth washed out with soap. Shut up!"

But Freddie was too far gone to heed the warning, and she only started to yell louder. Abruptly, Nat's head came down, and he silenced her angry cries by sealing her mouth with an angry kiss.

They both knew that the kiss was anything but loving. When Freddie first felt the hard line of his lips against hers, she stiffened in protest. But her resistance only made Nat more determined. The kiss went on and on. His mouth covered hers insistently, making it hard for her to breathe. At last she actually felt deprived of oxygen. Too dizzy to resist any longer, Freddie went limp beneath him, the fight finally knocked out of her.

Still, his lips remained sealed to hers. For Nat, the kiss was taking on a new character. He was only human. From the first he'd found Freddie physically attractive, and although her body struggling beneath his had made him angry, the line between anger and sexual excitement quickly blurred for him. His lips softened and began to move coaxingly.

Freddie, too, was becoming aware of Nat's body in a new way. As his lean hips pinned her, his insistent pressure awakened an instinctive reaction in her. She fought against it, but it took her enough by surprise that she couldn't resist it. Undeniable currents of electricity crackled between them. Suddenly, for Freddie his hard flesh pressed against hers held excitement more than threat. When his tongue filled her mouth, her hands, which had been shoving him vainly, curled around his shoulders and unconsciously drew him closer.

Pinky continued to issue staccato barks, but as he circled the two figures locked in the grass, there was a puzzled expression in his small eyes. Even he could sense the change.

Neither Freddie nor Nat was prepared to welcome what was happening. When she felt a new pressure against her hip that she couldn't help but recognize, a fresh dart of fear shot through her. Moaning, she tore her mouth from Nat's. She turned her face away from his and closed her eyes tight, as if to deny everything. The rejection forced him back to self-consciousness. For several long, tense moments, he lay on top of her, shuddering as he fought the tide of desire that had started to drag him under.

"I'm sorry," he finally rasped. "I didn't mean that to happen."

Freddie squeezed her eyes tighter and didn't answer. She was drowning in embarrassment and confusion. They were both aware that she had responded to his kiss and that in another moment or two the kiss would have turned into something far more compromising.

When Nat rolled to one side and she felt herself free of him, she finally opened her eyes. He stood up and aimed a sharp command at Pinky, then gazed down at her. He silently offered her his hand. She ignored it and, not meeting his eyes, struggled to her feet unaided.

Once she was upright, Freddie wrapped her arms around her chest and shivered. Her blouse, which had been in a sorry state before, was now nothing but rags. She looked down at herself and thanked God she hadn't worn one of her lacy, transparent bras. It was bad enough to be standing in front of Nat with her breasts covered only by a stained white cotton undergarment.

He picked up his rifle and then motioned her ahead of him. "We'll go back to the field now."

"What are you going to do?" she mumbled.

"Just what I started to do in the first place. I'm going to take your glider apart and hide it."

"Please—"

"It's no good," he interrupted brusquely. "I have no choice. Now start walking. I want to get this over with before nightfall."

Her shoulders sagging, Freddie stumbled back along the route they'd just taken. All the nervous energy that had been firing her had evaporated. She felt so limp, she could hardly hold up her head. Nothing seemed to matter anymore. She could hardly even work up the energy to protest when Nat lowered her to a sitting position in front of a sapling at the edge of the field and told her to put her hands behind her back.

"What for? You aren't going to tie me to this tree, are you?"

"Yes, I am."

She lifted her head and stared at him. Despite her own sorry condition, she noticed that there were ugly welts on his cheek where she'd scratched it. As he took what she realized was Pinky's leash out of his back pocket, his face was devoid of any expression. Nevertheless, she sensed that he wasn't particularly happy about what he was doing—although that didn't change the fact that he was going to do it.

"Is it really necessary to tie me to a tree? Don't you think that's a little ridiculous?"

"Lady, ever since you dropped out of the sky, I've felt like the bad guy in *The Perils of Pauline.* But yes, with you, I'm afraid it's all necessary." He knelt down behind her, and she felt his sinewy fingers on her wrists. "I can't trust you not to try some dumb stunt, and I want to work on that plane of yours without interruption."

"That plane is private property. If I ever get out of here, I'll report your assaults on my person and your acts of vandalism to the police."

"If I were really the villain you imagine, that wouldn't be a very smart thing to say to me, would it?"

Realizing how right he was, Freddie clamped her lips shut and made no further comment while he finished tying her wrists together. When at last he stood up and walked away, she tested the knots gingerly. They were strong, but they weren't painful. He'd taken care that the rope didn't cut into her flesh or cause her unnecessary discomfort.

But Freddie was in no mood to be grateful. Wearily, she leaned her head against the tree trunk and watched through half-closed lids as Nat set about finishing the job on her glider. The late afternoon sun was hot, and he soon worked up another sweat. He removed his shirt and dropped it on the ground. Freddie's eyes widened as she caught her first glimpse of his broad, uncovered back.

"You're really good at that," she called out. "I bet you liked to tear wings off flies as a kid."

"No, but I liked playing doctor. How about you?" Freddie shut up.

Methodically, Nat removed the other wing and carted it off, disappearing into the trees for what seemed like hours. She wasn't left alone, though. Before he left, he told Pinky to stand guard.

"Just a precaution. In case any wild animals decide to investigate, my dog will scare them off," Nat informed her. "I don't know how you got him to let you go before, but I'm pretty sure you won't be able to teach him how to untie those knots."

Freddie wasn't amused. She sighed as Pinky sat down on his haunches to watch her. Eventually, he stretched out full length in the grass, his troubled gaze pinned to her face.

"I wouldn't have shot you, or even your master for that matter," she told him in the friendliest tone she could muster. "It was all just a bluff."

His tongue lolled out, but he still looked suspicious.

When Freddie's captor finally came back and started to wheel the glider's wingless body through the rows of marijuana and toward the edge of the woods, she croaked, "I'm thirsty. Can I have a drink?"

"I haven't got anything with me but my hat, and that wouldn't hold water long enough for me to carry it from the stream."

"There's a cup in the plane."

"I'll see what I can do."

To her surprise, he brought a cup of water when he returned. Squatting down, he held it to her lips. As Freddie sipped, she tried not to look at his chest with its thatch of stiff gold hair growing between his light brown nipples. Once again she was uncomfortably aware of her own breasts. She knew their shapes were clearly visible beneath her shredded blouse.

Embarrassed, she avoided Nat's eyes. But she finally did fix her gaze on his face, which was very close to hers, and then she saw that he didn't look as if he were aroused by the sight of a half-dressed woman. He was pale beneath his tan, and there were lines of exhaustion around his eyes and mouth. The scratches on his face that she'd noticed earlier were an angry red, and for a moment she felt almost contrite about all the trouble she'd caused him—which was, of course, ridiculous.

It wasn't easy for Freddie to drink water in this awkward manner. As he tipped the cup up so that she could get the last of the cool liquid, some water dribbled down her chin and then fell in tiny drops to the cleft between her breasts. Nat's gaze followed their progress, and she felt herself go warm all over. Leaning forward, he gently brushed the moisture from her chin.

"Couldn't you untie me now?" Freddie whispered.

"In just a few minutes. I want to see if I can save any of the bushes that your plane crushed when you landed."

The statement made Freddie's expression harden. For a moment she'd been feeling almost grateful to the man. Now she reminded herself that he was a criminal who was holding her captive.

When at last he did untie her and pulled her to her feet, she almost toppled over. Her legs felt like water, and waves of exhaustion seemed to be sloshing back and forth in her head. "I'll never be able to walk back to your campsite," she said.

"You'll have to try. I can't leave you here." He put his arm around her shoulders and half-dragged, half-carried her out of the field and back onto the faintly marked woodland trail that led to his base. Although at first she had no choice but to lean on Nat, her pride soon took over, and as soon as her restored circulation made it possible, Freddie pulled away and staggered along behind him under her own power.

It was close to twilight, and shadows were thick among the tall trees that all but blotted out the sky. Although she was almost too tired to think, Freddie did wonder how Nat managed to see and find his way. As silent as an Indian, he picked an unerring path.

"We made it," he said as they entered the clearing where his tent was pitched.

"I don't know how you found it," she mumbled. It was pitch black now, and there was no light from the moon or stars. In the final minutes of the day the clear sky had clouded over abruptly.

"My homing instincts are pretty strong by now.

Here." He took her arm and guided her toward the tent.

The grip of his hard fingers on her flesh sent a thrill of alarm rocketing through her. "What are you going to do now?"

"I'm going to find my flashlight for you. Then I'm going to give you my first aid kit and some privacy," he explained shortly. "You should take care of some of the scratches you acquired this afternoon. I'm also going to give you one of my shirts. What you're wearing now doesn't cover much."

Freddie felt herself blush. So he had noticed her dishabille. She'd known it, of course, yet he hadn't responded to the fact that a half-dressed female who was entirely under his power was parading around in front of him. In fact, he'd treated her with amazingly dispassionate stoicism, considering that she'd attacked him and threatened his life earlier. How long would that last? she wondered. And what would happen when they spent the night together in his tent?

To cover her confusion, she asked, "What about you? You have some pretty bad scratches, too."

He laughed shortly. "Thanks for your concern, but I'll take care of those after I get the camp stove going and heat us up some water. I could use a cup of coffee."

Inside Nat's small tent a few minutes later, Freddie aimed the flashlight beam around and took stock of the situation. There were a rolled sleeping bag and a heavy-looking backpack in one corner. Nearby she saw the first aid kit, some shaving supplies, and a loose pack of cigarettes. There was no sign of the drug paraphernalia she'd expected to find.

After she applied antiseptic to her cuts and put on

Nat's flannel shirt, she crawled over to the backpack. Maybe she'd find some helpful clues about her captor in it. But just then, he stuck his head in through the flap and motioned her outside. He cleared his throat and gave her a stern look.

"The bathroom facilities, as you might imagine, are nonexistent around here. I'm going to let you take a ten-minute walk with Pinky."

Freddie's sigh of relief was audible. She'd been wondering what to do about that.

"Don't be so stupid as to take advantage. If you try to run off, Pinky will help me find you. And believe me, you're a lot safer with me than you are on your own in three thousand acres of wilderness. I wasn't kidding when I mentioned those wild animals."

Freddie was too tired and too needy to do anything but nod. Besides, Nat was right. Now that Pinky's suspicions had been reawakened, there was no way he would help her escape a second time. And where would she escape to?

When she returned to the clearing a few minutes later, Nat was sitting cross-legged before the blaze of a small fire. Stripped to the waist, he was applying antiseptic to the scratches inflicted by her nails. Arrested by the picture he made, Freddie paused just inside the trees and stared. The firelight playing warmly over his broad naked shoulders, contrasted sharply with the pitch darkness that surrounded him. She could see every detail of his upper torso, the play of every muscle and sinew as he arched to find a difficult-to-reach spot. She could see the indentation of his spine where it tracked from his strongly modeled neck down to his narrow waist and then disappeared beneath his denim waistband.

"Here, let me help," she said without thinking, and went forward to kneel behind him.

Over his shoulder he gave her a startled look. "What are you doing?"

"There's a long cut on your back that you won't be able to reach. I'll take care of it for you."

He lifted an eyebrow, then wordlessly handed her the antiseptic. Carefully, she spread it over his wound. "You didn't get this gash from me, did you?"

"No. I think that came from the tree this morning." He shivered slightly and reached for his shirt. "You can be gentle when you want to, can't you?"

"Of course. Most women are gentle." She rocked back on her heels and handed the medicine back to him.

"I would never have known it this afternoon. You fought like a wildcat."

"What did you expect? I was defending myself."

Buttoning his shirt, he turned toward her. "Look, I know you're scared."

Freddie swallowed. "Is it so obvious?"

"No. You're a gutsy lady, and you're putting on a good show." He grinned. "I have the scars to prove it. Where did you learn all those names you called me?"

"I work at a radio station around disc jockeys."

"Ah, that explains it."

He chuckled, and Freddie stared at the sudden warmth in his face.

Nat said, "What I'm trying to say is that there's no need to be afraid. Just relax. It may take some time, but as long as you don't pull any more stunts like the harebrained stuff you tried today, you'll be okay."

In that moment Freddie believed him. But later,

after they had eaten and she was crawling into the sleeping bag inside his tent, she called herself a fool. Of course the man would try to lull her fears, she told herself. A docile, cooperative prisoner would be a lot easier for him to handle. No, she couldn't fall under the spell of a man like him. She couldn't wait patiently until he saw fit to release her—if indeed that ever happened. She had to find a way out of this situation.

Suddenly, she was distracted from her thoughts by the sound of music. It was a faint, plaintive melody that seemed to be coming from somewhere close. Wonderingly, Freddie peered out the tent flap and blinked. It was Nat. He had a small harmonica pressed to his mouth. Amazed, she stared for a minute, then closed the flap and retreated.

Back in the sleeping bag, she lay with her eyes wide open and listened to the simple yet beguiling melody Nat played. It seemed to wander through the corridors of her mind. She didn't know what the tune was, but now that she'd heard it coming from Nat Steele's harmonica, she knew she'd never forget it.

Outside, Nat hunched over the dying fire and softly finished the song while he heated himself another cup of coffee. His mind was on Freddie. What a hell of a situation. And what a hell of a woman!

A sudden warming image of how she'd looked panting beneath him—her breasts had heaved inside the thin covering of that cotton bra—forced him to acknowledge that she was going to be a threat in more ways than one. He asked himself again if he should try to gain her cooperation by telling her the truth. But finally he took his harmonica away from his lips and shook his head. There were just too many ways she could throw a monkey wrench into the works. He was going to have to find some other solution. He was going to have to get her out of his hair— soon.

CHAPTER FOUR

An hour after Nat had lain down near Freddie in the tent and had propped his head against his backpack, drops of rain began to patter on the outside of the tent. When it was falling steadily, Pinky whined at the flap to be let in.

Nat got up to let the dog in, then once more lowered his head to the lumpy backpack and pulled his jacket around his shoulders. Pinky stretched out next to him, wet and smelling none too attractive, and Nat was even more uncomfortable than he'd been before. But, he reflected hopefully, once the animal dried off, his warmth might take some of the chill out of the damp night air.

He glanced to his right, where Freddie lay rolled in his nice warm sleeping bag, breathing like a baby. It hadn't been easy to part with the bag, but he couldn't very well let her spend the night with nothing but his jacket around her shoulders. He was worried enough about her already. What if she got sick? That would really complicate matters.

Nat shifted his weight and sighed. She was a tough little nut. He really didn't think she would get sick on him. Putting his arm behind his head, he smiled, remembering how she'd looked brandishing that gun today—like the wrath of God and a frightened little girl all rolled into one.

There were still some details to work out, but he'd decided what he was going to do with Frederica Davenport in the morning. She needed to be safe and out of the way, and she needed someone to keep an eye on her—someone who knew just how tricky she could be. That person was obviously him. She'd behaved tonight, but Nat didn't for a moment believe that would last. As soon as that little lady got a few hours' sleep—in his sleeping bag—she'd try some new shenanigan.

Yet he couldn't just abandon Project Parker and traipse off with his uninvited guest. It was close to harvest time, and he had to keep a close watch on the fields. Frowning, Nat put his other hand under his head and stared up at the tent ceiling. The rain fell against it with steady persistence. That might be the answer, he reflected. As long as it was raining, there would be no harvest. What he needed was a weather report.

Once again, he glanced over at Freddie. From what he could make out of her dark shape and the sound of her breathing, she seemed to be sound asleep. She'd had a long, rough day, after all. On the other hand, she might just be playing possum. Grimacing, Nat decided that he'd have to chance it.

As noiselessly as possible, he withdrew his slicker from the backpack. Pinky raised his head. Nat quieted him and slipped out of the tent into the rain. After a quick backward glance at the silent tent, he made his way across the clearing and through the trees. Fifty paces into the woods he stopped and knelt in front of a large, half-dead oak. He'd hidden his shortwave radio in its hollow, where it was protected from the weather and safe from prying eyes. Although it was always possible that someone might stumble across his tent, there wasn't a chance in a million that anyone would guess what was in this tree.

After unwrapping the radio, Nat made some necessary adjustments, turned it on, and tuned it to the proper frequency. Briefly, he explained his situation with Ms. Frederica Davenport to the operator, Al, and then asked that a check be made on her and that a local gliderport owner named Hank Pritchard be notified that she was safe and that no search party would be required.

"Will do," Al's voice assured him.

Nat grinned. That took care of one problem, anyway. "What's the weather report for up here?" he asked.

There was a pause and then Al said, " 'Fraid you're going to get wet. A low has settled in over those mountains. The weather bureau predicts forty-eight hours of rain."

Better and better, Nat thought as he signed off. Just then, some sixth sense made him turn his head and search the darkness with narrowed eyes. Was that a rustling noise? But he neither saw nor heard anything, so he turned back to put the radio away.

Twenty feet off, Freddie quietly slipped back through the woods and across the clearing to the tent. She grinned as she gave Pinky a reassuring pat, then hastily crawled back into the warmth of the sleeping bag. She was grateful that the animal liked his sleep. He'd lifted his head when she'd followed Nat outside but had made no other move to stop her.

Shivering, Freddie pulled the quilted material up around her neck.

Her clothes were soaked, and her wet hair was plastered down over her forehead. If her jailer were to touch her when he came back, he'd know right away what she'd been up to. She waited with bated breath, but when he pushed the flap back a few minutes later and slipped silently in, he didn't even look her way. Instead, he took off his slicker, quickly wrapped his jacket around his shoulders, and stretched out next to Pinky's warmth. As Freddie stopped shivering beneath the thick layers of Nat's comfortable sleeping bag, she almost felt sorry for the man. Almost, but not quite.

Her eyes were wide and bright in the darkness. So he had a shortwave radio hidden away! She hadn't gotten close enough to hear who he was talking to or what he was saying, but it didn't matter. Just knowing he had a radio changed the whole picture. Now that she knew where to find it, she had a chance. Shortwaves were no mystery to her. She worked at a radio station, after all. What she had to do now was get to the thing and make a call. It was only a matter of finding an opportunity.

However, much to Freddie's chagrin, no opportunity to use Nat's radio arose. A couple of hours later that night she sat up with the idea of sneaking back outside, but Nat turned toward her abruptly. Seconds earlier, he'd seemed to be sleeping heavily, but now he was wide awake.

"What are you doing?"

"I have to go to the bathroom."

"Bad enough to have me come along with you?"

"What?" she protested.

"I don't want you wandering out there alone in the dark."

Freddie sank back down into her sleeping bag.

"That's right. We have another long day tomorrow, so get some rest." Rolling over, he hunched his shoulders and laid his head back down on his pack.

What had he meant by that remark? Freddie wondered tiredly. What kind of a long day did he have planned for her?

When the first faint gray streaks of light penetrated the tent, a gravelly voice whispered in her ear, "Time to rise and shine." Her lids popped open, and she found herself staring up into Nat Steele's unshaven face and slightly reddened eyes. The scratch marks on his cheeks were still fresh, and with all the other signs of not having passed a particularly pleasant night, he was not looking his best. It didn't seem to matter. He was still one of the most attractive men she'd ever met—or slept with.

Of course, it would be hard to imagine anything less romantic than the tense, soggy night she'd just spent with Nat Steele. His crowded little tent had been intended for one person, not three, if you counted Pinky—and there was no way you could leave the dog out of the picture. Perhaps because he sensed the disquiet in the atmosphere, he had been restless. During the wee hours of the morning he'd gotten up every now and then to sniff first his master's face and then Freddie's. Nat had just batted the animal away, but Freddie was still wary of him. Each time he'd put his incredibly sinister-looking mug next to her face, she had awakened with a frightened jerk.

In addition to that nuisance, the wet tent had taken on a peculiar smell from their soggy bodies and the mud and wet leaves that had been tracked all over the floor during the night. No, she decided, it wasn't exactly a suite at the Ritz.

"I want to make a quick breakfast of it and get going," Nat said.

"What do you mean? Get going where?" Frowning, Freddie propped herself up on her elbows.

"Never mind that." He started to move away on his knees. "Just get your pretty little self out of my sleeping bag. I'll heat what's left of the coffee on the camp stove. There's a package of biscuits we can eat."

Since it was still raining, Nat did the breakfast preparations inside the tent. Freddie was forced to put herself together in front of him. Of course, she was fully dressed from the night before. Still, it made her feel vulnerable and self-conscious to crawl from the covers rumpled, with her eyelashes stuck together from sleep.

"Bathroom's that way," he said, pinning back the tent flap and pointing in a direction opposite to the one in which his radio was hidden. "Pinky will accompany you, and you can wear my slicker."

"Thanks." Freddie slipped on the rain gear and went outside. She was thinking that she could circle around to the radio, but when she tried it a few minutes later, Pinky suddenly started to bark because Nat had called his name. Hurriedly she retraced her steps and jogged back to the tent.

Nat was standing outside wearing an impatient expression. Water had plastered his hair and moustache down so that they looked almost dark brown instead of their natural pale gold.

"You're going to catch something if you stand out in the rain like that," she told him.

He eyed her wryly. "I've already caught something I don't need, and I'm going to be a lot wetter before the day is through."

Freddie didn't reply, but as she huddled inside the tent and sipped coffee, she shot Nat a speculative glance. She wished she could figure him out. He obviously regarded her as a nuisance, which wasn't surprising since she'd messed up his plans and threatened him with his own gun. But he didn't have to give her his sleeping bag last night or his slicker this morning. He was sharing his food and medical supplies equally, and except for the incident over the glider's wing, he'd done her no physical harm.

That made Freddie think back to yesterday's kiss. It had begun as a punishment, a way to keep her quiet. But she knew, and so must he, that it had quickly turned into something quite different. Whatever she might think of his life-style, Freddie was too honest not to acknowledge that she was attracted to him physically. After that kiss she had to believe the feeling was mutual. Yet he was keeping her at arm's length. The more she saw of Nat Steele, the more of a puzzle he seemed.

He stood up, tossed the remains of coffee outside, and began methodically to stow gear in his backpack. "Time to get ready and go," he told her.

"Go where?"

"For a nice long walk." He rolled up the sleeping bag and stuffed it into a waterproof cover.

"A nice long walk in the rain?"

"Yep." After he'd lashed his bedroll to the bottom of the backpack's aluminum frame, he picked up the damp slicker and handed it to her. "Don't worry. I'll be the one getting wet, not you."

"A person would have to be inside a time capsule not to get wet out there." Reluctantly, she put her arms through the sleeves of the protective garment. A few minutes later, Nat struck the tent, and they set off through the dripping forest. Other than his hat and light jacket, Nat had no protection from the downpour. Freddie guessed that the pack he'd shouldered must weigh close to a hundred pounds.

"Don't get cute and try to use this on me," he warned when he stopped to find her a walking stick. "If you do, I'm likely to break it over your head. After the night I had, I feel about as good-natured as a porcupine with an itch."

Freddie had to smile. "I won't," she promised. She'd learned yesterday that using anything less than a machine gun against Nat Steele would get her nowhere.

As they continued on, Freddie tried not to think about how miserable she felt. As if the cuts and bruises she'd acquired yesterday weren't bad enough, she was now stiff all over from the night spent on the damp ground. With the overcast skies and rain, the temperature had dropped sharply. She could feel her goosebumps sprouting goosebumps. Her light canvas sneakers hadn't been built for hiking in the mountains during a monsoon. The morning had barely begun and already they were sodden lumps.

For the first couple of hours, Nat and Freddie walked in relative silence. Even Pinky, plodding along with his head down, seemed subdued by the weather. From time to time Freddie surreptitiously checked her compass heading and kept a lookout for landmarks, of which there were plenty. She was particularly struck by an outcropping of rock that looked almost like a castle. Beyond it a gorge plunged to a rushing river. As she struggled to get her bearings, she wondered if it was the same river she'd seen when she was looking for a place to land her glider.

Even in the fog and rain the area they were traveling through was wildly beautiful. Enormously tall pines loomed like sentinels, and beneath them the stony terrain was carpeted with laurel, oak scrub, sourwood, and dogwood. Except for the noises they were making while hiking, a steady drip from the trees along with an occasional bird call were the only sounds. Freddie supposed it all had a kind of surreal charm, but at last she wearied of the oppressive silence and tried to engage her captor in conversation.

"Why won't you tell me where we're going? Are you planning to push me off the top of a waterfall or wall me into a cave?"

He answered without breaking his steady stride. "Nothing like that. You'll have a warm, dry bed to sleep in tonight. And so will I, thank God!"

"As long as it's not the same bed."

From under his hat he shot her a caustic glance. "You like to play with fire, don't you?"

"What?"

"Don't look so innocent. You know what I mean."

Freddie did know, and she regretted her unconsidered remark. She wasn't sure why she had made it. It was almost as if she were trying to goad Nat into approaching her sexually. But surely she couldn't be so foolish as to want anything like that. "I wasn't flirting," she said.

"Weren't you?"

"No, I wasn't."

"Well, keep it that way. You're safe from me as long as you want to be safe. But bear in mind that right now I have a short fuse."

She cocked her head and caught a drip of water on her nose. "Why? Because you didn't get much sleep last night?"

"Because of a lot of things." He stopped, casually reached out, and brushed the water away from her nose and then looked to his left. "There is a cave around here, as a matter of fact. I'd like to take a break and have something to eat before we push on."

That sounded like an excellent idea to Freddie. She'd been too proud to admit how rotten she felt, but she was ready to drop. Gladly, she followed him toward a sharp rise that was covered with scrubby growth. The cave turned out to be nothing more than a hollow, but it provided enough protection from the steady downpour that Freddie could brush back the hood of Nat's slicker, unsnap it, and pull its clammy neckline away from her throat.

"Why don't you take that thing off?" Nat asked as he struggled out of his backpack. "I know it's not comfortable when you have to wear it a long time."

"I'm cold."

He frowned. "Yes, of course you are. I'd offer you my jacket, but it's soaked."

It was, too. Underneath his sodden clothes, the man must be wet to the skin, Freddie thought. "You're probably feeling a lot worse than I am."

"I'm all right. I would like something to eat, though. There's bread and smoked meat in my pack. How about putting together a couple of sandwiches?"

This was the first time Nat had asked her to do

anything useful, and Freddie had mixed feelings about complying. Since she was an unwilling participant in this wretched journey, she felt as if she should refuse to cooperate whenever possible. On the other hand, was there anything to be gained by balking at making sandwiches that she'd be eating as well as he? Finally, she muttered, "Okay," and undid the pack.

"I wish we could have a fire," she remarked a few minutes later. Nat was sitting with his back against the cave wall, his long legs stretched out before him. In his hand he held the sandwich she'd just made, which was no more than two roughly hacked slices of homemade bread with a slab of meat jammed between. She squatted down opposite him in the narrow passage and took a bite of her own. It tasted delicious.

"As wet as it is, I'd have a devil of a fight getting a blaze started," Nat responded to her statement. "Besides, we don't really have the time."

"You're in a big hurry to get where we're going, aren't you? Will you break down and tell me where it is?"

While he chewed on a large bite of sandwich, he eyed her expressionlessly, and Freddie found her gaze lingering on the golden stubble that roughened his face. From what she could see of his mouth beneath his moustache, his lips were not full. In fact, his mouth had a rather ascetic cast to it. But it hadn't felt ascetic when it had been pressed to hers the day before.

"You know, most women with any sense in your situation would just shut up and hope for the best. But not you," he said after he'd swallowed. "You never stop pushing, do you?"

For reasons she didn't understand, Freddie felt insulted. "Are you calling me a pushy female? Listen, I have every right to know what you're planning to do with me."

He looked up at the cave's ceiling and laughed. "I feel sorry for your boyfriend. You can't be an easy woman to live with."

Nat waited for one of the sharp retorts he'd learned to expect from his feisty captive. But this time she said nothing.

Surprised, he looked at her sharply. She had turned her face away so that he had a clear view of her profile with its firm jaw, full lower lip, and small, straight nose. He knew she wasn't wearing any makeup and that he was seeing her under the most unfavorable of circumstances, yet she looked damned good. He liked those dark brows of hers that guarded her expressive deep-set eyes. And he liked her tousled curls. This morning, she hadn't been able to do anything more than finger-comb them and they were damp from the rain, yet they looked delicious. She looked delicious.

"Did I hit a nerve?" he asked. His gaze went to her hands. "No rings, I notice, so you're not married. But I figure a girl as pretty as you must have a boyfriend."

"I'm a woman, not a girl."

"All right." He finished off his sandwich and put up his hand in a conciliatory gesture. "You look about fifteen right now, but you're a woman. And a very pretty one," he added. "I wasn't kidding about that."

Ignoring the compliment, but at the same time taking note of it, Freddie said, "I don't have any boyfriends at the moment."

"Why? Did one of my sex do you wrong?"

She shot him an angry look. "Yes, as a matter of fact. Although I don't know why I'm answering you. It's certainly none of your business."

"You're right," he agreed. He gave the remains of his sandwich to Pinky. "But you're the one who wanted to talk. There's really nothing else to have a conversation about but the weather." He pointed out the mouth of the cave at the gray downpour. "Would you like to discuss the rain?"

"Of course not."

"Then maybe we'd better get going." He dusted his hands off and then got to his feet. "We've already stayed here too long, anyway. I'm beginning to stiffen up."

Feeling miffed as well as uncomfortable, Freddie pushed herself up off the ground, too. "After spending the day in the cold and wet like this, it'll be a miracle if we both don't need to be hospitalized. Or are you actually trying to give me pneumonia?"

Nat only laughed. "You're too mad at me to let a bug get you right now."

After she'd refastened the slicker and he'd hoisted the pack, they resumed their journey. For a while they hiked along with only the squish of their soggy shoes between them. Now and then Nat shot Freddie a quick look. She trudged beside him with her head down and her brows knit. He sensed that she was angry—not just because this trip was such an ordeal, but also because of the personal questions he'd asked while they were having lunch at the cave. And on both counts she had a right to be irritated. The hike was unavoidable, but the questions hadn't been. He didn't know what had gotten into him back there. Last night, he'd promised himself to keep as much distance from Ms. Frederica Davenport as possible.

Nevertheless, curiosity nagged at him. What man had done her wrong? And what had she meant by that, anyway? Finally, he cleared his throat, and against all his better judgment, he commented, "Since we're stuck with each other, we might as well know enough so that we don't step on each other's toes. You're not wearing any rings now, but I gather that you were engaged or married at one time."

It was a moment before Freddie answered. "Neither of those. I was living with someone."

"I see." Although his voice was cool, this information created a disturbance in the vicinity of Nat's gut. He definitely didn't like the mental image of Freddie in another man's arms that his imagination had instantly conjured up.

Freddie read disapproval in his tone. "Since you know nothing about it, you can't 'see' anything," she retorted defensively. "I'm not the sort of person who's casual about living with a man. I was serious about Carter."

Pinky suddenly veered off into the woods after a squirrel, and Nat stopped to shout after him. When the dog trotted back, Nat turned toward Freddie.

"By 'serious' you mean that you were in love with him, or that you wanted to get married, or both?"

"All of it—everything."

He eyed her. Not many women were so forthright about what he had long ago concluded was their genetic drive to lasso a man. "Haven't you heard that marriage is a passé institution?"

"Now you sound like Carter." Her voice was scornful. "I've had it up to here with that shallow line, and I've seen enough open relationships to know what a lot of malarkey they are." She dabbed away some drops of water that had gathered in her long black eyelashes like tiny jewels. "As far as I'm concerned, marriage, home, and family are not out of fashion."

"You're a lady who knows what she wants."

"I'm twenty-five years old." She sniffed. "I should have some idea about that by this time, don't you think?"

"And marriage, with a rose-covered cottage thrown in, is it?"

Her jaw had taken on that mulish cast that, against all logic, he was beginning to find appealing. "Yes. I want a life with someone who's going to care enough to stick around and build something with me."

"But your boyfriend, this Carter guy, couldn't see things your way?"

"No. He wanted to keep his freedom. So I told him he was welcome to it—without me." Freddie plodded along, unconscious that her lower lip was sticking out again and that her blue eyes were sparkling with bitter emotions. She told herself she must have just about recovered from her year with Carter. If she could talk about him and feel angry instead of wanting to throw herself on the ground and weep, then she'd made a lot of progress.

"Who was this guy?" Nat demanded gruffly. "A disc jockey, by any chance?"

"Yes."

"I should have guessed you'd fall for someone like that."

"What do you mean, 'someone like that'? He was as witty and charming as they come and almost as good-looking as his voice made him sound."

"All right, all right. What happened to him?"

There was another little silence. "After we split up, he left the station for bigger things in New York City." Freddie's expression grew remote. She was remembering her ex-lover's parting words: "Good-bye, blue eyes. If you get to missing me, all you have to do is pick up the phone."

She had suffered after their breakup. It had been like losing a vital part of her body. Love was like that, she told herself. It could make you ecstatic, but it could also flay you. That was why a woman had to be careful about who she loved. That was why, even though she'd sat home alone for months after Carter left, she'd never picked up the phone.

Freddie squared her shoulders and lifted her head. "You've been giving me the third degree," she said to Nat. "How about your love life? Are you married or engaged? Do you have someone special?"

"No to all three."

"A good-looking guy like you?" She shot him a disbelieving glance. "What are you, the love them and leave them type?"

"I guess you might say that. Haven't got much choice in the matter, actually."

"What do you mean?"

His gray eyes were amused. "In my line of work, you can't afford to make too many commitments."

Freddie stiffened. Again, she'd almost forgotten who and what this man was. "I'll bet," she said coldly.

After that all conversation ceased. As the afternoon lengthened, Freddie was too tired and wet to do anything but put one foot in front of the other. At one point she stumbled and fell into a pile of soaking leaves.

"Watch your feet," Nat said as he helped her up.

She gave him a scathing look. "That's about all I can do. I don't think these cold wet things attached to my ankles really belong to me anymore—I can't feel them."

She had expected a sarcastic retort, but instead his expression was sympathetic. "I know. It's been a rough day. But it's just about over."

"What do you mean?" A dart of fear pierced Freddie's breast, and her gaze went to the rifle that he held loosely in his left hand. What if she'd misjudged him? What if his lack of aggression toward her had merely been an act, and he'd brought her deep into this wilderness so that her lifeless body would never be found?

"We're nearly there," he told her, still supporting her elbow.

She tugged free and shivered. "Nearly where?"

"You'll see." He guided her toward a slope fringed at the top with a row of pines interspersed by dogwood.

Freddie's numb feet had dragged before, but now they were lead weights. By the time they reached the top, Nat was almost carrying her. As he all but hauled her through the trees, her teeth chattered. Then he stopped.

Her eyes widened, and she stared. "This is it?"

"This is the place."

CHAPTER FIVE

From the high ground where Freddie and Nat stood, the land dipped into a small, misty valley. She could just make out several buildings through the grayish veils that hung in the air. As she surveyed the eerie scene, she thought of Brigadoon, the ghostly Scottish village that rose out of the fog every hundred years.

She cast Nat an inquiring look. "Someone lives here?"

"The Parker family. This is their land."

"But you said we were in the Cohutta Wilderness."

"We are. There are a few isolated parcels of privately owned property in the Wilderness." He pointed down into the fog-shrouded valley. "This is one of them. The Parkers have owned this land since before the Civil War." He took her hand. "Come on. There'll be a warm fire and a roof over our heads down there. No sense staying out in the rain any longer than we have to."

Freddie agreed with that in principle. Nevertheless, as they made their way down the slippery terrain, she hung back, her gaze fixed nervously on the complex of low, dark buildings ahead. Who was inside them? A bunch of hoodlums, drug people like Nat—only less civilized?

"Come on," Nat urged as they approached the largest building. "Nobody's going to hurt you, if that's what's making you drag your feet."

"I'm dragging them because they're so numb they don't feel as if they belong to me anymore," Freddie retorted stoutly, although her heart was thudding in her chest.

The building was the simplest of structures—nothing more than a big log cabin. It had a sagging porch and roughly glazed windows through which light flickered. When she and Nat stepped up onto the low porch, a dog started to bark and several hounds appeared, seemingly from nowhere. It was obvious from the way they faced off with Pinky but still kept their distance that they knew and respected him.

Nat threw a few curt words in their direction and they slunk away. Just then, the cabin's front door was thrown open, and a tiny old woman stood framed in the light. Her gray hair was done up in a thin braid coiled on top of her head like a crown. She wore a limp dress that was faded from many years of washing and a black sweater that had been made for a person twice her size. Still, with her straight posture and bright eyes, she was a regal figure.

"Nat Steele!" she cried. "I thought you might be scramblin' back this way." Her gaze went to Freddie's forlorn shape, and she cocked her head. "My land, what kind of a fish have you caught yourself?"

"Let us in where it's dry, and I'll tell you all about it," Nat said.

"Step yourselves into the house this minute. Isn't fit out there for nothin' but frogs and nightcrawlers." So saying, she moved to one side. But when Pinky tried to sidle into the cabin, she held up a forbidding hand. "Not you, you ugly critter. You go back to the shed with the other mutts. There's a fox been sniffin' around my henhouse. Maybe your ugly face will keep those no-account hounds from sleepin' through its next visit."

Unhappily, Pinky turned back.

"Why are you so mean to my dog?" Nat protested. "He's cold and wet, too."

"Because, as you very well know, it gives a body the creeps to look at him," she said, closing the door with a decisive thrust. "And when he's wet, he smells like a skunk! Beats me how a handsome man like you can stand to own anything so sinful-looking."

"Beats me how an old lady like you can be so pretty and ornery at the same time," Nat answered, giving up the argument. He kissed her on the cheek.

Freddie stood listening to this exchange in a kind of trance. The old lady was so different from what she had been expecting that she felt disoriented.

"Well, don't stand there gapin', girl. Take off that wet coat and come over here by the fire where you can get yourself warmed up." The woman turned her attention back to Nat. "Lordy, you're wetter than a drowned slug. Take off them soggy clothes this minute, do you hear?"

Obediently, Nat removed his hat and then stripped away his jacket and shirt. As Freddie moved over to the fire that was crackling cheerfully in a potbellied stove that protruded from an open hearth, her hostess disappeared into a back room. Almost immediately she returned, laden with towels and a pile of dry clothing.

"Nat, you young fool, don't you think you should

introduce me to your lady friend?" she scolded as she began to sort through the garments.

"Freddie," Nat began, "this is Granny Parker, the toughest seventy-year-old in the state of Georgia. And Granny"—he swept a bow at Freddie—"this is Ms. Frederica Davenport, who by the time she's your age will probably run a close second in the tough-old-lady department."

Chuckling, Granny turned to Freddie, who was still shivering in front of the stove. "Delighted to meet you, Miss Davenport."

"Oh, call me Freddie, please."

"I'm proud to welcome you, Freddie. Now, just to save Nat's modesty, come on with me into the back room, where I can get some dry things for you, too."

Freddie cast a quick look at Nat. Naked to the waist, he had just bent over to remove his shoes and socks. His wet jeans clung to his narrow flanks and muscular legs like a second skin.

"Granny, you know I have no shame," he said, glancing up and slanting a wicked wink in Freddie's direction.

Averting her face, Freddie followed her hostess out of the main room and into a small back bedroom. When she was alone with Granny, she wondered what to do. Should she throw herself on the old woman's mercy and beg for protection from Nat? But why would he have brought her to this place if he didn't regard Granny as an ally? Then again, he wasn't actually threatening her. Freddie decided to hold her tongue until she got a better fix on the situation.

Granny's bedroom was simply furnished with one crudely constructed pine chest and a bed to match.

The furniture and walls were unpainted. A faded but still lovely homemade quilt provided the only color.

"It's beautiful," Freddie murmured, fingering the intricately pieced-together spread.

"Made it for my bride bed many a year ago," Granny supplied briskly. "Now, let's see what we're to do about you." Critically, she scrutinized Freddie's shorts and scratched knees. "Lord, that Nat has no sense takin' a gal out walking in such an outfit on such a day. But he's a man, don't you know."

Freddie smiled. "Does that explain it?"

"It explains a lot of the foolishness in this world."

Granny opened the chest and, after rummaging around, withdrew an old sweater and dress similar to the ones she wore. On top of this she placed a pair of long woolen stockings and a flannel nightgown. "You put this on," she said, tapping the nightgown, "and climb under that quilt for a spell. Supper's not for a couple of hours yet, and you look about to drop."

Freddie received the suggestion with a nod and a grateful smile. She hadn't realized how exhausted she was until she'd seen the large, inviting bed. Now she felt as if she couldn't keep her eyes open another minute. Plopping down on the edge of the quilt, she struggled to push off her shoes.

"Look at them things!" Granny exclaimed. "They're all in tatters. You'll never get those on your feet again."

It was true. The light canvas sneakers had all but dissolved. They hardly looked like shoes anymore, and they fell to the floor in shapeless lumps.

Sighing with disgust, the woman picked them up and held them out at arm's length. "These things aren't good for anything but to get throwed away."

She squinted down at Freddie's feet. "You got long toes on you. None of my shoes or Vandy's would fit you, but maybe one of the boys has something."

Freddie's eyes were all but closed, and she was too tired to even ask who Vandy or the boys were. Mumbling her thanks, she allowed her hostess to tuck her under the warm quilt. Then, like stepping off the edge of a cliff blindfolded, she plummeted into oblivion.

Granny gave her unexpected guest one last look, shook her head, and pursed her lips. Then she shut the door and went back out to the cabin's main room. There, after dumping Freddie's ruined shoes into a trash bin, she descended on Nat.

"Now, just tell me what you've been up to," she demanded. "Who in tarnation is that girl?"

Nat, who had changed into the loose-fitting pair of jeans and faded red flannel shirt that Granny had supplied, was standing with his hands stretched out to the fire in the stove.

"It's a long story."

"And I'd relish to hear it." She sat down on a low wooden stool and folded her hands expectantly.

Nat chuckled and then gave a brief account of his meeting with Freddie.

"Well, if that don't beat everything," Granny exclaimed when he finished the story. "Flew in on an airplane with no motor! Now I've heard it all." She cast a backward look at the closed bedroom door. "She's right pretty, don't you think?"

When Nat didn't comment, Granny shot him a sharp look. "Right troublesome, too, I'm thinkin', showing up just now when everything's hanging by a thread."

"You could say that."

"I just did. Now tell me what you're planning to do about her."

Nat turned and folded his arms over his chest. "I can stay until the rain lets up. I wanted to be here for the music, anyway."

"Just where will she be sleepin'?"

"In my cabin."

Granny eyed him.

"She needs watching, and I'm the best one to do it," he pointed out.

"And after you're gone?"

"Then someone else, maybe Jeremy, will have to keep an eye on her. I'll speak to him about it." He rubbed the back of his neck. "It's only going to be a matter of a few days."

Granny sighed. "I surely hope you're right. This business has put more gray hairs in my head than forty years of married life." She grimaced. "Vandy sure isn't going to like you taking that Freddie girl off to your cabin."

"Where is Vandy?"

"Down with Marshall and Lou. If she knew you was warmin' yourself by the stove here, she'd be up in a flash." The old woman pinned Nat with an interrogative look.

"I'm thirty years old," he answered her unspoken question gently. "Vandy is only fifteen."

"That's old for a mountain girl," Granny snapped back. "Why, I was younger than that by a year when I married her great-grandpa, and I made him a good wife."

"I don't doubt it. But I'm not looking for a wife."

Granny sighed again. "Poor Vandy. I don't know what's to be done with her. Seems like she gets one dream after another in her head, and none of them has the least chance of coming true." The old woman looked off into space for a moment, then shrugged philosophically. "Oh well, we all have our disappointments in life. Now, I have work to do. Supper'll be here tonight, and that means, counting you and Miss Freddie in there, ten mouths to feed. You have some work to do yourself," she added, rising to her feet. "You need to set up an extry bed in your cabin and get a fire going to dry out this infernal damp."

Freddie awoke with a jerk. A candle was shining in her face, dazzling her so that she couldn't see who stood at the foot of her bed.

"Food will be on in just a mite," a female voice informed her coolly. "I'll leave my cousin Jeremy's shoes here by the bed." There was a thud as the shoes were dropped to the floor. Then the candle was placed on the pine chest and whoever had spoken glided out of the room and shut the door behind her.

Blinking, Freddie struggled up onto her elbows. It was a full minute before she even knew where she was. Then it all came back: Nat, the marijuana field, the horrible hike in the rain, and this place—whatever this place was. Groaning, Freddie rubbed a hand over her forehead. All she wanted was to crawl back under the quilt and pull it up over her head. But that was impossible. It was time to find out where she was and just what this was all about.

Throwing back the covers, she crawled out of bed and stood up. Through the walls she could hear the drone of male voices. Putting her ear against the door, she listened intently. There were definitely men out there, but how many? After Granny Parker's kindness, Freddie was less inclined to believe that she was in immediate danger. But she wasn't about to make any naïve assumptions.

The clothes Granny had gotten out for her lay neatly folded on top of the pine chest. Freddie held the faded dress up and grimaced. Even in the candlelight she could see that it was about as shapeless as a flour sack. Yet she needed a change of clothes, and her hostess might be insulted if she ignored her offering.

Shrugging, Freddie pulled the nightgown up over her head and stepped into the tired old dress. Then she slipped on the sweater and stockings that completed the outfit. At least they were warm—an important consideration in this damp chill. Once dressed, she looked around for cousin Jeremy's shoes. When she spotted them, she put a hand over her mouth to muffle a laugh.

They were a pair of men's army boots—a small size to be sure, but still army boots. She would look like she'd just stepped out of Dogpatch, Freddie thought as she slipped her feet into the sturdy clodhoppers.

Actually, they weren't a bad fit. Straightening, Freddie twirled around. The boots clumped noisily. She wished there were a mirror in the room so that she could see herself. But she could guess what her appearance must be.

"Well," she murmured under her breath, "now that Cinderella is dressed for the ball, it's time to summon her coach and be off."

Throwing back her shoulders, Freddie opened the door and stepped out into the main living area. Her emergence was greeted by seven pairs of curious eyes.

On the left side of the room, three husky-looking young men, all of them wearing tattered jeans and badly in need of haircuts, lounged in front of the stove.

Freddie guessed that their ages ranged from somewhere around seventeen to perhaps twenty-five. To the right a middle-aged couple sat side by side on a wooden bench. The woman was knitting and the man was whittling at what looked like some sort of musical instrument. Nearby, Nat and a young boy of about fourteen played a game of checkers.

Nat saw her and pushed back his chair. As he got to his feet, he looked her up and down. Then a slow smile spread over his handsome features, and he crossed the room toward her.

"Sleeping beauty has arisen."

"Yes, my lord, fresh from her latest cover for *Vogue.*" Freddie managed a curtsy, then allowed Nat to take her hand and lead her farther into the room. As he did so, her gaze darted nervously between the small groupings of strangers staring back at her. She considered blurting out her true predicament and begging for help, but her instincts warned her not to do that. She decided to bide her time.

"Frederica Davenport, I'd like to present you to Mr. and Mrs. Jim Parker and their son Jeremy," Nat said. "Jim is Granny's youngest son."

"Pleased to meet you, Miss Davenport." The older couple nodded and smiled, and the boy dipped his head shyly.

"Oh, please call me Freddie."

"And you can call us Martha and Jim," the woman told her with a sweet smile. Her husband had gone back to his whittling, but she seemed eager to carry on the conversation. "We live in the whitewashed cabin back yonder. You'll find me there most anytime. I'd be proud to have you stop by and share a cup of tea."

Touched, Freddie assured Martha that she would. Yet where she would be staying herself, and for how long and under what conditions, was still a mystery. To the boy she said, "I guess I have you to thank for my shoes."

He blushed violently. "Weren't nothin'."

"Well, I thank you for them."

Angling her toward the fireplace, Nat presented the three young men. "And these are Marshall and Lou Parker. They live in their own cabin, too. Their friend, Hap Morgan here, is just visiting. He works in Atlanta."

Freddie studied the three faces uneasily. With varying degrees of male appreciation, they gazed speculatively back at her. The two Parkers, with their brown eyes, reddish sandy hair, and lanky builds, bore a striking family resemblance. Their friend, Hap, was stockier, with a squarish face and gray eyes. It seemed to Freddie that he was studying her with a mixture of suspicion and leering amusement. Freddie looked away. Suddenly, she wondered just what Nat had told these people about her.

A moment later, Granny and a beautiful young girl came into the room bearing platters of food.

"Supper's on," Granny called out cheerily. "Find yourselves a seat, and don't be shy."

As Nat escorted her to the table, Freddie looked around curiously. When she'd first stepped inside Granny Parker's cabin, she'd been too exhausted and apprehensive to notice much. Now she studied her surroundings with interest.

It was a simply built cabin with a large main room. The two back rooms consisted of the bedroom where Freddie had slept and what she guessed must be a kitchen. Although it was rustic in the extreme, the main living area had charm.

It was dominated by the enormous, open-hearth stone fireplace from which the stove protruded. Close to the kitchen entry a long trestle table, around which the family now crowded, had been set up. A few simple rag rugs lay scattered on the floor, which, although it had never been waxed, was very clean. The pictures tacked on to the walls were a whimsical mix of old family photographs and pages cut from magazines. Except for one ragged overstuffed chair and matching sofa, the furniture looked homemade. The untreated wooden walls and floor had acquired an appealing patina from time and living. And the fire in the open stove cast a homey glow.

"Oh Lord, for what we are about to receive, we thank you," Granny said. Then everybody dug in.

The meal, too, was simple: fried chicken, mashed potatoes, corn muffins, home-preserved green beans, and tomatoes. To Freddie, who hadn't seen decent hot food in two days, it was a banquet. Like everyone else around the table, she concentrated on loading her plate.

It wasn't until she had filled most of the emptiness in her stomach that she looked up from her food and focused on the young girl who she guessed had brought Jeremy's shoes into her bedroom earlier. She was seated almost opposite Freddie, eating from her earthenware plate with the natural grace and daintiness of an untutored princess. She was also staring at Nat as if he and not the fried chicken were the most delicious thing at the table.

Disturbed by the observation, Freddie put her fork down, adjusted her skirt, and sat up straighter in her chair. The movement attracted the girl's attention away from Nat just long enough for her to shoot Freddie a jealous glare.

Freddie's eyes widened. Then her teeth clenched as her earlier suspicions were confirmed. Nat must have told the Parkers she was his girl friend. That was the only explanation for the poisonous look she'd just received from this young mountain beauty who obviously cherished an adolescent crush on him.

Guardedly, Freddie studied her. This must be the Vandy Granny had mentioned. She really was a beauty. Her eyes, although brown like the other Parkers', were large and the rich color of milk chocolate. Her skin was creamy, and her thick, straight hair, which hung down past her waist, had a reddish cast that caught and held the flickering lights from the oil lamp in the center of the table. She was already lovely, Freddie mused. It wouldn't be long before she was an absolutely stunning woman.

Freddie turned toward Granny, who sat at the head of the table ladling out second servings of mashed potatoes. Had the old woman ever been as pretty as her granddaughter? Looking at her lined face, such fresh beauty was hard to imagine. She might be spry, but she showed all the signs of having lived a hard life.

The platter was passed down to Hap, who sat at the foot of the table next to Lou and Marshall. Glancing his way, Freddie observed that he was staring at Vandy with the same kind of concentration that Vandy was directing toward Nat—only where her expression was worshipful, his was avid.

"Vandy, you planning on favoring us with a song tomorrow night?" Hap asked, breaking the silence that had been punctuated only by the clink of active knives and forks.

Tearing her gaze away from Nat, the girl gave him a startled look. "Why yes, I expect so."

"What song are you planning on singing?"

Vandy's expression became hooded. "I haven't made up my mind about that yet."

"How about 'Down by the Garden Gate My Love Lies Waiting'?"

Flushing with anger, Vandy averted her face. "That's not a song I cotton to." Deliberately ignoring Hap, she turned back toward Nat. "Will you play something for us?"

"I guess." He caught Freddie's puzzled expression and explained. "Tomorrow night, you're in for a treat. There's going to be a concert. It's an annual event in these parts. Several mountain musicians will be trekking in from as far away as South Carolina just to play their brand of old-time music."

"Old-time music?"

"Yes. Not the canned stuff you hear on radio, but the real thing."

"They're going to hike into these mountains in this weather?" Freddie was incredulous.

"A mite of rain never stopped a tough old banjo picker like Pete Lorden," Granny interjected. "And nothing short of Judgment Day would keep Bill Hooper away, either."

Next to his mother, Jim Parker chuckled good-humoredly and tugged at his thick, grizzled beard. "I sure am looking forward to seeing that old son of a gun. Now, he's one prime fiddle player."

"No better than you are on the autoharp," Martha chimed in stoutly.

When almost everyone at the table loudly agreed to that, Jim beamed with pleasure.

"Why, he's just comin' because you make the best fiddles in the mountains," Martha added.

"Best fiddles anywhere, for that matter," Marshall sang out. "Now, how about passing that fried chicken down this way again?"

Everyone chuckled, and the platter once more began its journey toward the end of the table. When it finally came back, the serving dishes were empty and so were the plates. Coffee and several sweet potato pies finished up the banquet. By that stage of the meal Freddie was so stuffed that she had to refuse the scrumptious-looking dessert. Nat, however, dug in with gusto.

"Granny, that was delicious," he finally said, wiping his mouth with his napkin and then patting his stomach. "And you too, Vandy," he added, looking across the table at the teen-ager. "I'll bet you made those corn muffins."

She nodded eagerly and blushed. "It's a special way I have. I put honey in them and some mashed-up cranberries."

"Well, they were wonderful. If you don't mind, I'd like to take some home with me so that Freddie and I can have them for breakfast tomorrow."

Instantly, the pleased look on Vandy's face was wiped away. She looked from Nat to Freddie and back. "Is she going to be staying in your cabin tonight?"

"Yep." As if sensing the protest Freddie was about to sputter, he grabbed her hand under the table and squeezed it hard. Above the table where everyone could see, he put a loverlike arm around her shoulder. "Freddie and I have been sweet on each other for close to a year now, haven't we, honey?" Leaning over her, he stared meaningfully into her face. There was a smile on his lips but a warning in his gray eyes.

Swallowing her objection, Freddie stammered, "Why, yes. In fact," she added on a sudden inspiration, "I wouldn't be surprised if we got married soon."

That was greeted by a raucous guffaw from the young men at the foot of the table.

"Why, Nat, you old devil you," Marshall crowed, jabbing Lou in his ribs. "I'll be damned if I ever figured you for a marrying kind of man. All this time, I thought you just liked to play the field."

Nat shot Freddie one last glittering look and then answered Marshall. "That's what I thought, too, but then I met Freddie here, and she turned my world upside down. Didn't you, sugar?"

"I sure hope so," she returned sweetly. "I know that's exactly what I'd like to do."

While everyone else at the table chortled, Nat gazed back at Freddie. Vandy stared down at her plate, her expression stormy. Suddenly she pushed back her chair with a scrape so abrupt that it toppled over backward. Ignoring it, she fled the room.

"Now where in creation is that crazy girl going?" Martha complained. She craned her head and stared after her.

"Just never you mind," Granny retorted, standing up and starting to bustle about the table. "You men go over by the fire and leave us women alone here to clean up this mess."

After a few more teasing remarks, the males ambled away, and Granny, Martha, and Freddie were left with the dishes. As Freddie helped carry platters and bowls back to the kitchen, she thought about what had just happened. Putting herself in Vandy's place, she felt sorry for the young girl. It was obvious that her romantic illusions had just been cruelly shattered. How could Nat be so insensitive? Freddie wondered.

Granny Parker's kitchen was almost as primitive as the rest of the house. An unvarnished wooden table dominated the center of the room. Crudely made pine cabinets lined the walls, along with another wood stove, where water for washing the dishes had been heating in a large kettle. There was a pump over a tin sink and a vintage icebox.

"We got an ice house and a generator out back for when we want to play the radio," Granny explained as Freddie set down a stack of dishes near the sink.

"I think you do very well for being so cut off from things," Freddie commented politely.

"I used to think so myself." Granny put a pan in the sink and poured soap powder and hot water into it. "But these young'uns . . ." She sighed. "They all want city things, don't you know. The Parker family ain't what it used to be. Why, there are two empty cabins out back now. Them cabins used to be full up with my grandkids."

"They come back to visit Thanksgiving," Martha pointed out as she scraped bits of food into a pail.

"Is Vandy your granddaughter?" Freddie asked.

Granny threw her head back and laughed. "Lordy, no. Vandy is my great-grandchild. I had her grandma when I wasn't but sixteen. She's dead now, and her daughter run off when Vandy wasn't but a baby." She pulled a dish out of sudsy water and handed it to Freddie to dry.

As Freddie polished the cracked plate, she tried not to let her face reflect her feelings. At twenty-five she was just now beginning to think seriously about marriage and children. These mountain women were grandmothers before they were thirty.

"Where are your other children?" she asked.

"All gone away to the city. Marshall and Lou are my second daughter's grandbabies and they got left behind for me to raise, too." Granny accepted a freshly scraped stack of plates from Martha and plunged them into the soapy water. "Jim's the only one that stayed on. When his first wife died without giving him any young'uns, he married Martha here and she had Jeremy." She glanced over her thin shoulder at Martha. "I shore hope you all don't take it into your heads to up and leave me by myself. I know Marshall and Lou are itchin' to go down to Atlanta to stay and probably will one of these days."

"We aren't going anywhere," Martha said, giving the old woman a reassuring pat on the back. "Where else but here in the mountains could a dreamer like my Jim live? You know all he wants to do is whittle on his instruments and take long walks in the woods hummin' to himself."

Granny chuckled. "You're right. He was never good for nothin' much but dreamin'. Just like Vandy." She shook her head.

At that moment Nat poked his head into the doorway. He was holding the slicker that Freddie had worn during their hike.

"You three have got this place clean already. Haven't you left anything for me to do?"

Granny snapped a dish towel at him. "You scalawag, don't try and sweet-talk me. You know you waited until there wasn't nothin' left. Just like a man!"

Grinning, Nat stepped forward and gave the little old woman a hug. Then he turned toward Freddie. "My love, it's time to say thank you and good night. We both had a long day and need to get some shut-eye." While Freddie stood goggling at him, he put his arm around her shoulder and drew her into an iron grip that looked affectionate but felt otherwise.

"Did you get a fire going in that cabin of yours so you won't freeze yourselves to death?" Granny demanded.

"It's warm and comfy, with plenty of extra blankets." As he spoke he helped Freddie put on the raincoat. Then, saluting the two older women, he led her out the back door and into the rainy night.

CHAPTER SIX

"Just what do you think you're doing?" Freddie hissed. Nat had practically carried her out into the night.

"What I said. Taking you to my cabin so you can get some sleep. You need to rest up from your terrible ordeal."

She glared up at him as he strode by her side. His arm was still clamped around her waist. "Why can't I sleep at Granny's?"

"Three reasons. For one thing, there's no room. For another, tricky as you are, you need someone like me to stand guard over you."

"And the third reason?"

Nat's teeth flashed, and he steered her toward a low structure that had suddenly appeared before them. "Vandy might murder you in your sleep if you stayed at Granny's," he said, firmly guiding her through the door.

It was a one-room cabin. A small fire crackled in the stone fireplace on the left, and a rustic table and chairs were arranged in front of it. Several stringed musical instruments, including a guitar, were leaned against the wall opposite the door, and above the mantel there were others supported by hooks. Freddie stared at them curiously. She remembered the way Nat had played the harmonica and wondered if he could bring forth music from these as well.

On the right side of the cabin, catercorner to each other, two narrow cots had been made up with old army blankets. She was pleased to see the separate sleeping arrangements but was displeased by what Nat had just said. Arms akimbo, she turned and confronted him.

"I resent you giving those people back there the idea that we're lovers."

Nat took off his hat and shook it, scattering raindrops around him. Then he unsnapped his coat. "I'm sorry if you think I've compromised your reputation. But take my word for it, the Parkers will be a lot friendlier to you if they think you're my girl friend than they would if they got the idea you're spying on them."

"Spying on them?" Freddie's jaw dropped. "Why would they think that?"

"The Parkers are marijuana farmers. If it hadn't been so dark when we got here, you'd have seen that the gardens in back of their houses are full of hemp." Having dropped this bombshell, Nat pulled an ancient wooden rocker up in front of the fire, sat down in front of it, and stretched out his legs.

Freddie didn't know what to say. Given what she knew about Nat, she supposed she shouldn't have been surprised. But that didn't change the fact that she was. She could picture those three young men growing pot—but Granny Parker?

"And while we're on the subject," Nat continued, "don't start getting any ideas when Granny's guests arrive tomorrow."

"What do you mean?"

"I mean," he said, aiming a pointed look at her from under his fair eyebrows, "don't start asking any of them to help you escape. Believe me, you'll only be making trouble for yourself. These are mountain folk, with family ties so complicated that even they can't figure them out. They also have an inbred irreverence for the law. To their way of thinking, growing marijuana is in the same category as running a still, and they've been manufacturing illegal liquor in these mountains for generations. If it looks like you're here to make trouble for the Parkers, their friends won't take it kindly. They could even get nasty."

While Freddie contemplated this warning, she undid the slicker. She hung it on one of the several rusty hooks screwed into the wall near the door, and then stood with her arms wrapped around her chest.

The fire warmed the cabin, but not nearly enough. Slowly she walked toward it, her gaze fixed resentfully on Nat, who had turned away from her. "You were using me back there, weren't you?"

Warily, he glanced up. "What do you mean?"

"That girl, Vandy, is infatuated with you. You used me to hurt her."

Nat's brows snapped together. "Hurting her was the last thing I wanted to do. But it's high time she got over her crush. Surely you don't think a man my age should be encouraging a fifteen-year-old?"

"No, but you needn't have been so cruel. You could have let her down gently."

He scowled into the fire. "I've done everything I can think of. She's as persistent as a cat with a mouse. Once she even followed me into the woods, and I had to climb a tree and hide in the leaves to get away from her."

The image made Freddie laugh. She took another step closer so that she could look down at the top of his burnished head. "Poor man! Is Vandy unusual, or do all women find you so irresistible that they chase you up trees?"

"I've been pursued before," he allowed, "but never by a female so young and so tireless. As far as the irresistible part goes—" Suddenly, he swiveled and reached up. Seizing Freddie's hand, he gave it a tug, and she found herself tumbling into his lap. "You ought to be able to answer that," he said as he grinned down into her surprised face. "Am I irresistible?"

She could feel her cheeks burning. "Not to me!" She struggled to get up, but he held her tight.

"You say that now, but yesterday in the woods when I kissed you, you kissed me back."

Her skin grew even warmer, and she looked away. "If you were a gentleman, you wouldn't mention that. It was just a mistake."

"By now you've figured out that I'm not a gentleman. And if that kiss was a mistake, it's one I've remembered with pleasure through most of last night and today." When he finished the sentence, he turned her face back to his and kissed her again.

Freddie knew she shouldn't allow it. He was holding her tightly, but not so tightly that she couldn't escape. Yet for the moment, at least, she couldn't move. Her bones seemed to have dissolved. She wasn't sure why she'd responded to that punishing kiss in the woods, but she knew why she liked this one. It was entirely different in character—warm, caressing, even friendly. Freddie had been around enough men to be able to recognize expertise. Nat Steele knew how to kiss a woman, how to mold his lips to hers and express with gentle and sensitive movements a special realm of new feeling.

The contact of his warm mouth with hers was so pleasant that she wanted the kiss to go on, wanted to see where it would lead. It was almost physically painful to draw away. Nevertheless, she managed it. In the firelight, their gazes locked and neither said a word. It was he who finally broke the thick silence.

"We do that well together, you know."

"It doesn't mean a thing."

"I know it doesn't." Leaning back, he took his hands from her waist and shoulders so that she was free to scramble off his lap. When she was on her feet, he stood up as well.

"I expect you'd like to go to bed," he said, as if nothing had just happened between them. "I'm afraid you'll have to make one more trip in the rain. The outhouse is around back. While you're getting ready for bed, I'll wait on the porch to give you some privacy."

"You don't have to do that."

He cocked his head. "You don't mind undressing in front of me?"

"I didn't mean any such thing!"

Chuckling, he crossed the room and picked up the guitar by the neck. "Remember," he warned as Freddie tossed on his slicker and headed out the door, "I'm going to time that trip to the outhouse. Don't try anything cute."

A few minutes later, Freddie came back around the

cabin. She found Nat sitting in a rocker on the sagging front porch. He was strumming his guitar.

"Where's Pinky?" she asked as she stepped up onto the weathered boards. "I thought he'd be here waiting for you."

"No, he's in the barn with the rest of the dogs. Sometimes he prefers his own kind. Though," Nat added dryly, "I can't say the same for the others. They usually stay about as far away from Pinky as they can get."

"Why? Is he as mean as he looks?"

"As long as you don't make him mad, he's as gentle as a lamb."

"And when he's mad?"

Nat shook his head and tightened a string on the guitar, plucking at it experimentally with his thumb. "His father was a pit bull. If one of those hounds were foolish enough to make Pinky mad, it wouldn't last more than ten minutes. Maybe that's why they give him plenty of room. They have sense."

Freddie wondered if by that he meant she didn't have sense. Saying no more, she went inside and shut the door. For a minute or two she stood in the center of the small room looking around. All right, she told herself, the safest thing was to go to bed. But no way was she going to take off anything more than she had to. Removing Granny's sweater and Jeremy's boots, she left the dress on and slipped under the ragged army blankets.

The fire continued to crackle, sending flickers of light across the ceiling. But as Freddie lay staring up at it, with her arms folded behind her head, she was hardly aware of the patterns of light and shadow dancing above her. Her mind was on the man outside and the sound of his guitar.

He was playing a ballad, effortlessly weaving the haunting melody through the chords. Then she heard him sing in a low, resonant baritone.

"Come nigh to me, the dawn is breaking.
My love, come nigh. It's almost day.
Stay not behind locked doors and windows.
Say you'll be my wife, and come away."

It was the same plaintive song he'd played on his mouth organ the night before. The melody was etched in her brain, only now she had words to put to it. She listened intently as he continued the song into the second verse.

"She shook her head and locked her window.
'Oh no, John Haynes, I'll say ye nay.
Though your face is fair, your land is lonesome.
I'll not be yours on my wedding day.' "

It was obvious that there must be a third verse. But Nat didn't sing it. Instead, he ran his hands across the strings and then started a new tune, one that was familiar to Freddie.

There were several verses to "Go Tell It on the Mountain," and as Nat sang them, Freddie found herself smiling and whispering the words along with him. He was good on that guitar, she thought—close to professionally good. His voice wasn't bad, either. Maybe she'd suggest that he give up the marijuana business and take up a career as a folk singer. He might make it.

For several minutes Nat strummed his guitar without singing. Then he began to croon another evocative ballad.

"It's hopeless," Freddie muttered, pushing back her blankets and swinging her feet down to the floor. She couldn't just lie there listening any longer. She put the sweater and boots back on, then crossed over to the door and opened it.

The rain fell in an opaque black curtain all around the little cabin. Nat sat on the narrow, roofed porch, rocking gently, his feet propped up on a post. He was singing "In the Pines," one of Freddie's favorites.

When he came to the refrain, she joined him. Her clear soprano blended with and underlined his deeper tones. He didn't look back, just continued to play. When the song was over, he turned and surveyed her.

"I thought you'd gone to bed."

"I tried, but I couldn't sleep."

"My singing bother you?"

"No." Freddie sat down on the porch next to him and wrapped her arms tightly around her tented knees. "I like your singing."

"I like yours, too."

Pleased, she bobbed her head in a shy acknowledgment. "You're pretty good on that guitar. I heard you on the harmonica the other night. How many instruments can you play?"

"All the ones in the cabin are mine, and I can get tunes out of them."

"All? Even the recorders?"

He nodded. "Just fair to middling, you understand. I'm not a virtuoso on any one of them."

As he ran his fingers softly over the guitar strings, she studied his shadowed profile curiously. "What was that tune you played on the harmonica last night? I heard you singing it a few minutes ago."

"Which?"

" 'Come nigh to me, the dawn is breaking.' "

"Oh, that." He ran through a series of quiet chords and then strummed the first few bars of the now-familiar melody. "It's an old mountain song I've been trying to put together."

"You mean you're writing it?"

"No. Collecting vintage tunes from these parts is a hobby of mine. I got the first verse of that one from an old lady who runs a general store and the second from a guy at a gas station who remembered his granddaddy singing it. I'm hoping to pick up another verse tomorrow night. Bill Hopper knows most if not all of the old mountain ditties."

"What do you do with these songs after you collect them?"

"Write them down so they won't be lost."

Freddie blinked and then turned her face up to his. "You mean you're a . . ." She searched her mind for the right term. "You're an ethnomusicologist?"

He laughed and reached over to ruffle her hair. "That's an awfully big word. I'd prefer to call myself a guy who likes to collect old songs."

And grow illegal marijuana, Freddie thought, her gaze straining up at him through the darkness.

"Do you know 'The Miller's Daughter'?" he asked.

"Yes."

He tightened a string and then strummed a lively chord. "All right, then. 'There was an old miller by the Northland sea . . .' "

Her voice joined his, and together they sang the many verses of the ballad, which, despite its rollicking tempo, dealt with betrayed love and murder. When it was over and the last note had died away, Freddie stared out into the rainy night. What was she doing singing folk songs with her jailor? She excused herself and slipped back into the cabin. Once again, she removed her shoes and sweater and crawled beneath the blankets.

But after she'd pulled them up around her chin, she still didn't sleep. A half hour later, when Nat came in, her eyes were wide open. She closed them as he glanced in her direction. But when he turned away to bend over the fire and bank the last dying embers, she studied him through her lashes.

Lord, but he was a handsome man. He was built the way she thought a man should be—tall and lean, without an extra ounce of flesh anywhere. In the past she'd been attracted to dark men, but as Nat's golden hair caught the last reddish streaks of the fire's dying light, she acknowledged that she was coming around to a different point of view. She focused on his profile. It was clear-cut and hard, but it held sensitivity, too. Freddie had heard that quality tonight in his music. No one could sing and play with such delicate passion and not have some poetry in his soul.

Fascinated, she watched as he unbuttoned his shirt. He apparently had none of the reservations about undressing that she'd entertained earlier—or maybe he believed she was asleep. More likely, he just didn't care. Once he'd removed his shirt, he unzipped his jeans and stepped out of those as well. He walked toward his bed wearing only briefs.

Freddie closed her eyes tight and listened to the springs creak as he got in beneath the covers. She didn't need to look his way anymore. His image was larger than life in her head now and just as vivid—his long, muscular legs and trim buttocks so clearly defined . . .

What was she doing? she asked herself in disgust. Drooling over a man she knew couldn't be trusted. She thought she must have some very strong self-destructive impulses.

Rolling over so that she faced the wall, she put her hand up to her forehead, remembered Nat's marijuana field, and winced. Out on the porch she'd been tempted to ask him point-blank why he was involved in such a business. Now she was glad she'd held her tongue. All right—so he was handsome and charming. She'd been seduced by that kind of man before. Surely she was smart enough to have learned something from the experience—wasn't she?

Carter was handsome and charming. His every other word had been witty, and his smile devastating. Maybe he hadn't sung her any obscure romantic folk songs, but he'd known how to do just the kind of thing that would endear himself to a woman who was ready to fall in love. He'd bought her balloons with funny little messages printed on them, sent her stuffed animals accompanied by cards that pleaded, "I was meant to be squeezed," and shown up at her place with a romantic midnight picnic for two.

She'd been charmed, all right. She'd fallen like a lead weight dropped off the Empire State Building. But it hadn't meant a thing. When the man had realized that she wanted a future with him as well as a present, he'd fled with hardly a backward glance. It had been a painful lesson, one she'd certainly suffered for. But she was back to normal now, with a very clear idea of what to avoid in a man.

Freddie rolled over, trying to find a more comfortable position. The move made it possible for her to peer through the darkness at Nat. Under his blankets he was nothing more than a huddled shape, but with only the sound of the rain disturbing the cabin's silence, she could hear his quiet breathing and imagine his warm body—which she shouldn't be doing.

Maybe there was no such thing as Mr. Right, but the man under those army blankets was definitely Mr. Wrong. Once again, Freddie rubbed her aching forehead. Be honest, she thought. Right or wrong, she was attracted to him. And if she was alone with him like this much longer, he'd get to her. She'd go off the deep end just the way she had with Carter. Dear God, she harangued herself, for all she knew Nat Steele could be planning to push her off a cliff. And what was she thinking about? About his kiss, and the way it felt when he took her in his arms!

Freddie felt an urge to scream. Bubbles of hysteria rose in her throat, and she had trouble controlling her breathing. This situation was absolutely crazy! Not only was she being threatened physically, she was being undermined emotionally. This sort of thing couldn't be allowed to happen. She had to get out of there—and suddenly she knew she had to do it tonight!

Beneath the blanket, her body was stiff and cold. As if looking for a bolt hole, her gaze darted around the dark cabin. Calm down and think clearly, she almost whispered aloud. Taking several deep breaths, Freddie struggled to clear her mind.

Actually, tonight might be her best chance to escape, she told herself at last. After that long, miserable hike, Nat wouldn't expect her to do anything but collapse. The rain was keeping everyone inside and would muffle the noise of her departure. Since Pinky wasn't there, he wouldn't give the alarm to his master. Nat had to be just as exhausted as she, and judging from his even, quiet breathing, he was already deeply asleep.

Freddie's hand went to the pocket of Granny's dress, where she'd secreted her compass. It was still there. With a little maneuvering, she'd be able to make her way back to Nat's shortwave radio. And once she found the radio, all she had to do was call for help and hide in the woods until it came.

Nothing could be simpler. The only tricky part would be sneaking out of the cabin without waking Nat. Taking another deep breath, Freddie decided to let another hour pass before she attempted her escape.

In the meantime, she lay tensely on the cot, counting up all the things she would need—the slicker, the boots, Granny's sweater. Hiking on a moonless night through the pouring rain wasn't going to be pleasant, but if Nat didn't wake until dawn and if she had a good head start, she'd have plenty of time to make her call and then choose a hiding spot. Of course, when he came looking for her, he'd have Pinky with him. Yet with all this rain, surely her scent wouldn't be easy to find. Maybe she'd even take a lesson from Nat and climb a tree.

While the minutes crawled past, these thoughts whirled through Freddie's mind. Finally, she could wait no longer. Once again she peered tensely through the darkness in Nat's direction. He sounded truly dead to the world. It was now or never.

Pushing back the covers, she swung her bare feet to

the floor and inched her weight from the cot as silently as possible. All the while, she watched her captor intently. There was no sign that he was disturbed.

Breathing a little more freely, Freddie picked up the boots and socks, padded across the floor, and removed the slicker from the hook. The next thing was to open and shut the front door without letting it creak. Since it was sticky and the wood was swollen from the rain, that turned out to be impossible.

Cursing the faint groaning noise it insisted on making, Freddie closed it behind her and peered beyond the shelter of the porch and into the darkness. It looked about as inviting out there as a swamp in the rainy season. Bravely, she slipped the stockings onto her feet and stepped into the boots. Then she pulled on the raincoat and lowered herself off the porch.

It wasn't easy to tiptoe in army boots, but that was what she tried to do as she navigated among the dark buildings. As she passed Granny's cabin, she cast a longing look at the kitchen door. It would be wonderful if she could steal some of that leftover food. Right now, her stomach was full from dinner, but if she had to spend the next couple of days hiding in a tree, it would be smart to pack along some food. She took a step toward the kitchen door, but then stopped. Was it worth it? Yes, it was.

The decision made, Freddie approached the door swiftly, removed her boots, and slipped inside. There were several chicken legs in the icebox. These she appropriated and stuffed into her pockets along with some corn muffins. Heart beating as if it were about to jump out of her chest, she went back outside, replaced the boots, and headed toward the woods. About fifty yards from Granny's cabin a mud puddle the size of a small pond had developed. She was hesitating in front of it when the fine hairs on the back of her neck stood up. With hideous conviction, she knew that someone or something was directly behind her.

"Oh, no you don't," Nat whispered as he reached for her shoulder.

But it was too late. With a muffled squeak, Freddie jumped a quarter of the way across the puddle. When she landed, the mud was even deeper and stickier than it looked. Her boots were sucked into it and held immobile. For several seconds she wavered back and forth like an anchored punching clown.

A few moments before, Nat had awakened with a jolt. When he'd seen that Freddie was gone, he'd dashed out of the cabin barefoot, wearing only jeans. Now he leaped after her with a grunt of rage. Freddie went down, and Nat followed immediately behind. Furiously, they rolled about in the slop. The snaps on the slicker soon gave way. Mud coated Freddie's legs and soaked through her dress. It covered Nat from head to foot. When he finally rose from the muck dragging a struggling, spitting Freddie with him, he looked like a perambulating clay statue.

"You little fool!" he exclaimed. "Just what the hell did you think you were doing?"

"Escaping from you," she snapped back. Close to tears, she tried to take a swipe at him.

Grasping her roughly by the shoulders, he turned her around. Then he clamped a hand around the back of her neck, captured her flailing arms behind her waist, and marched her back toward his cabin. "You're stupid, do you know that?" he grated behind her ear. "You aren't smart enough to know when you're well off."

"I'm smart enough to know that I need to get away from you!" she retorted through her tears.

"Judas!"

Bodily, he lifted her onto the porch and then shoved her through the front door. In angry silence he lit an oil lamp and set about rekindling the banked fire. When it blazed up, he turned, looked her up and down with a caustic eye, and then dragged her back outside through the front door.

"What are you doing?" she protested.

"You'll see."

With quick, efficient movements, he removed the ruined slicker and dropped it. Then, reaching down, he peeled her muddy dress and sweater up over her head and tugged them off.

"Hey! Hey, stop that!" When she realized what he was doing, Freddie danced around, frenziedly trying to obstruct his movements. It was useless. In a twinkling she was standing on the porch in nothing but her bra and soggy panties.

"You're a monster!" she railed, desperately attempting to cover herself with her arms. "You belong in a nuthouse!"

"Right! Bedlam is where I've been headed ever since I met you!" he gritted. As he spoke, he lifted the full bucket of water that had been sitting next to a corner post and dumped half of it over Freddie's head.

She gasped, blinded by the icy liquid in her eyes and disoriented by the shock. "Are you trying to drown me?"

"You need a bath, and so do I." Nat stripped off

his own muddy jeans and sluiced himself down with the rest of the water. After that, he pushed the still blinded and sputtering Freddie back in through the door and toward the fire. She was furious and shivering violently.

"Stop wasting your energy. Wrap yourself up in this." Nat shoved a blanket at her. Then he stalked back outside to retrieve their clothing.

When he returned, he was wearing a grim expression and little else. Since his wet briefs were practically transparent, they hid nothing. Freddie, who had managed to wrap the blanket around her and wipe the water from her eyes with a corner of it, averted her gaze and huddled closer to the fire.

"My slicker is full of soggy corn muffins and muddy chicken legs," Nat accused. "Nice. What did you do, go back to Granny's place and steal her food?"

Through her wet lashes, Freddie shot him a defiant glance. Standing there all but nude in the firelight, his feet planted wide apart and his fists bunched on his hips, he looked like an angry but magnificent young god.

"I had no choice. I knew I was going to need something to eat." Once again, she tore her eyes from him and stared back into the leaping flames.

"What will it take to make you behave like as sensible human being?" he asked in disgust. Plucking a blanket off his cot, he wrapped it around himself and strode toward the fire.

"I am behaving sensibly. Trying to get away from a crazy person like you is very sensible."

Nat rolled his eyes upward and raked a hand through his damp hair. "This situation gets more bizarre by the minute. Do you realize that it's two o'clock in the morning and that fifteen minutes ago you had me rolling around in the mud with you out there?" he asked, jerking a rigid thumb toward the door. "We'll probably both come down with pneumonia!"

Freddie gazed back at him. "It was your fault that we landed in the mud."

"My fault?"

"You're always finding excuses to jump on me, and I wish you'd stop it."

For a moment, Nat was speechless.

"I never saw anything more ridiculous than the way you looked covered with mud," Freddie continued. "You looked like the thing from the swamp that time forgot."

He continued to regard her in outraged silence. "I couldn't have looked more absurd than you after I poured that bucket of water over your head," he finally commented. He reached forward to flick a spot of dried mud from the end of her nose. "The phrase 'madder than a wet hen' comes to mind."

"A rotten trick like that would make anyone mad," she shot back.

"Lady, when it comes to tricks, you can hold your own." As he spoke, his expression altered subtly. He no longer looked angry. Suddenly, to Freddie's surprise, he started to chuckle.

"It's not funny."

"Sure it is." Tipping his head back, he began to laugh. She could see the long line of his throat and the bottom of his square jaw. Beneath his moustache, his chin was peppered with gold stubble. If he didn't shave soon, he'd begin to look like a bearded Viking.

"I'd like to bury you in that mud out there," she muttered.

"You damn near did." He began to roar louder.

Freddie stared at him and struggled to control the corners of her mouth. But they seemed to have taken on a quivering life of their own. Suddenly, she couldn't help herself.

"This is stupid," she managed to get out between chortles.

"We're a couple of fools," he agreed, then collapsed against the back of the chair, his hand against his hairy chest. The blanket had slipped so that she could see the top of his waistband. To her relief, his briefs had dried and were once again opaque.

When the last of their laughter finally died away, they stared at each other.

"Are you dry?" Nat finally asked.

"Yes, I think so."

"Good. That bra of yours is transparent when it's wet."

Freddie felt her cheeks glow and decided not to mention his underwear. "What now?" she asked instead.

"Now we go back to bed and try to get some sleep."

"Good." She stood up. Pulling the blanket tightly around her, she started to hobble toward her cot.

"Not there."

"What?" She glanced back at him over her shoulder.

"Now that I know you're given to midnight rambles, I've decided you're going to be spending the rest of the night with me in my cot, Ms. Davenport."

CHAPTER SEVEN

Freddie stared at him. "What are you talking about?"

"I'm talking about getting some sleep. I'm not interested in lying awake the rest of the night waiting for you to try sneaking off again." Nat took the blanket off and replaced it on his cot. Then he reached for her blanket.

Backing away, she clutched the covering to her more tightly. "I'm not going to try another escape tonight. I promise."

"Sorry. I'm afraid your promises don't mean a hell of a lot to me." He strode over and took her arm.

"I refuse to spend the night with you on that cot." She shot it a scathing glance. "Why, there's hardly enough room on it for one person, much less two."

Amusement gleamed in Nat's gray eyes. "Maybe by morning it will have made better friends of us."

Freddie stiffened. "If you think—"

"Look, I'm not going to seduce you. I just want to sleep." He looked around the room. "Would you rather I tied you up in a chair? I could do that."

She was horrified. "Of course not!"

"Well, then." He grasped her wrist. "Come along peacefully. And let me have that blanket. We'll both be warmer with two over us." He divested her of the army blanket and propelled her toward the cot.

Freddie was in a state of something near shock. Once again she was wearing nothing but her bra and mud-streaked panties. And he was covered only by his briefs.

"Aren't you going to put on more clothes?" she protested as he pushed her down on the mattress.

"I don't like sleeping fully dressed. Besides, my jeans are still wet. So are your things. Don't worry, I have no plans to molest you. I just intend to make sure that you don't go anywhere." As he spoke, he crawled in and pulled the blankets up around both of them.

Freddie tried to move away, but there was no room. "Can't you see this isn't going to work?" she hissed. "If we each lie flat, we'll fall out of bed."

"Then we'll spoon."

"Spoon?"

With a low chuckle, he flipped her on her side. Then he wrapped a muscular arm around her waist and hauled her close so that her backside fit symmetrically against his front. In the dark, Freddie's eyes widened. She tried to move away, but Nat only drew her closer and found a place in the hollow of her neck to rest his cheek.

"Now," he murmured, "lie still and let me get some shut-eye. I'm beat."

Freddie waited tensely, hardly breathing. In only a few minutes, his breathing evened out, and she felt the slow, regular rise and fall of his chest against her back. The man was actually sleeping!

Suddenly, Freddie was as irritated by that as by everything else that had happened. She told herself that it was going to be impossible for her to get any rest with her body crammed up against his. The hair on his thighs tickled the backs of her legs, and his warm breath on her neck sent little shivers down her spine. Around her waist his arm was heavy—and disturbing. She tried to inch away. But even in his sleep, Nat was a determined captor. His grip tightened, and she knew that escape was hopeless. Like it or not, she was going to be spending the rest of the night cradled against Nat Steele's long, hard body.

Gradually, however, she became accustomed to the feel of the masculine body shaping itself to hers. The blankets created a warm, comfortable cocoon. Exhaustion took over, and she closed her eyes.

For a long time she drifted in a semiconscious state. Scenes from the past blended with the present. Carter was the only other man with whom she'd ever slept. She now knew that she'd fallen in love with an illusion and that he hadn't been the man she'd believed him to be. Still, when he'd abandoned her, she'd been human enough to miss the shared intimacy of their nights together. Freddie's fierce independence masked a personality that was vulnerable and very hungry for the warmth of a loving relationship. She had liked the taste and touch of love, the feeling of caring and being cared for—of being truly part of another person. As she sank deeper into unconsciousness, she whispered Carter's name and turned toward Nat. Her head burrowed into the crook of his arm and her hand found its way to his hip.

He was usually a heavy sleeper, but not that night. His eyes snapped open. As he heard the other man's name, he frowned. But when Freddie snuggled her near-naked body against his, the frown disappeared and he began to struggle with another reaction. His hand moved from her waist to her shoulder. Her skin was like satin beneath his palms, and the sweet smell of her hair filled his nostrils. He smiled as a curl tickled the end of his nose, and he adjusted his position so that his chin rested lightly on top of her head.

"Mmm," she murmured, and her hand moved down the flat plane of his hip until it stopped on his thigh.

Nat sucked in his breath. His chest was suddenly alive with the delicious pressure of her breasts. He told himself to lie still, to close his eyes and use a meditation technique to clear his mind. But although he was normally good at this, it wasn't working now. His body seemed to have its own ideas—and they no longer included relaxation. Slowly but purposefully, his left hand slipped down and around until his fingers grazed the soft roundness of Freddie's breast. With a slight adjustment, he could feel her nipple against his forefinger. Gently, he rubbed its tip. It began to stiffen. Her mouth opened slightly, and she moaned and clung to him even more provocatively.

Instantly, an urgent ache burgeoned in Nat's groin. As he struggled with himself, he tipped back his head and stared into the darkness. There were only two or three hours left until dawn. He suspected they were going to be some of the longest hours of his life.

As gray tendrils of first light found their way into Nat's cabin, Freddie awoke in slow stages. Because she was afloat in a wonderfully pleasant welter of sensations, she had no desire to awaken and resisted it. Nevertheless, gradually some of the sensations began to sort themselves out. There was a hand on her breast, stroking with delicate precision so that the tips tightened in a delicious ache. Instinctively seeking the source of this pleasure, she moved closer, molding her curves to the strong masculine body sharing the blankets with her.

Cooperatively, the body pressed her into the mattress, and she felt lips begin to nuzzle the sensitive place beneath her ear. Her arms reached around a broad, naked back and explored the structure of hard bone and muscle beneath satin skin. Eyes still tightly shut, she turned her face and breathed a clean, masculine fragrance. "Carter," she whispered. And then her mouth sought and found his.

At the same time her hands moved upward, wanting to riffle the crisp curls she remembered. But when her fingers began to winnow through her companion's hair, it was straight and silky. Her lashes started to part and prisms of light invaded the darkness.

"I'm not Carter," a masculine voice whispered against her ear. "But right now I'd like to be."

Freddie's eyes opened wider, and her fogged blue gaze encountered a laughing gray one. But far more unnerving was that she recognized desire mingled with the amusement. "What—"

"Don't talk. Don't wake up. Close your eyes and let's go back to sleep and take up where we left off," Nat ordered huskily. "What we were doing was much too nice to interrupt." His head came down, his blond hair tangled with her dark curls, and once more his lips moved over hers.

Carter's name was no longer on Freddie's lips. He wasn't the one she wanted, she realized—it was this man and only this man.

"Nat," she whispered, and obediently closed her eyes and gave herself up to the persuasive kiss.

But it wasn't just the kiss. It was the feel of his body, his chest and hips covering hers, his hairy, muscular legs entwined with her shorter, smoother ones. She lay with her arms bent at right angles on either side of her head. Nat's were a mirror image. He pressed his palms flat to hers, and their fingers locked together.

Instinctively, she wriggled beneath him, which produced an immediate and very disturbing reaction.

"I want to make love to you," he whispered thickly. "I feel as if I'm on fire."

Freddie knew exactly what he meant. Right now, a complementary flame was spreading through her. But his words also jarred her out of her semiconscious complacence. Once again her eyes opened, but this time they were focused and beginning to be alarmed. "We shouldn't be doing this."

"I know, but telling myself that doesn't seem to make a damned bit of difference." Curling his fingers even more tightly into hers, he began to drop kisses along her hairline. "My God, but you feel good. Carter was a fool."

Freddie let her lids flicker shut, and she fought her inclination to submit. "Nat, you have to stop it. Last night you promised."

"What did I promise?" His mouth moved down the side of her jaw, nibbling. "I can't remember any of it. I'm only human, you know. There's just so much provocation a man can stand."

"You said you wouldn't molest me."

"Molest?" He lifted his head. "Why do you use

that word? My God, woman, you've been rubbing yourself against me for the past three hours."

At last Freddie was able to think clearly enough to martial an obvious argument. "That's not my fault. You're the one who insisted we sleep together like this."

"Freddie, let's stop kidding around. We're attracted to each other. I knew it from the first, and so did you."

When she remained stubbornly silent, he smoothed the curls from her forehead. He bent his golden head to whisper playfully in her ear, "Your body contradicts the things you say with your mouth. Bodies don't lie, and yours broadcasts that you want to make love with me. Be honest for a change and admit it's true. We've both wanted it since that tussle we had in the grass a couple of days ago."

She tried to avoid meeting his eyes, but they drew her, and when she looked into their clear depths, she couldn't lie. "All right, I am attracted to you. But it's not what you think."

He blinked. "What is it, then? Maybe you'd better explain this to me."

"It's clearly a case of prisoner syndrome."

"Prisoner syndrome?" He stared down at her. "Just what the hell do you mean by that?"

"It's something I've read about, and once we had a psychologist on a talk show at the radio station who discussed it." Nervously, she cleared her throat. "When someone is taken prisoner, out of sheer self-defense they become psychologically dependent on their captor. And sometimes that dependence can take the form of . . ."

"Yes?"

"It can take a sexual form," she finished, glaring at him.

He continued to stare down at her. "And you think that's what's happening here between us?"

"Yes, I do. That's the only explanation for it."

"It is, is it?" Nat rolled over on his side and put his head back on the pillow. "You're a woman in a million." He started to laugh. "Prisoner syndrome." He whooped. "Now I've heard everything!"

Freddie looked at him uncertainly. The dangerously sensual mood of a few minutes earlier had been broken, but she wasn't sure she liked hearing him laugh at her. "It's not funny."

"It is. Woman, you are a barrel of fun. A very nicely shaped barrel." As he spoke, he drew her close. Wrapping his arms tight around her, he gave her an affectionate hug. Then he loosened his grip and tipped her face up to his. "Maybe we'd better have breakfast."

"That sounds like a good idea." Despite her brisk reply, she couldn't help feeling a twinge of disappointment. She didn't really want to get out of the cozy bed she was sharing with Nat. It was still cold, gray, and rainy outside. And who knew what lay in store for her today?

But he'd already swung his feet down onto the bare wood floor. He stood up and stretched, his joints cracking slightly. Then he began looking around for his clothes. "You might as well stay warm under the covers until I get the fire going," he told Freddie.

He pulled on his jeans and knelt down before the hearth to feed the embers with small pieces of tinder. Soon crackling flames were taking some of the damp morning chill off the air. Nat filled a coffeepot and set it on a hot brick. Then he put on his shirt and shoes and went outside.

When he was gone, Freddie reluctantly crawled out of bed and scampered across to the chair in front of the fire where her own things had been laid out to dry. The roll in the mud last night hadn't improved Granny's dress and sweater any, she thought as she pulled the bedraggled garments over her head. Jeremy's army boots weren't exactly a charming sight, either. Although Nat had given the tops a cursory scraping, the bottoms were still caked with mud.

Nevertheless, she stepped into them, slipped on Nat's slicker, and went to visit the outhouse. On her return, Nat was waiting with an accusing expression on his face, which, except for his moustache, was now cleanshaven.

"Since you stole all of Vandy's corn muffins and then turned them into mush in the mud, we won't be having them for breakfast," he informed her curtly.

"I already apologized for that. And you know why I took them."

"Oh yes, your wilderness survival kit. I was looking forward to those muffins." He stalked over to the table and started to tear open a package. Inside was a round brown loaf and a small jar. "Granny was good enough to give us some of her homemade bread and apple butter."

That sounded fine to Freddie. Perking coffee filled the cabin with an enticing aroma. While Nat poured the dark brew into mugs, she removed his slicker and sat down opposite him at the table. Although she had eaten a huge dinner the night before, she was suddenly ravenous and eagerly tore off a hunk of the coarsely textured bread.

"Prisoner syndrome certainly hasn't ruined your appetite," Nat remarked wryly. He eyed her over the rim of his mug as he took a sip of coffee.

"No, why should it? I have to build up my strength."

"For your next escape attempt?"

"Possibly."

Nat sighed. "Well, you can forget about trying anything like that today. You're going to be far too busy."

"Doing what?" Freddie took a bite of the bread that she'd spread with thick apple butter. It was absolutely delicious.

"Helping out the womenfolk." His eyes, she noticed, had started to twinkle mischievously.

"What's that supposed to mean?"

"How should I know? Cooking, I suppose, and cleaning. All the things that good women do to make life easier for their hard-working men."

"Well, you're not my man, nor do I approve of your work, so why should I try and improve the quality of your life?"

"In this case, out of pure self-interest. It's important that the Parkers go on thinking you're my sweetheart. After breakfast I'm going to take you over to Granny's, where you can apologize for stealing her food."

"Apologize?" Freddie winced. "What sort of explanation should I offer?"

"Just say you got hungry. She'll understand that."

"After that meal she fed me, she'll think I'm a glutton!"

Nat shrugged. "Sometimes escape artists get themselves into awkward situations. You can handle it."

"Thanks. What happens after that?"

"You stay and help Granny, Vandy, and Martha get ready for this musicale."

"What are you going to be doing?"

The corners of his mouth twitched. "The kind of stuff menfolk do—chopping wood, tending to the animals, pitching hay—"

"Oh, sure." Freddie snorted. "I bet that means you'll be playing cards and drinking beer with the Parker boys."

"Maybe a little of that, too," Nat agreed with an unrepentant grin. "Only make it home brew. I think I already mentioned that there are a lot of stills around here to go with the marijuana fields."

A little later, on the walk over to Granny's cabin, Freddie saw that Nat hadn't been kidding about the marijuana in the Parkers' gardens. Behind each house were row upon row of the tall, spiky bushes. It gave her a very different feeling about the isolated enclave from what she'd had the night before. Maybe Nat was right. Maybe she should do the best she could to play the role of his doting girl friend.

Having to stammer an apology about the food didn't make it any easier to play that role. But except for a cocked eyebrow, Granny accepted it gracefully. Vandy was a different story. Freddie already knew that the girl had taken a dislike to her. Her making off with the muffins in the dead of night only fueled Vandy's disfavor, and the scowl on her cameo face emphasized the fact.

"While Vandy stays here to tend to the stove, we'll go down to the church to sweep up," Granny explained.

"Is that where your musicale will be held?" Freddie asked.

"Yep. That's where it's been for almost twenty years, and that's where it'll be tonight."

Freddie was still having trouble believing in this backwoods concert. Who in their right mind would trek through the mountains in such weather just to play some old folk songs? But instead of expressing her doubts, she went along with Granny, Martha, and Jeremy through a path in the woods to a small, deserted log church.

"This place used to be kept neat," the old woman commented, swiping at a thigh-high weed. "But that was in the old days when the family stuck together. Now . . ." She shrugged eloquently and turned to Jeremy. "You set about knockin' down these pesky weeds."

As Jeremy attacked the overgrowth, Freddie asked, "Did your family attend church here?"

"Used to. Don't no more since the preacher stopped comin'. Those no-account boys up yonder are more interested in figurin' ways to get down to Atlanta and get into mischief than they are in their own home. Grass is always greener, don't you know."

"Now, Granny," Martha protested. "It ain't so bad as that. Jim and Jeremy and I are here with you."

"Humph. You all and Vandy are the only Parkers worth a penny now," Granny muttered.

As Freddie watched the old woman mount the church's sagging steps and push open the door, there was a sympathetic look in her blue eyes. It must be awful to live such a hard life, only to end it by wit-

121

nessing the gradual dissolution of your family. Freddie hadn't seen Marshall, Lou, or Hap since the night before, but judging from her first impression of them, Granny was right. What was their relationship with Nat? she wondered. Somehow, she just couldn't picture her tall blond captor really getting along with those three shiftless young men. For one thing, he was much more mature. And for another, she thought as she followed the old woman, he just seemed cut from a different mold.

Inside, the church had a forlorn air and was badly in need of a sweeping and airing. "Needs a drop or two of elbow grease," Martha commented.

"More like a peck," Granny retorted. Using the brooms, mops, and dust rags they'd brought along, the three women set to work.

"It'll be nothin' but cooking this afternoon," Granny said as she reached for the cobwebs that were festooning a crossbeam, sending a family of industrious spiders scuttling. "Before we come down here for the music, we'll fill everyone's belly up with good food. The music will sound all the better for that."

"Couldn't we hear the music in your cabin?" Freddie asked.

"Nope." Granny shook her silvery head. "It's tradition to come here, you know. But it's somethin' else, too." She looked about reflectively. "Music sounds better in a place like this. I don't know how to explain it."

Freddie nodded. She was beginning to grasp how important this annual concert was to the old woman. Naturally she wanted the setting to be right.

"Now you be sure and eat plenty at supper, so you won't get hungry again and have to go gallivantin' about in the middle of the night," Granny said, giving Freddie a sharp look.

"I will," she replied guiltily, averting her eyes and dusting a pew quickly.

"You sleep all right otherwise?" Granny continued, studying Freddie with eyes that seemed to see a great deal.

"Fine."

"Stop pesterin' that poor girl," Martha protested. "Can't you see she's turning so pink she looks like she's being boiled alive?"

But Granny persisted. "You know, I think Nat Steele is a mighty worthy young man. The gal who persuades him to propose marriage will have done a fine piece of work."

"I'm sure that's true." Freddie jammed her dust rag into a murky corner.

"Course, it won't be easy. Like most men worth their salt, he's skittish about settlin' down. He'll come to it, though," she added slyly, "when a smart girl says and does the right things."

Doubtless, Freddie thought. But that wasn't going to be her—oh no, not a chance!

Returning to Granny's cabin later that afternoon, they found that Vandy had been busy. As they stepped inside the back door, they were greeted by the aromas of baking bread and savory bean soup simmering on top of the stove. They were also hailed by a jolly masculine voice that was unfamiliar to Freddie.

"Well, if it isn't the prettiest passel of women in these mountains. How about givin' this old coot a kiss for luck?" A short, bearded man with gaping teeth and laughing eyes stood inside the kitchen. After Granny and Martha flew into his outstretched arms, they introduced him to Freddie. It was Bill Hooper, the fiddle player she'd heard spoken of the night before. She could tell right away why everyone had looked forward to seeing him. Freddie guessed he was somewhere in his sixties, but he exuded vitality and good cheer. Despite the rainy weather, his presence in the cabin seemed to make everything bright and cheery.

It wasn't long before all Freddie's doubts about the audience for the forthcoming concert were set to rest. During the remainder of the afternoon mountain folk carrying musical instruments and baskets of food streamed in. Most of the men left to spend the time before dinner in Jim's and the other Parker boys' cabins. But the women stayed at Granny's to gossip and help with the enormous meal that was gradually taking shape.

Such a large number of guests made it impossible to serve a sit-down dinner. Instead, when eating time was finally announced, everyone filled their plates from the bounty on the table and stood talking and laughing in the crowded room, which was now almost overheated from the sheer press of bodies.

The table was loaded with different kinds of food. There was ham, fried chicken, venison, and breads and muffins of every description. Several squash and vegetable medleys brightened the groaning board, and at one end a dozen delicious-looking pies and several cakes beckoned to those who'd finished the main courses.

As Freddie came into the room bearing a freshly loaded platter, she noticed that the jugs of liquor that many guests had brought were being rapidly emptied.

Her gaze gravitated toward Nat, who was carrying on what looked like a jovial conversation with Bill Hooper. Nat, too, sipped occasionally from one of those jugs, she observed. He'd been bad enough last night when he was stone-cold sober. What was he going to be like tonight with all that illegal whiskey warming his blood? And why couldn't she stop thinking about him? Every time she caught a glimpse of his burnished head, her pulse leaped.

Turning away, she began gathering up abandoned dishes. But as she worked, she shot speculative glances at the people around her. Nat had warned her not to appeal to any of them for help, and it was true that no one appeared in the least concerned about the illegal plants growing in the Parkers' gardens. Yet they all looked like decent people. There must be someone among them who would help if she explained her situation. Tomorrow, she told herself, she'd find an opportunity to see if there was.

By the time dinner ended, the whole assemblage was in a merry mood. The long, wet trek to the church didn't seem to dampen it in the slightest.

"Old Felix said there was a man aplayin' 'Black River Banjos' on an excursion boat a few years back," Jim was telling Bill Hooper. "Felix told me he'd run many a mile just to stay alongside so he could learn the tune from the bank. Now that's really wantin' to pick up a new song, ain't it?"

"Shore is." Bill laughed. "Isn't no better banjo player than Felix. But wait till you hear my grandson Billy play this old fiddle. When he was big enough to hold it, I gave him the fiddle and said, 'Buddy, you're going to learn to play it.' Now he's just fifteen and winnin' prizes at all the county fairs."

Jim slapped his friend on the shoulder and said, "Wish I could say the same for Jeremy. He don't seem to take to anything."

"But you got your niece, Vandy," Bill countered. "My Lord, but what a pretty thing!"

"Maybe too pretty for her own good," Granny dropped into the exchange.

Freddie looked up at Nat, who was walking by her side. His guitar, wrapped in a cover to protect it from the drizzle that still persisted, was clasped loosely in his right arm. His other arm was around her waist. Did he think Vandy was too pretty for her own good? Freddie wondered. All evening, the girl had been casting longing glances in his direction and shooting poisonous looks in hers. Freddie felt sorry for her. She obviously fancied herself in love with Nat and was too young and inexperienced to hide her feelings. Would she herself be any better at hiding her feelings if she were in love with him? Freddie wondered. Suddenly, she admitted to herself that all through dinner her gaze had been drawn to Nat's tall figure just as Vandy's had been. The realization made her shiver.

"You cold?" Nat asked.

"No."

"The church should be warm. About an hour ago, Lou and Marshall went down to get the stove going."

"Where's Hap?"

"There." Nat pointed in Vandy's direction, and Freddie spotted Hap trying unsuccessfully to take the girl's hand. Irritably, she slapped him away and ignored him until he finally abandoned the effort.

A few minutes later, when Nat held the door open and Freddie walked inside the old building, she gazed around in surprise. With the candles lit and a fire blazing in the potbellied stove, the place looked entirely different. In addition to the light and warmth, there were the bright, expectant faces of Granny's guests. As they filed in and took seats in the rows of pews, the sound of their laughter and cheerful gossip suffused the place with vitality. Already the musicians who were going to lead off the evening's entertainment were tuning their instruments and gathering around each other.

"I've been to a lot of concerts, but I've never seen anything quite like this before in my life," Freddie whispered in Nat's ear. "It's so different from a big-city performance."

He nodded. "Music means something different in these mountains. People turn to it for release. It can be important in a life that owes you nothing and sometimes gives you less. That's what you'll be hearing tonight. That's what old-time music is all about."

When the audience settled down, Bill Hooper got up in front to lead off. "He's a purist," Nat whispered in Freddie's ear as the old man tuned his violin one last time and then winked at the audience. "He's over seventy now, but he started playing when he was nine. He told me he turned off the radio when he was growing up because he didn't want it to ruin his ear."

"I'm going to play first like an average fiddler," Bill announced, his grizzled cheeks cracking into an impish grin. He played timidly, with short, shallow draws of the bow. "Now I'll play the way you do when you've learned better and can put more notes in," he informed the audience. They laughed and clapped. This time, the tune vibrated to life, louder, clearer, and brimming with power. "Now I'll really play," he shouted over the sound of the foot-stomping music. He fiddled native pieces and old Celtic tunes. In a style all his own, he played with keen precision and ease. To Freddie, his fiddle sounded like a waterfall, tumbling and sparkling with life.

The excitement in Bill's music was only the beginning. He was followed by a small, middle-aged woman named Katy Hughes who wore a loose yellow dress that bloomed with flowers. She was a banjo picker from North Carolina.

"This banjo was made for me by my cousin," she told the audience, holding up her distinctive instrument. "He fashioned it from a 1956 Buick transmission ring. And that's what it does—it rings like a church bell. Listen here." Although her voice had been timid and her smile shy, she attacked the strings in a confident drop-thumb style.

The next performer played the same kind of instrument as Katy, but in an entirely different way. "I prefer this old S.S. Stewart banjo my grandaddy gave my father to any I've found since," a wiry little man named Harlie Hamilton said. His gray hair was swept back from his forehead, and his face bore the lines of good years spent singing and laughing. He had an economical manner of speech, and his voice carried words up and down, just the way tunes climbed hills and valleys on the steel strings of his instrument. His style, Nat told Freddie, was strictly old-time frailing.

After Harlie left the performer's spot in front of the pews, Bill walked up front with a blushing Vandy behind him. "I think it's time we heard some good singing, so I'm persuading this pretty little gal to give us a tune." He grinned down at the teen-ager. "How about it?"

"All right," she agreed shyly. Then her gaze flew

to Nat. "But I'll need someone to play the guitar for me. Nat, will you do it?"

"Why, sure." Everyone else on the pew made room so he could slide out and walk to the front of the church. Her heart in her lovely brown eyes, Vandy watched him approach. Then, when he'd arranged his length on an old folding chair and balanced his guitar on his knee, she leaned down and whispered something in his ear. Nodding, he bent his head and tightened a few strings.

"I'll sing 'Go Tell It on the Mountain'," Vandy announced.

Freddie watched all this closely. Her gaze went back and forth between Nat and the dark-eyed mountain girl. They made a handsome pair, she noted with an undeniable pang. Nat's tall fairness was the perfect foil for Vandy's youthful good looks. But when Nat struck a chord and Vandy opened her mouth and began to sing, Vandy was more than merely goodlooking. Suddenly she was vibrantly beautiful.

The girl had a perfectly gorgeous voice. Freddie stared across the audience and drank in the crystalline purity of her tones. But it was more than just her voice. Singing seemed to transform Vandy. She was no longer merely a very pretty mountain girl. Suddenly, she was something rare and bright. The audience recognized it. They listened to her song with profound attention. No one moved or made a sound that might disturb its magical effect.

When it was over, they clapped and stomped until Vandy sang another. Nat accompanied her without missing a beat, almost as if they'd practiced their routine for hours.

Vandy's second song ended, and applause burst out

so enthusiastically that it echoed from the little church's rafters. Still glowing from her impassioned performance and the audience's appreciation, Vandy turned to Nat. Again, she had her heart in her eyes, and her smile as she looked into his handsome face was incandescent.

How could he not fall in love with her? Freddie wondered. How could any man not fall in love with her? Right now she was irresistible.

The smile Nat returned held warmth and admiration, but it didn't have that special sparkle that Freddie knew was the look of love.

He turned away from Vandy and gazed out into the audience in Freddie's direction. His clear gray eyes engaged hers in a long, intensely personal scrutiny that made her catch her breath. At that moment Freddie knew in her heart why Nat could look at the beautiful young creature at his side with merely brotherly indulgence. She couldn't really admit it to herself yet, but she knew.

CHAPTER EIGHT

The playing and singing in the old church went on until the wee hours of the morning. And all of it was fine. But after Freddie saw that look in Nat's eyes, nothing else made much of an impression on her.

It was crazy, she told herself. She was imagining things. But deep within, she knew that that expression was the way a man looked at a woman who was special to him. And it had been directed at her alone. Despite all logic, every cell in her body responded to the secret knowledge of it. When Nat took her hand in his and walked her back to the cabin, it was all she could think of.

"Well, how did you like the music you heard tonight?" he asked as they strolled through the wet grass. "I suppose, working at a radio station as you do, you're light years away from this kind of backwoods singing and playing."

Freddie took a deep breath. The rain was now only a fine mist, and though the stars and moon weren't yet visible behind the scudding clouds, there was a freshness in the air. It promised that sometime tomorrow the sun would shine again.

"I liked it," she answered his question. "Yes, it was

very different from what I'm used to. But I enjoyed it."

"It's hard for us to understand what music like this meant to people in the old days," he commented after a moment. "Radio took it off mountain porches and spread it around. Country-western packaged the sound and bluegrass up-tempoed the tunes. There aren't many who play the old stuff anymore."

"It certainly sounded alive and well in Granny Parker's church tonight."

Nat chuckled. "Oh, it's still around. If you take the time to travel and listen, old-time music is still deeply rooted in West Virginia, Kentucky, Alabama, and out in the Arkansas Ozarks. It differs from place to place, and it's frayed around the edges and patched in places, but it still endures."

She gazed at him curiously. "You certainly sound as if you know what you're talking about. Have you been to all those places collecting songs?"

"I get around," he responded evasively.

They approached the porch of the little cabin, which was now shrouded in fog. It looked mysterious and yet welcoming. She was beginning to think of this place as home, Freddie mused, which just showed that a person could get used to anything.

This was all too true in the case of Nat Steele. She was rapidly becoming very accustomed to him. It seemed perfectly natural for his arm to be around her and for her to lean close to him as they made their way through the fragrant woods. She felt nothing strange about letting him lead her into his dark little cabin. It seemed right to watch expectantly while he lit an oil lamp and then knelt before the hearth to blow the coals back into dancing flames. Soon they gave off light and heat, creating a cozy intimacy in the small room.

"Want to sit in front of the fire and warm up for a bit?" he asked.

She nodded and drew a chair up. "You and Vandy made a very good team tonight."

"She'd sound terrific no matter who was playing for her. The girl has a lot of talent."

"Yes," Freddie agreed. "But you performed very smoothly together. Have you—" She paused. "Have you played and sung together a lot?"

As he settled back into a rocking chair, he looked at her shrewdly. "When I first started visiting here, she'd come around and sing while I played. It seemed harmless enough. Now I guess it was a mistake, because that was how she developed this infernal crush."

"It's not surprising," Freddie commented in what she hoped was a neutral tone. "She's young and so isolated up here. I don't suppose she gets to see many eligible young men."

"None except for her cousins and their friend Hap. He fancies her, but she's taken a dislike to him. That remark about the garden gate at dinner last night probably meant he tried to kiss her down by the henhouse. There's a fenced-in patch around back of it." Nat shook his head. "She won't go there alone now."

Freddie couldn't blame Vandy for that. Hap hadn't particularly appealed to her, either. Freddie looked through the warm shadows at Nat. Although his posture was relaxed, he seemed tense. She told herself to drop the subject of Vandy, but somehow she couldn't get that scene in the church out of her mind.

She realized that the image of Vandy's glowing face after she'd finished her song would be imprinted in her memory for a long time. Indeed, the past forty-eight hours had been crowded with memorable moments. As she stared into the fire, images flickered through her mind—Nat tending her wounds, kissing her in the grass after their struggle, asking her questions while they ate their lunch in a damp cave. With an effort, she forced her thoughts back to the concert.

"Vandy was so beautiful while she was singing, and the way she looked at you afterward—" Freddie shook her head. "I don't know how you could resist her."

"Don't you?" His voice was surprisingly gruff. "Don't you really?"

"What do you mean?"

"I mean that it's not hard to turn your back on a teen-ager who isn't really responsible for what she's doing when you're being driven crazy by a beautiful woman who knows exactly what she's about."

Freddie raised her head. "Are you talking about me?"

"You little witch, you know very well that I mean you."

As he spoke, he rose from his chair and stepped toward her. His expression held purpose, but for Freddie it was also packed with excitement. When he grasped her shoulders and slowly drew her up to her feet, a little thrill of alarm shot straight down to the soles of her feet, and she stared up into his set features as if she were mesmerized.

"What do you want?" she asked breathlessly.

"A kiss—what do you think?"

When his mouth claimed hers, she made no complaint. There was nothing rough or demanding in his caress. Freddie could not have stepped from the circle of his arms if she had wanted to. Despite herself, she was learning to want Nat's kisses, and as his lips explored hers with a studied delicacy that belied the compelling intensity burning in his eyes, she surrendered.

"It's time to go to bed," he whispered in her ear.

"No," she murmured huskily. "We can't sleep together on that cot of yours tonight. You know we can't."

"No choice in that matter." His lips moved against the tender place just below her lobe. "Who knows what you'll get up to if you're not with me? You're a very tricky lady, Frederica Davenport—maybe too tricky for your own good."

"No, it's impossible. Nat, I can't let this happen."

"Where's that prisoner syndrome you were telling me about?" he questioned. "Prisoners are supposed to humor their jailors."

"Or else what?"

"Or else the whole system breaks down."

"I'm not afraid of you."

"That's because there's nothing to be afraid of," he agreed with a sleepy smile. "Tonight we'll be like two babes in the woods, just rolled up together to keep each other warm."

Freddie didn't believe that for a moment. Yet when he began undoing her dress, she didn't say any of the things that might have made him stop. In a moment the loose garment was pulled up over her head and dropped lightly onto the back of a chair.

When she stood shyly in front of the fire wearing only her bra and panties and Jeremy's army boots,

Nat started to chuckle. "You're quite a calendar girl in that getup. I wish I had a camera."

"I can imagine."

Still smiling, he knelt and ran his hand along the curve of her bare calf and down to her ankle. Gently he lifted her foot out of the mud-encrusted boot and paused a moment, cradling her instep in his palm. Mesmerized, Freddie stared down at the top of his fair head as he took the other boot off.

"You have a beautiful body," he murmured. "Instead of that old dress and these clodhoppers, you should be wearing silk underwear and Italian shoes with high heels that look too fragile for walking. I wish I could see you dressed that way."

Freddie's eyes widened, and when Nat tipped his head back and looked up into her flushed face, they were inky blue.

"But don't get me wrong," he added softly. "I'm not complaining about the way you are now." He rose in one smooth movement and gathered her body to his. Then, as if it were his right, he lifted her in his arms and carried her to the bed.

Wordlessly, Freddie stared at him as he laid her down on the narrow bed and pulled the blankets up around her. Their eyes were still fixed on each other as he unbuttoned his shirt. After dropping it on the floor, he unzipped his pants and stepped gracefully out of them. She flushed even more, seeing the very evident effect she'd had on him.

"Yes. I'm only human, after all, and this situation has gotten to me," Nat told her in a voice that seemed a note deeper. "Don't worry about it."

But that was just the problem, Freddie admitted to

herself, she wasn't worried about it—not at all. And she should be. It was crazy not to be.

An instant later he was beside her, pulling the covers up around them both and enfolding her in his arms. With a sigh, she closed her eyes and moved close to him, pressing her length against his. It felt so good. Their bodies seemed to conform as if they had been made for each other. Which in the grand design of nature, Freddie reflected a little dizzily, they had been.

"This is torture," Nat murmured. "But it's very, very sweet torture."

"You could always let me sleep in the other cot."

"Never. I want you right here where I can do more research on this prisoner syndrome. I think I'm beginning to like it." Nat's lips found her temple and rested there. This was their last night together, he thought. It had all but stopped raining, and tomorrow he'd have to go back to his campsite. Given the nature of his work, who knew when he and Freddie would meet again? Certainly they weren't likely to be seeing each other under such provocative circumstances as these.

That knowledge should have made him draw back. This wasn't fair to Freddie, he admonished himself. Yet instead of pulling away, he tightened his embrace. There was just so much that flesh could bear, and he had passed beyond that point.

Freddie's reaction was no different. She could lecture herself all day that Nat Steele was Mr. Wrong, but she was only human, too. Everything conspired against her—the emotional charge of their peculiar situation, the night with its cloaking intimacy, the look she'd seen on his face when his eyes had sought hers in the audience back at the church. What woman could not respond to that? The feel of his arms enfolding her was so exciting. She wanted to wrap her own arms around his muscular back and never let go. Against his chest her breasts tingled, and a fierce heat grew between her thighs.

"The hell with being a gentleman!" she heard him mutter. Then they were kissing. It was no gentle, exploratory caress. Their hands clutched, and their mouths came together urgently. For days they'd wanted each other. Now that pent-up desire tore through its bonds.

When his lips moved in quick, possessive forays from her mouth to her jaw and then to her throat, Freddie tipped her head back in wordless acceptance. It was an instinctive gesture of submission on her part. With a groan, Nat accepted her decision. His lips sought and found the pulse that throbbed at the base of her unguarded throat. At the same time his hands went to her shoulders and slid away the straps of her bra.

"I've been wanting to kiss you like this," he murmured. "I've had dreams about it." As he spoke, he bent his head to the V between her breasts, nuzzling the lush softness he found waiting for him there.

Freddie didn't say anything. She couldn't tell him that she'd wanted it, too. But her body spoke for her. Arching her back, she abandoned herself to the increasing intimacy of his caresses. When he unhooked her bra and pushed it away altogether, she shivered with anticipation. How could she object when her whole body seemed to be on fire? His lips began tugging gently, first on one stiffened nipple, then the other, and there was no way she could deny the pleasure that shot through her. She moaned as his tongue swirled around them. When he began to suckle, she arched back even further in sensual delight.

Her fingers curled at his narrow waist, feeling his taut male strength. While his mouth continued its urgent, teasing caresses, his hands cupped her buttocks and drew her hips close to his. She felt the hard thrust of him against her belly, and her eyelids fluttered open.

"Nat," she managed to gasp on a fragile thread of caution.

But his mouth came up and silenced hers. It was an easy victory. Shuddering, she sank once more into the warm, inviting depths of their mutual desire. While her lips opened beneath his and his tongue invaded her receptive mouth, his hands fondled the smooth, soft curves of her bottom. In a moment his fingers had slipped beneath the elastic of her panties. She felt them stroke and knead the curve of her hip. Then he pulled back just enough to allow himself access to the sensitive area between her thighs.

Freddie's mind tumbled with confusion. This man was already her lover. In a moment his body would join with hers. Both of them were aflame with excitement. It spiraled between them, mounting higher and higher, demanding satisfaction. But it was a mistake, a mistake, part of her warned, even as her thighs parted and a honeyed softening answered the summons of his knowing fingers.

He tore his lips from hers and cradled her head in his palm. She opened her eyes and made out the shadowed shape of his face, so close she could feel his warm breath fanning her cheek. As they twisted together, they were like one being, yet so different.

There were so many unknowns. Even as her fingers foraged through his hair, Freddie struggled to marshal her wits. But it was impossible to drag herself back from the brink. Nat's hands still moved on her, feeding the flame his kisses had first ignited. Suddenly, it burst into a bright clear plume of light and heat.

"Oh!" Freddie gasped as her body stiffened and then shuddered in a fierce release.

During the seconds she lay lost in sensation, Nat kissed her deeply and held her close. "I want to make love to you," he whispered against her mouth. "I've been going crazy these last couple of days."

As the final thrilling slivers of ecstasy died away, Freddie lay in his arms, feeling like a lost soul. When he wedged one of his legs between hers, she offered no resistance. Yet he sensed something was wrong and looked down at her face, which in the darkness was only a pale glimmer of forehead and rounded cheek.

Lingeringly, he kissed her cheeks and her brow. "Freddie, I can't just take you like this," he whispered thickly. "I need to hear you say you want me."

"I can't," she finally answered, her voice uncharacteristically faint.

"Why not? You do want me now, you know you do!"

"Yes, yes, but I . . . I can't . . . I don't know you!"

A pulse throbbed in Nat's temple. "You can't mean that you're still afraid of me—not after this!"

"I don't know you!"

It sounded more like the wail of a confused child than one of the feisty, passionate young woman to whom Nat had started to make love. His first selfish instinct was not to listen. It wasn't as if she'd been unreceptive, he told himself. He knew when a woman was sincerely trying to be discouraging, and that hadn't happened tonight. The imperative ache in his groin demanded satisfaction. The thought of going without it at this stage was almost too painful to consider. He knew that physically she was ready for him now, that he could take her without real protest.

Rigidly, he lay on top of her, her head clasped between his palms while he struggled with himself, breathing deeply.

Freddie heard Nat draw several long, harsh breaths. Then, to her astonishment, he rolled off her body and turned away from her, breathing like an exhausted athlete after a marathon. She stared at the wall of his heaving shoulders and struggled with her own emotions. They lay around her in ruins, and it would be hopeless to try to piece them together. Part of her had rebelled, but she had wanted him and still did. That he had drawn back at the last moment amazed her. And now that the passionate mood between them had been irretrievably broken, she wasn't even sure how she felt about it, whether she was glad or sorry.

"Nat," she whispered, "I know that was partly my fault."

"There are ways a woman can let a man know when she really doesn't want him—ways that she should use a little earlier on."

"I know, I know." She extended a hand toward his shoulder, then paused uncertainly. "It's just that everything is so confusing. I can't seem to think straight anymore."

"It's pretty clear that we want each other. There's not much confusion there."

"Yes, but—oh, can't you understand how I feel?" The tears that had been burning in her eyes began to dampen her cheeks. Nat heard them in her voice and turned back toward her.

"I understand," he said gruffly. "It's my fault. I should never have started this."

That made her tears flow faster. "Do you want me to sleep in the other cot?"

"No." He took her back into his arms and pulled her close. "You'll sleep here with me tonight." Amusement crept into his voice. "I still don't trust you."

"Oh, but—"

His hand stroked down her back. "Don't worry, I won't try anything. I'll just hold you for a while. We're both in need of comfort, wouldn't you say?"

"Yes." Freddie sighed and pressed her wet cheek against his chest. She felt grateful down to her bones. And he was as good as his word. Although his hands stroked her shoulders comfortingly and his fingers played gently with her curls, pushing the silky strands back from her forehead and away from her ears, he did not approach her again that night. Freddie closed her eyes and relaxed against him. His warmth and strength cocooned her, and she finally fell asleep.

It was a long while after that before Nat closed his eyes. He cursed himself for what had happened—or almost happened. Maybe he wasn't exactly a perfect gentleman, but it didn't require a Beau Brummel to know that he'd had no business taking advantage of this situation with Freddie. Even though she had wanted him to make love to her, she still thought he was a criminal.

At that moment the temptation to wake her up and tell her the truth was very strong. But he knew he couldn't. Outspoken and headstrong as she was, too many things might go wrong if she knew the whole story. He had no right to betray Granny's trust or jeopardize the net that had taken many weeks to put into place. No, he'd have to wait until this case was closed before he explained the facts to Freddie. That shouldn't be too long from now, he consoled himself.

The next morning, Freddie awoke with a start. She knew even before she opened her eyes that something was wrong. Nat was gone. Sitting up, she stared around. It was early, but the light stealing through the windows looked different from the way it had looked the past couple of days. Strands of gold played among the dust motes. The sun really was going to shine today, she realized. But welcome as that prospect was, Freddie didn't dwell on it. She was thinking about Nat. Where was he?

Of course, he might be just outside. Or he might have gone over to Granny's to pick up some food for breakfast. But an instinct told her that neither of those things was the case. Suppressing a shiver, she got up, wrapped one of the army blankets around her, and prowled about the room. Nat's clothes were gone, and so was his pack. Then she found the note.

It was a scrap of paper in the center of the table written in a large, slanting scrawl. As she picked it up, her heart beat double time. The words she read did nothing to quiet it. "Dear Freddie, I had to go. I've asked Jeremy to keep a watch over you. Trust me enough to be good, and in just a few days everything will come out all right. Nat."

Freddie felt her blood freeze. Still holding the note and clutching the blanket around her, she hurried to the front door and threw it open. Jeremy sat on the front porch, whittling. He wore a straw hat pulled down low so that his straight brown hair hung in jagged points over his eyes. Although he was just a boy, he was bigger than she. When he turned in the old rocking chair and looked at her curiously, Freddie felt herself sink inside.

"Where's Nat?"

"I don't know. Said he had to go."

"Go where? When is he coming back?"

"Don't know," the boy responded, and judging from the frank expression in his round brown eyes, he was telling the truth. But Freddie knew where Nat had gone. He was back at his campsite near the marijuana field. He'd left it only long enough to get rid of her. Now he'd accomplished that. Unconsciously, she pulled the blanket closer and twisted her fingers together at her breast. He must have been planning to abandon her all along. So what had last night been about? He'd called himself a love-them-and-leave-them sort of guy. Then why hadn't he finished what he'd started and really loved her before he left her? An attack of conscience?

The speculation did nothing to improve Freddie's mood. Drawing back, she shut the door and looked around bleakly. With Nat gone, the place was about as appealing as a prison cell. Her gaze fell on the rumpled cot, and she reviewed the events of the night before. Had it really happened? Had he come close to making love to her and then turned away at the last moment out of what she had to suppose was consideration? And had she then lain in his arms the rest of the dark hours pressed to his heart while he comforted her with kindly hands and gentle words?

If he cared enough for that, why hadn't he told her he was leaving? Why had he stolen away and left her alone in this alien place with these people that she couldn't begin to understand? Even after all that had happened, he was still a stranger. Really, she knew no more about him now than she had that first moment when she'd opened her eyes to find him looking down at her. In some ways she knew less, for each piece of information she'd managed to glean about Nat Steele seemed to contradict the one before.

When Freddie dressed and walked back out onto the porch, Jeremy was still patiently waiting. "I'm to take you over to Granny's," he told her.

She had no choice but to follow. A few minutes later she sat down to a hearty breakfast with several other of the concertgoers she'd met the previous evening.

"There's ham, and grits, and more of Vandy's corn muffins on the table," Granny told her cheerfully. "Help yourself to all you want."

The cheery atmosphere in Granny's crowded cabin was much different from the air of desertion that now prevailed in Nat's. In addition to Freddie, there were five other people at the table—a family of three and a young couple. "Don't expect to see Pete Lorden or Bill Hooper until sundown," Granny said with a rich chuckle. "Last I heard, they was both snoring away in a church pew, overcome by melody and corn liquor."

"A powerful sleepy combination," commented an older man who'd introduced himself as Milt.

Freddie peered around and noted that several other guests were still asleep in Granny's living room, stretched out on chairs and benches or curled up on blankets in front of the stove. Those who were up and eating breakfast ignored the others. In lively tones they talked of last night's concert and the trips they had to make back to their homes today.

As Freddie split a muffin, she remembered her resolve to appeal to someone for help. She gazed speculatively at Loretta, Milt's redheaded wife. She had a kind face and looked as if she might be willing to play Good Samaritan. Freddie decided to risk approaching her if she could find a minute of privacy in which to do it.

"Can't you stay on a day or two?" Granny asked as Loretta served a generous portion of ham to her bearded, thickset husband.

"No, there's so much doin' back home, and it takes such a while gettin' there. 'Sides, you got more people than you know what to do with here. You should be pushin' us out the door, not invitin' us to stay on."

Granny set down a platter of freshly scrambled eggs. "Oh, I enjoy the company. Sometimes it gets mighty lonely up here."

"I expect it does," Loretta agreed.

As Freddie spooned some eggs onto her plate, she silently concurred. What was it like in winter? she wondered. And how would Granny stand up to the isolation when the rest of her family had deserted her and her health began to fail? Suddenly, Freddie felt almost guilty about her own plans to leave. It was strange how she had become involved in the lives of other people so quickly, she mused. Two days ago she hadn't even known this place existed. Now she was worried about whether or not Granny and Vandy were lonely.

Nevertheless, when Loretta, Milt, and their lanky teen-age son Josh set off, Freddie excused herself to visit the outhouse and then circled around to intercept them. To her annoyance, Jeremy had followed her and was no more than fifty yards away when she tapped Loretta on the shoulder and made her appeal.

"Can you help me?" she asked after blurting out what she knew was a garbled and highly unlikely-sounding story.

Loretta's sandy eyebrows rose into sharp, suspicious points. "Help you? My land, girl, don't start tellin' me no bad tales about Nat Steele and the Parkers. They're finer folks than you'll ever know, and if they want you to stay here, it's for your own good."

"Damn right," Milt growled, coming up behind his wife and glowering at Freddie.

"But—" Freddie sputtered. She looked from one hostile face to the other. "You can see the marijuana growing around their houses. It's a controlled substance."

"Looks mighty healthy to me," declared Loretta. "Now, get your hand off my shoulder before I go back and tell Granny all about this foolishness!"

At that moment Jeremy approached and snagged Freddie's elbow. "You're wanted back at the house. There's lots of chores need doin'."

"I should hope so," harrumphed Loretta, shaking herself free and turning to stalk away with the rest of her family.

Her shoulders slumping, Freddie allowed herself to be led back to the house. During the rest of that morning and late into the afternoon, she was kept busy with the cooking. It was a nonstop job, for all through what remained of the day people continued to wake up hungry. At unlikely hours they straggled in from the barns and the other cabins, rubbing their eyes and looking around for a hot cup of coffee and a plate of food.

Twice more Freddie found an opportunity to beg for help. On both occasions, she met even more hostility than Loretta had shown. At last she admitted to herself that Nat had been right: none of the Parkers' guests would help her. And if she kept on asking, she risked getting herself into even more trouble. She was going to have to think of something else. Frowning, Freddie went back out to the kitchen.

"You been gettin' to know folks?" Granny asked as she prepared to scramble another dozen eggs in her big iron frying pan.

Freddie's emotions were so tangled that she couldn't quite meet the spry old woman's inquisitive gaze. To cover her confusion she commented brightly, "Goodness, that's the tenth batch of eggs you've scrambled. You must have a lot of hens."

"Nope, I just been collecting for a spell," Granny explained as she stirred the golden mixture. "I knew I'd have some people to feed, so whenever those hens started cacklin', my ears upped like a rabbit's and I run out with my basket. Now, give me a hand with this, would you?" She held the platter while Freddie spooned the cooked eggs onto it. Then Granny went out to serve the food and chat with her guests, leaving Freddie alone in the kitchen with Vandy.

All day the girl had been withdrawn, going about her tasks in moody silence.

Freddie cast her a sympathetic look and cleared her throat. "Vandy, I've been meaning to tell you how much I enjoyed your singing last night."

"Thank you."

"You're very talented. You have a really beautiful voice."

The girl was bent over a mixing bowl. Although she didn't look directly at Freddie, the compliment softened her expression slightly.

"I like to sing," she finally answered. "And I always sing better when Nat plays for me. We make an extra special good team, don't you think?"

"Yes, I do." Actually, Freddie thought that Vandy would sound good with any accompanist. Nat played very competent guitar, but so did a lot of other musicians. Vandy's voice, on the other hand, was extraordinary.

"I work for a radio station," Freddie added after a moment. "So I've heard a lot of country singers. To my ears, you are as good as any."

Dropping the large wooden spoon with which she'd been desultorily stirring batter, Vandy turned and stared wide-eyed at Freddie. "You work for the radio? I've always wanted to sing on the radio. Could I come and sing on your station?"

"I'm afraid it's not as simple as that. You have to make a record for a record company, and then a deejay has to want to play it."

Vandy's face fell. "I wouldn't get the chance to do nothin' like that up here."

It was true, Freddie realized. With all the talent in

the world, Vandy didn't have a chance as long as she was hidden away in these mountains.

Just then Granny came bustling back in. "I swear, these folks have stomachs that won't quit. And that no-good Pete Lorden just came in lookin' to be fed." She put down her empty platter, her gaze darting around the kitchen. "Vandy, why don't you and Freddie go over to Martha's? I know she's been feedin' a peck of people over there, but you might see if she's got any extra eggs. If she don't have any, you can show Freddie the henhouse and look for some that might've been laid since last night." Granny patted Vandy's shoulder. "Now that it's stopped raining tomcats and hoe handles, it's time you two girls got out of this kitchen for a breath of fresh air."

Her great-grandmother took over at the mixing bowl, and Vandy untied her apron. Freddie followed her out the door. It really had turned into a beautiful day. Without the rain and overcast skies, the little valley looked entirely different. The sparkling-clear air was crisp with the promise of autumn, and all around scarlet and gold threaded the velvety green of the thickly wooded hills.

Martha and Jim's cabin turned out to be a fascinating place. When Vandy and Freddie arrived, Martha was in the kitchen talking with some friends, but Jim was alone in the living area, perched on a stool and carving at a piece of walnut. All around, musical instruments hung on the walls in various stages of completion. While Vandy went to the kitchen to speak to Martha, Freddie walked around examining the instruments.

"How long have you been making them?" she asked Jim.

He tugged on his beard and adjusted the feathered straw hat he wore. "I started when I was thirteen, and the first one took me three solid weeks. See that banjo there on the wall?"

Freddie turned to examine the smoke-blackened instrument.

"That was my first," Jim said. "With my grandaddy's help, I sawed the wood with a keyhole saw, made a bridge out of a piece of bucket, and cut up a washtub to make the circle for the head. I used the hide of a rabbit for a soundboard."

"It still rings true," Freddie commented, plucking one of the strings.

"Yep, but it's not as good as the work I do now. Over the years I've learned a thing or two. That's why they still come from all around when they want a really fine instrument."

Freddie believed him. The truth of what he said was in the pride on his face and the rich, smooth glow of the wood he fashioned so lovingly.

"No eggs here," Vandy declared, coming back into the room. "Let's try the henhouse."

Together they set off for a ramshackle building a couple of hundred yards away. As they walked, they passed a large plot of land planted with row upon row of hemp bushes. At one point Freddie stopped to finger one of the long, serrated leaves and look inquiringly at Vandy.

"You know what that is, don't you?" the girl queried.

"Yes, I do. It's marijuana."

They walked on in silence for a moment before Freddie finally asked the question burning on the

151

edge of her tongue. "Why are you all growing it around your houses like this?"

"Didn't Nat tell you?"

"No, he didn't."

Vandy sighed and scuffed a toe in the grass. "It was Hap's idea. He and Marshall knew a man in Atlanta who said he'd sell it for us and give us a lot more money than we could make growing anything else. He was right," she allowed with a shake of her head, "but now that we've had so much trouble over it, I don't think we'll plant it after this year."

"What kind of trouble?" Freddie asked as they paused outside the henhouse.

But Vandy's expression closed up. "I've already talked too much," she said. "Granny would have my hide if she knew. I don't want to speak about this no more."

CHAPTER NINE

"Get off, Pinky!" Brushing the inquisitive dog away, Nat knelt in front of the old oak and peered into its hollow. To his relief, the radio was still there. Carefully, he withdrew it and unwrapped it. Then he opened the case and made the necessary adjustments. A moment later, he was speaking with his contact.

"There's no sign of them yet," he told Al. "The fields haven't been disturbed."

"Not for long, judging from the weather report," Al's voice crackled back. "It's supposed to stay warm for the next couple of days, but there's a cold front coming in Wednesday morning and a prediction for frost that night. Headquarters is betting your playmates will turn up within the next forty-eight hours."

Nat's eyebrows elevated, and he glanced down at the rifle lying near his feet. "Got you."

"Here are your orders: Call us the minute anything happens, and then stay as clear as possible. When we hear from you, we'll be on top of the situation with a small army."

"I'll be ready and waiting."

"Keep your eyes peeled."

"I'll do that."

"Oh, and speaking of playmates, any trouble with that female glider pilot who dropped in?"

Nat's mouth twisted wryly. Words couldn't begin to describe the trouble Ms. Frederica Davenport was generating, he thought. Aloud, he said, "No. I've tucked her away with the Parkers. She should be okay until this operation is tied up."

"I hope so. Turns out her brother is a bigwig lawyer with a lot of connections. Anything happens to her, and we'll have hornets in our pants. You sure know how to pick 'em, buddy."

"Don't I though," Nat agreed.

After the call was concluded and the radio carefully restored to its hiding place, he rocked back on his heels, pushed his hat up on his forehead, and reflected on what he'd just learned. Freddie hadn't said anything about her family. She'd been too busy spitting like an angry cat and defying him at every possible turn. He remembered her words last night: "I don't know you."

She had been right, he acknowledged ruefully. They really knew almost nothing about each other. They'd been too busy fighting the attraction exploding so inconveniently between them to find much out. Now Nat regretted that. During the long, solitary hike back to his campsite, he'd thought about her. His mind had posed questions to which he frustratingly had no answers.

It had just about killed him to leave Freddie that morning. All night, she'd been curled against him like a kitten. Only instead of spitting and hissing with anger, she'd purred contentedly and wrapped her soft, cuddly body around his. With a physical ache that was pure torture, he remembered the curve of her full breasts and the supple roundness of her hips pressed to his. Her face in the shadows had been so sweet to look at, with the curls clustered around her forehead and the long lashes sweeping her cheeks. She was such a bundle of contradictions—part little girl, part spunky adventuress, and all woman.

Nat wished he could resolve some of those contradictions. Oh yes, he wanted to know more about her. But it wasn't just the big blanks that he felt the need to fill in—her family background, her education, her convictions and prejudices. In some ways he was less curious about those than he was about the little things. What was her favorite color? What kinds of food did she like to eat? Given a choice, how would she want to spend a Sunday afternoon? And how would it be to spend that Sunday afternoon in her arms, undressing her with slow deliberation and then making love to her while the waning light played over her beautiful body?

Nat guessed he knew the answer to that. Even though they hadn't consummated their physical union, they'd come close enough for him to know how it would be. That was going to make the next few vigilant days alone in this wilderness very tough indeed.

While she worked in Granny's kitchen, Freddie almost had the illusion that she was part of the family. Everyone seemed friendly, and Granny treated her with the same casual motherliness that she showed Vandy and the rest of her kin. But there was a difference. Every now and then, Freddie caught the old woman casting sharp, speculative glances her way. Busy as she was, Granny kept an eye on her, and there was no time when Freddie was left to her own devices.

Even when she and Vandy had gone out to hunt for eggs, Jeremy hadn't been far behind. He hadn't joined them, but he hadn't lost sight of them, either.

The night after Nat's departure, Freddie wasn't allowed to sleep by herself in his cabin. Vandy joined her, and when Freddie got up in the middle of the night to peer out the window, she saw that Jeremy was on the porch rolled up in a sleeping bag. No doubt about it—she was a prisoner.

That realization had a chilling effect. Of course, she'd known it all along. But somehow, now that Nat was gone, things seemed much worse. With an aching heart, she acknowledged that while he'd been with her she'd really felt more threatened by her attraction to him than by her awkward situation. Now she was forced to assess what was happening objectively. It wasn't pleasant.

She'd been taken captive by a handsome rogue who'd abandoned her without a backward look. She was now the prisoner of people who were breaking the law. Freddie liked Granny and Vandy, but she didn't have much confidence in the Parker boys and their friend, Hap. Who knew what they would eventually do with her? She'd already behaved like a crazy fool with Nat. It would be insane to accept the assurances he'd written in that note. Of course he'd tell her not to worry—he'd say the same thing to a turkey he was about to behead for Thanksgiving.

"I've got to get out of here," Freddie muttered under her breath. "And this time, I've got to be clever enough to succeed."

The next morning, Granny sent Freddie and Vandy

out together again to collect eggs. As they rooted around in the fetid-smelling henhouse, Freddie searched for a way to begin the conversation she'd decided to have with Vandy. Finally, she just opened her mouth and started in.

"Vandy, what did Nat and Granny say to you about me?"

"How do you mean?" Vandy shot her a quick, startled look, then glanced away.

"I mean, it's obvious that you and Jeremy are watching me. Did Granny and Nat tell you to do that?"

"Nat didn't say nothin'," Vandy mumbled, "but Granny said I was to make sure you didn't go nowheres." Obviously embarrassed, the girl straightened and began to examine the contents of her basket. "Maybe that old fox that sneaks around here made these hens nervy. They ain't layin' half what they should."

Freddie refused to be distracted from her purpose. After they'd walked back outside, she stopped and gazed searchingly into Vandy's pretty young face. "Do you know why Granny doesn't want me to leave?"

Vandy shuffled her feet. "No. But I figure it's got somethin' to do with Nat. Maybe you're his girl friend, but there's somethin' funny about it."

"You're right. But I wouldn't do anything to hurt him." Which was the absolute truth, Freddie realized. Although she was aware that she should report everything she'd seen here to the police, she knew she wouldn't. All she wanted now was to get away. She paused. "Vandy, how much do you want to sing on the radio?"

The girl stared. "What do you mean?"

"I mean that if I were back in Nashville where I work, I might be able to arrange an audition for you. Would you like that?"

Vandy's face lit up. "Do you mean it? Would you really do that?"

"Yes, I would." Freddie looked her straight in the eye. "But first you have to do something for me."

"What's that?" Suspicion clouded Vandy's radiant expression.

"Help me leave here tonight." Freddie put up a quick hand to forestall the negative answer she saw coming. "You wouldn't have to do much. You'd just have to distract Jeremy long enough for me to get out of the cabin tonight without him seeing, and then not tell anyone that I'm gone until the morning."

The girl stared back silently, her brow puckered. "Granny would skin me."

"You could say I slipped away while you were asleep. She couldn't really blame you."

"You don't know Granny."

"Isn't getting the chance at an audition worth a risk or two?"

Vandy considered. "You sure you don't mean Nat no hurt?"

"None. I promise. And as soon as I'm back at my job, I'll start calling people I know about getting you that audition." Freddie held her breath and waited. It was obvious that Vandy was tempted.

"What are you going to do out there in the woods by yourself?" Vandy finally asked. "There's big animals in these parts. You might never find your way safe."

"I've got a compass. I'll make it."

158

Vandy looked doubtful, but now there was a calculating glint in her beautiful brown eyes. Vandy was young and naïve, but she wasn't stupid. Freddie guessed she might be reflecting that no matter what happened, she would be the winner. If Freddie made it back to Nashville, she'd have an audition. And if she didn't—well, in that event Vandy would no longer have a rival for Nat's affections. Then Freddie felt ashamed of herself for thinking so ill of the girl.

Whatever her motivations, a few minutes later Vandy agreed to Freddie's scheme. "All right," she whispered harshly. "As soon as everyone's gone to bed tonight, I'll look the other way so's you can skedaddle. But you better not forget your promise. You better get me that audition."

Freddie stuck out her hand. "I won't forget, and I will do it. You have my word on that."

Vandy quickly shook the proffered hand. Then she self-consciously shifted the half-filled basket of eggs onto her round, lightly freckled arm. "Then it's fixed. Now we'd better get back to the kitchen afore Granny thinks there's somethin' funny going on and comes out lookin' for us."

By sundown that evening Freddie was so nervous, she was ready to jump and run whenever a burning log crackled in the stove. She wasn't only anxious about whether her escape tonight would be successful, she was also wondering what she would do if it were. Would she really be able to make her way safely through the wilderness and find Nat's radio?

It didn't help that Granny's cozy cabin was now a very pleasant place to be. All the concert guests had left to return to their homes, and Marshall, Lou, and

Hap had taken the dogs and gone hunting. For almost two hours after dinner had been cleared away, Freddy, Vandy, and Granny sat around the old stove in what was mostly a companionable silence. Granny's wooden knitting needles clacked while Vandy put in small, neat stitches on a sampler. Freddie struggled with some socks she'd been given to mend.

"My goodness girl, you're surely making a botch-up," Granny commented, looking over the top of her spectacles. "Don't you know nothin' about darning socks?" The woman clicked her tongue disapprovingly.

"Where I live, when you get holes in your socks, you just throw them away."

Both Granny and Vandy looked horrified.

"These city folks is wicked," the older woman finally exclaimed. "Well, I hope you learn better here. You'll never get a man wantin' to marry up with you when you have such wasteful ways."

Freddie smiled and shook her head. "Maybe I don't want one."

"Tush, girl! Don't give me that nonsense. Any gal worth her salt is lookin' for a good man to make a home with. That's the way the Lord made us. And a fine thing, too. If it wasn't for us women holdin' 'em down, these no-account men would be gallivantin' all over, makin' a fine mess of things."

Freddie didn't argue. Actually, she realized, Granny's sentiments were not so far from those she'd expressed to Nat on that long, rainy hike up here. Had that really been only three days ago? Now it seemed to have happened in another lifetime. Everything had been turned topsy-turvy, and she hardly felt like the same person anymore. Freddie wasn't sure what she believed now. She needed time to sort it all out again —which she wouldn't be able to do until she was safely back in Nashville. No two ways about it: If there was any chance she could leave this place tonight, she had to try.

A short time later, she and Vandy strolled back to Nat's cabin to spend the night. Jeremy was already there. He'd built a fire and was sitting before it whittling and waiting. After he'd taken his sleeping bag out onto the porch, Vandy turned to Freddie.

"You'd best hold on until about an hour after the lights turn off in Granny's cabin," Vandy whispered. "Then I'll go out and get Jeremy."

"What will you say to him?"

"I'll tell him I heard a noise out by the henhouse. There's been a fox skulking around. I'll make him walk back with me to check. While we're gone, you can sneak out and into the woods."

"That sounds like a very good scheme," Freddie complimented. Now that Vandy had agreed to help, she seemed almost enthusiastic and had obviously thought out her plan with some care.

"I brought some things you might need," Vandy went on. She surprised Freddie by unrolling a small bundle that she had concealed in her apron. It consisted of a wool army shirt in which a flashlight and food had been wrapped. "It's only bread and some dried beef, but I thought you might like to have it."

"I certainly will. Thank you very much." Freddie was touched by Vandy's unlooked-for consideration, and she was particularly grateful for the flashlight, which she was pleased to discover had a live battery. Although the sky was clear and the moon and stars were out, it would be dark among the trees. In that rough terrain a thousand obstacles would present themselves for stumbling over. The flashlight would be invaluable.

Slipping the army shirt on over Granny's sweater, Freddie carefully tucked the food and flashlight into her pockets and lay down on her cot to wait.

The minutes crept by, but after what seemed like hours, Vandy glided across the floor and tapped Freddie on the shoulder. Then the girl went outside, where she roused young Jeremy from what had apparently been a sound sleep.

"Get up, you lazybones!"

"What's wrong? What you pokin' at me for?"

As Freddie sat on the edge of the cot listening to their voices, her shoulders ached with tension and her heart thudded painfully. Grumpily, the boy agreed to accompany Vandy to check the henhouse. Everything seemed to be going according to plan. When she heard the two step noisily off the porch, she crept to the window and peered out. A moment after they had rounded the side of the house and their voices had faded, she slipped out the front door. Jumping off the porch onto the grass, she hurried in the opposite direction toward the dark shape of the looming forest.

The sea of mud that had stopped her earlier was now no more than a small puddle. She hopped across it easily. On the other side the ground sloped up sharply toward the trees. After a quick backward look, she began to climb, panting a little in her haste. As she labored up the incline, Freddie remembered coming down with Nat into this fog-shrouded valley. Back then, it had been a place of mystery. How would she think of it in the future? she wondered.

And just what kind of future lay in store for her tonight?

Her escape route took only a few minutes to cover, but it seemed like forever before the woods swallowed her up. At last she glided in among the shelter of the tall trees. There she was truly grateful for the flashlight Vandy had given her. The first thing she did with it was check her compass and take her bearings. Feeling vulnerable and utterly alone, she realized just how difficult this journey was going to be. But she didn't have much choice, did she? Squaring her shoulders, Freddie set off.

It was even tougher than she'd imagined—and not just because the difficulties of finding a safe route through the rocks, fallen trees, and roots made the uneven terrain even more formidable. Although Freddie had been told there were dangerous animals in the area, she hadn't taken that warning too seriously. In her hike with Nat she hadn't seen anything but birds and squirrels. But now, as she made her way through the darkness, flashing her light and checking her compass at regular intervals, she became painfully aware of the alien noises around her.

The mountain forest at night was anything but silent. Dry leaves fluttered and branches scraped. There were odd little squeaks, punctuated by whispers and scuttling sounds. Could those be coming from one of the wild boars Nat had mentioned, or even from a mountain lion who was stalking her? Although she strained her eyes and saw nothing, her nerves prickled. What a comfort it would have been to have Pinky at her side. But Nat had taken the dog with him.

Overhead, an owl hooted. Freddie shivered inside

her layers of clothing. The day had been warm, but the night was still chilly. She was glad for the army shirt Vandy had provided. She was also extremely happy to have Jeremy's boots. Without their sturdy protection, she would long ago have twisted her ankle or broken a toe. Then what would have happened to her? she wondered. Would she have lain in pain until some hungry wild animal discovered her?

The thought sent such icy fingers down her spine that she almost bumped into a tree. Gasping, she turned on her flashlight. To her horror, she saw that there was a sheer drop of some twenty feet on the other side. She'd been about to walk right over it.

"If I don't want to kill myself, I'd better stop and wait until morning," she muttered to herself. But where could she do that safely? Aiming her flashlight up into the tree, she saw that its branches forked about five feet off the ground. The place where the limbs separated looked like a perch where she could settle herself fairly comfortably.

Freddie was good at climbing trees. As a kid, she'd always been able to beat her brothers up all the oaks and maples growing on their property. This tree was a cinch. In just a few minutes she was leaning her head back against one of the two main trunks and stretching her tired legs out along a sturdy limb projecting parallel to the ground. After that, it was just a matter of waiting for dawn.

A moment later, she closed her eyes and almost dropped her flashlight. Stay awake, she told herself, staring wide-eyed up at the starry sky. Where was Nat now? she wondered. Most likely, he was sleeping like a log, not giving her a second thought. What would he do if he discovered her using his radio? She smiled, but then her expression quickly sobered. Of course, that all depended on her surviving this woodland ordeal long enough to find the thing. Freddie folded her arms across her chest and stuck out her chin. It couldn't be long before dawn, not more than an hour or two.

A few miles away, Nat sat up in his tent with a startled exclamation. He'd been dreaming about Freddie, dreaming that she was in terrible danger. Would he ever get that woman out of his mind? he wondered. Irritably, he scratched his stubbled chin. Then he felt around in the dark until he found his jeans. After he'd pulled them on and thrust his arms into his flannel shirt, he went outside to have a look around. Nothing stirred. The night was serene.

Serenity was something he hadn't been able to achieve for himself the past few days. Snapping an oath, he went back into his tent and rooted around in his pack until he found his cigarettes. Then he searched out a spot on the banks of the creek that gurgled nearby. There he leaned against a tree trunk and prepared to have one of his infrequent quiet smokes. After he lit up, he inhaled and then turned the cigarette sideways in his long fingers so that he could contemplate the ruby glow pulsing at its end. Where was Freddie now? he wondered. Safely tucked away in her cabin, of course. He sighed with relief and regret. At least he didn't have to worry about her. That made things a little easier.

The hours Freddie spent waiting for dawn were two of the longest she could remember. At last, thin gray streaks lightened the sky. When there was enough illumination that she could study the face of her compass without the flashlight, she ate some of the bread and meat Vandy had provided and then slid awkwardly down to the ground and resumed her journey. As she trudged along, Freddie was relieved to spot some of the landmarks she remembered from the trip up. So she hadn't lost her way, she thought, eyeing the rock formation that had reminded her of a castle. Hooray for her years as a Girl Scout and her pilot's training.

Around noon, she found herself in territory that looked particularly familiar. There was a stream on her right that she suspected was the same one that ran past Nat's campsite. It and the radio might be very close now.

After stopping to take a drink from the stream and to eat some more of her food, Freddie moistened the end of her finger and tested the wind. Luck was in her favor. If she followed the creek bed, it would put her downwind of the camp. If, as she suspected, the creek led her to Nat's camp, its gurgling water would help muffle the sound of her cautious footfalls. Twenty minutes later, she was peering through the trees at a familiar scene.

About sixty yards off, through the screen of leaves and trunks, she could just barely make out Nat's tent. At that instant, a flash of movement made her duck behind a bush and then squint through the weblike tracery of its delicate branches. She saw Nat. He was lying down under a tree, evidently taking an afternoon snooze. Pinky was stretched out beside him.

The sight of Nat's fair head made Freddie's heart squeeze, and she fought back a terrible temptation to walk out into the clearing and greet him. But that would be crazy. Dragging her gaze from him, she looked around, trying to spot the tree where the radio was hidden. It would be equally insane to try and use the radio now, she told herself. If Nat didn't hear the noise and wake up, Pinky surely would. No, the time for that was either at night when they were both asleep in the tent or, better yet, later this afternoon when they weren't around.

Once again, her eyes lingered on Nat's prone form. It was a shock to realize just how hungry she'd been for the sight of him. Was part of the reason for this crazy journey her need to see him again? But no. She shook her head. The perfectly rational reason why she'd undertaken her trip was to contact a rescue party and get away from here. And she wouldn't accomplish that goal if she stayed around here much longer gazing longingly at Nat.

Turning away, Freddie snuck back along the stream bank. The sight of Nat's sleeping form had produced several effects in her. One of them was to make her realize just how tired she was. For a day and a night she'd had almost no sleep. Maybe she should take a cue from Nat and get in an afternoon snooze. But where?

She walked a safe distance away from the campsite and looked around for some sort of shelter. It was useless to imagine that she could nap in a tree. She'd probably fall, and if she didn't break something, the sound of the crash might make Pinky's sharp ears prick up. What she needed was a little cave, like the one where she and Nat had eaten their lunch.

She hunted along both sides of the stream, but she saw nothing that looked appropriate. Not until she wandered farther afield toward a rock outcropping did she spot something that might do. There looked to be some sort of opening in a rock face beneath a huge old pine with projecting limbs that ran up its thick trunk almost like a stepladder.

Gingerly, she approached it, stopping every now and then to listen. What if it already had an occupant? She heard nothing, yet the fine hairs on the back of her neck were prickling. When she was within about five feet of the small, dark opening, she stopped and stared at it. Had she heard a noise, a soft grunt?

At that instant, she saw the gleam of an eye. A small, dark body spilled from the opening. It was immediately followed by another. Freddie's first wild thought was that she'd stumbled on to a cave occupied by gnomes wearing fur coats. She gave a piercing shriek and turned to run, but in her haste she tripped over Jeremy's clodhoppers and stumbled. She had just managed to leap to her feet when the gnomes were upon her.

Horrified, she felt furry arms clasp and cling to her legs. Looking down, she saw a long, pink tongue and uttered another bloodcurdling scream. And at that instant she recognized her assailants. They weren't gnomes, they were bear cubs. One was clinging to her leg for dear life.

"Oh, my God!" Freddie exclaimed as she tried to dislodge the furry arms. The clinging cub's sibling was less forward. Instead of attaching itself to her other leg, it circled around, making excited grunting and squealing noises. Still attempting to unwrap one creature's arms, she eyed the other nervously. Did bear cubs bite? So far, neither was making any effort to do so. Instead, the one glued to her leg was gazing lovingly into her face as if it expected her to take it up into her arms.

"Didn't your mother tell you never to talk to strangers?" Freddie asked. But that made her eyes widen in even greater chagrin. These cubs must have a mother someplace. Freddie might not know much about the ways of the wild, but she was sure that mother bears did bite. Especially if they found someone fooling with their cubs. She had to get away!

That wasn't easy to do. The toddler bear glued to her leg had a summer's growth on him, and he was strong. He was cute, too. But that wouldn't have stopped Freddie from cuffing him hard enough to make him let go if she hadn't thought it would change his affectionate mood to one of anger. Who knew what damage he could inflict or what distress signals he might send out?

She had just managed to unwrap one of his arms when she heard a roar of pure fury. Turning, she saw a dark shape running toward her through the woods.

Freddie emitted a shriek so piercing that the cub fell back in alarm. Springing over it, she rushed for the mammoth pine tree near the cave and began scrambling up its ladderlike limbs. The adrenaline of terror gave her the speed and strength of an Olympic gymnast. She was perhaps fifteen feet from the ground before she paused to look down.

What she saw did nothing to lessen her fright. The mother bear was at the base, glaring up at her, while the cubs cowered back. As high as she was, Freddie could still see red sparks of rage flickering in the animal's eyes. Letting out another scream, Freddie began to climb again. But the bear, her claws extended, was now mounting the tree, too.

Her ascent was nowhere near as hasty as Freddie's had been. Instead, it had an ominous deliberation.

"Oh, my God!" Freddie muttered under her breath. She shinnied helter-skelter up another five or six feet. Her heart was beating so fast and furiously, it seemed likely to fly out of her chest at any moment. As high as she was, it was becoming more difficult to climb. The branches were closer together, and their sharp needles tore at her skin and clothing. Dizzily, she turned to look back. The bear was still coming.

"I wasn't hurting your cubs. Stop! Go away!" she screamed, aware even as she yelled that her commands were useless and ridiculous. The animal didn't look as if she had any intention of turning back. Freddie was now so high off the ground that she felt nauseous when she glanced down. The dark shapes of the cubs who were observing the show from below swam before her eyes. How could she have imagined, even for an instant, that they were cute?

Overcome by terror, she clung to the branches. At this height they were much more fragile, and they swayed sickeningly under her weight. Her only hope was that the mother bear, with her much greater bulk, would break a branch and fall. But so far that wasn't happening. The animal, growling horribly and showing its fangs, was now no more than five feet away.

Freddie tried once again to climb. But she couldn't. Her muscles failed her. All she could do was brace her back against the trunk and look down in horror as the bear came closer and closer.

Then, at last, the bear too had some trouble. A branch broke under her, and she roared with fury as she struggled to save herself. The top of the pine tree swung back and forth like a pendulum. Nevertheless, the enraged creature managed to haul her bulk up another foot. Freddie could almost feel the bear's hot breath on her ankles. Suddenly, the animal took a swipe at her feet. Freddie kicked back and felt claws rake the soles of her boots. She once more thanked providence for Jeremy's clodhoppers. If she had been wearing her own canvas sneakers, she would now be missing her toes.

The bear continued to struggle for balance. With her heart in her mouth, Freddie watched for a moment or two. Then, gathering up what shreds of courage and resolution remained in her, she lowered herself slightly and jammed her boot hard against the top of the creature's head. The blow was enough to upset the bear's precarious balance, so that she slid down several feet, ripping off branches as she fell, roaring with frustration.

"Get away!" Freddie howled. "Go back to your cubs!"

At that moment another sound was added to the cacophony. Down below, barking furiously, Pinky barreled out of the woods. At the sight of him, the cubs began to scamper up the pine tree, too. But their progress was impeded by their mother, whose attention was no longer on Freddie.

Bellowing with rage, she descended hastily. As she went, she knocked her cubs out of the way and sent them sprawling back down to the ground. Pinky paid them no regard. All his attention was fixed on the mother bear, and all of hers was on him.

Growling, with his fangs exposed and his ears flat to his head, Pinky was a terrifying sight. But the mother bear was equally daunting. She was much bigger than the dog and was prepared to fight to the death for her cubs.

As Freddie stared down, she wrung her hands and thought that she was about to witness a senseless tragedy. She certainly wished the little family of bears no harm. If Pinky attacked the mother, he might inflict some serious damage, but he'd get his belly ripped open in the process. "Pinky!" she shouted frantically. "Pinky, no!"

CHAPTER TEN

The afternoon sun filtered down through the canopy of leaves. Under it Nat lay sleeping. Pinky dozed peacefully at his side. Stirred by a wayward breeze, dappled shadows moved softly over his face. His sleeping features were set in an unconscious smile. He was dreaming of Freddie again. In this dream she was perched in a tree, just out of his reach. Her face was radiant as she laughed playfully down at him. Beseechingly, he lifted his arms toward her.

Then, his pleasant dream was shattered by a sharp noise. His eyes snapped open. He sat up and looked around him groggily. The sound had come from Pinky. The dog was standing, sniffing the wind, his ears cocked and twitching.

"What is it?" Nat muttered. "Have they come?"

The dog paid him no mind. It was obvious from the growl rumbling low in his throat that he'd just heard something.

Nat's ears hadn't picked up a thing, but he trusted Pinky's hearing and instincts. Grasping the gun at his side, he scrambled to his feet. "Stay put!" he instructed Pinky. "I don't want you warning them off before I get a chance to reconnoiter."

Again, the dog seemed not to have heard. In the

next instant, barking wildly, he took off in the opposite direction from the one Nat had been prepared to investigate.

"Hell!" he exclaimed. The last thing he needed was to have his plan ruined because his dog had suddenly gone berserk. "Come back here!" he shouted as he started to race after the animal.

But Pinky was intent on some goal all his own. What the hell was bothering him? Nat wondered. He couldn't remember ever seeing him quite this frantic.

Cursing under his breath, Nat crashed through some prickly brambles that tore at his jeans. Then he heard it, too. He stopped, and his cheeks went white under their tan. *What was that?* It sounded like a scream. What was worse, it sounded like a woman's scream. As the realization of what that might mean penetrated, Nat burst forward, plunging after Pinky.

The dog had long ago outstripped him. But now Nat had not only the sound of a woman's screams to guide him but a chorus of bloodcurdling animal growls as well. When he burst into the clearing from which the screams and growls were coming, he was appalled.

"Pinky, back!" he commanded. He raised his gun and fired two rapid shots into the air.

The explosive sound of the gunshots distracted Pinky, who had been poised to spring. The mother bear, who had reared up on her hind feet, her claws out and teeth bared, was thrown off kilter by the sound of the gun and the sudden appearance of another human. Abruptly, she dropped back down onto all fours, gathered up her whimpering cubs, and rapidly shambled away in the opposite direction. When Pinky started to follow, Nat once again barked a sharp command. This time, much to his relief, the dog heard it and was smart enough to obey.

"Christ!" Nat muttered as he stared after the disappearing bear. Then he looked up into the tall pine tree under which she'd been cornered. "Christ!" he hissed again.

It was like a parody of the dream he'd been having. Freddie was in the tree. But instead of being just out of reach, she was clinging to a limb twenty feet off the ground. And instead of smiling playfully down at him, she was wide-eyed, as pale as a ghost. She had blood on her knees.

"Are you all right?"

"Yes."

He took a deep, shuddering breath. "What the hell," he called up to her, "are you doing?"

It was a moment before she answered. When she finally did, her voice quavered. "The mother bear chased me up here."

"The mother bear—" Nat stopped abruptly, staring at her incredulously. Then his face turned red. "What are you doing here? You're supposed to be with the Parkers. Why the hell aren't you?"

Freddie gaped down at him. "I snuck away."

"Snuck away?" Nat lowered his head and glared at the pine as if he'd like to rip off its branches. "God in heaven, there should be a law against women like you!" Then he looked back up at Freddie. "Get down here!"

"I can't."

"What do you mean, you can't? You got up there, didn't you? Come back down!"

"I've never been up this high before. My legs aren't working."

Nat realized that she was telling the truth. She was twenty feet off the ground, but he could see that her eyes were the size of dinner plates and that she'd wrapped her arms around the swaying trunk as if she never intended to let go. He guessed that after what she'd been through, shock had set in, and she really couldn't climb down.

"Freddie, you have to try," he told her a little desperately.

"I can't."

He glanced around the clearing and then at the gun clasped in his hand. What if he were to put it down and the bear came back? But that was unlikely. He had to get Freddie out of the tree. He set the firearm onto the ground and turned toward the pine. He began to climb it—which was not such an easy task now that the bear's rapid descent had broken off many of the branches.

When Nat finally reached her, their combined weight set the trunk to swaying once more. Nat was no gymnast, nor was he particularly fond of heights. Swallowing, he told himself not to look down. Instead, he focused all his attention on Freddie's small white face. "It's going to be all right," he told her.

She stared at him.

"Put your arms around my neck."

"I can't." Her blue lips barely moved, and her eyes had the blind look of a person in shock.

"Yes, you can." He reached out and covered one of her hands with his. It was ice cold. "Take hold of me."

She followed his instructions to the letter: she abruptly abandoned her death grip on the tree and threw herself at him. As a result, they both slid pell-mell down the trunk a good five feet. A large branch finally impeded their progress. Freddie screamed, Nat cursed, and down below Pinky barked frantically as he danced back and forth.

"My God, are you all right?" Nat asked when they came to a jolting halt.

"Yes." She had locked her arms around his neck in a hold so convulsive that he was having trouble breathing.

"Listen, put one arm around my shoulder this way, and one around my waist. Can you do that?"

"Yes—no . . . I don't know."

It took a little more persuasion, but he finally got her rearranged. Then, with Freddie clinging to his back and the woods resounding with Pinky's staccato barks, Nat somehow managed to inch his way back down to the ground. At last they fell off the tree and onto the needles that cushioned the area around the pine's base. Freddie's grip didn't loosen. Her tense and shaking body was still glued to his. Gently, Nat disengaged her and looked into her face.

"Are you all right?" he asked again.

"Yes."

But it was obvious that she wasn't. She was pale and trembling violently. Without another thought, he wrapped his arms tightly around her and gathered her up onto his lap. Sitting cross-legged on the ground, he gently rocked her back and forth. "It's okay," he crooned, tightening his grip. "It's going to be okay."

This time she seemed to believe him. Wordlessly accepting his comfort and seeking his warmth, she curled up, burrowed her head against his chest, and closed her eyes.

Rhythmically, Nat stroked her back and her curls. "Did you really climb all the way up that tree with a bear on your tail?" he finally asked.

"Yes." Freddie's eyes stayed closed. She rubbed her cheek against his shirt.

"What a woman! I wish I'd been there to see."

At that her blue eyes popped open. "It's not funny. I nearly got killed."

"Of course it's not funny," he agreed, "but you've got me so turned around that I don't know whether to laugh or cry, scream or curse. You're one very unsettling female."

She tipped her head up and met his gray gaze. There was a strange expression in his eyes: part wry amusement, part something much more serious, and part question.

"Shouldn't we get out of here?" she finally asked, lowering her lashes and focusing on his chin.

"Yes, I think we probably should. Can you walk?"

"I think so."

"Well, let's find out." Rolling her gently off his lap, he stood up and offered her his hand. When he had pulled her to her feet, it was obvious that she was still wobbly. "Here," he said, putting his arm around her waist, "lean on me. This is that mother bear's territory, and she'll be wanting it back."

"Not to mention the father bear," Freddie replied with a shaky laugh. "I suppose he's around here someplace, too."

"I wouldn't worry about him. From what I hear, father bears aren't good family men."

Freddie didn't answer. Instead, she leaned her weight against Nat's strength and looked down at the ground while they slowly made their way back to his campsite. She had gotten over enough of her shock that her brain could function again. She was thinking that all her escape plans were in smithereens. Yet it didn't seem to matter. Irrationally, with Nat's arm around her and his body supporting hers, she felt happy. And what was even crazier, she also felt safe.

When they arrived at the campsite, Nat propped Freddie against a tree. Then he brought out his medical kit and knelt down beside her. Carefully, he cleaned and dressed the new scrapes and scratches on her legs. As he worked, his fingers were amazingly gentle on her skin, but his expression was grim and more than a little withdrawn.

"Seems like I'm always cleaning your wounds," he commented. Freddie had taken off her clodhoppers and unrolled her torn wool stockings so that her legs were bare.

"Yes," she agreed, holding up one of the army boots. "See what that animal did to Jeremy's shoe?" Part of the sole had been ripped away.

Nat picked up the damaged boot and inspected it. Then he slanted a narrow look at Freddie. "That could have been your foot." His gaze lingered. "Tell me, did you get yourself into these kinds of situations when you were a kid?"

"I was never attacked by a bear in the mountains," she answered with a conscious little laugh. "But I guess I was a tomboy. I have two older brothers, and I was always trying to go them one better. My mother used to spend a lot of time moaning about how I would come to a bad end."

"I'll bet." Nat put away the antiseptic. Then he rested his hands on his knees. "Freddie, why are you here? Why didn't you stay with the Parkers the way I asked you to?"

She swallowed and looked away. "I couldn't. The only thing I really know about them is that they grow marijuana in their backyards."

"You were safe there with Granny, and she treated you like a guest."

"I wasn't a guest. I was a prisoner."

"I asked you to trust me for just a few days. Why couldn't you?"

"Don't ask me that. You know why."

The corners of Nat's mouth tightened. "So you took off? How did you get away?"

Succinctly, she recapped the story of her escape.

"You mean you fooled Vandy into helping you?" Nat sounded outraged, and Freddie began to wonder if his feelings didn't run deeper for the girl than he admitted.

"I didn't fool her. I made a deal with her, an honest deal. If I ever get back to Nashville, I really will try to get her an audition."

"And you wandered around in the woods half the night?" Nat's voice was still frosty. "Do you realize how crazy that was? Do you realize how easily you could have run into serious trouble? This isn't some kind of park with tame animals running around like in a petting zoo."

"Obviously, after what just happened, I realize that," Freddie answered. Her expression was growing mutinous. "But I'm here, aren't I? I got where I wanted to go, didn't I?"

Nat's eyes narrowed to slits. "Yes, you're here all right. But wanting to be here doesn't make any more sense than the rest of it. Just what did you have to gain by coming back to my camp? Are you going to tell me that you made the trip because you missed me?"

Freddie stared back at him. This was where she had to start lying, she told herself. Certainly, she couldn't tell Nat that she knew about his radio. Her thoughts tumbled like pebbles in a waterfall. Perhaps she should follow his lead and let him think she'd come here because she was infatuated with him. Maybe then he'd relax his guard long enough that she'd be able to get at that radio.

"I did miss you," she said.

He lifted a disbelieving eyebrow.

"Why do you look like that?" She tried to make her expression ingenuous. "Have you forgotten what happened between us that last night?"

"No, I haven't," he answered gruffly. "That much frustration tends to linger in the memory."

"You know there was more to it."

"I haven't forgotten that, either." He studied her face. Her smooth cheeks were streaked with dirt, but her pink lips were made to be kissed. Beneath her long lashes, her eyes were as clear as blue crystal and just as guileless. What was she up to now? he wondered.

Sternly forbidding himself to give in to his impulse to throw her on the ground and make unrelenting love to her, Nat stood up. "Well, since you're so fond of yours truly, you won't mind giving me a hand with chow tonight."

"Of course not. What would you like me to do?" Freddie was suddenly the soul of cooperation.

"You could bring some water from the stream and load up the coffeepot. I'm afraid I've eaten all the fresh food Granny gave me. But I've got some packages of freeze-dried stew. We can have that." When Freddie wrinkled her nose, he laughed at her. "It's not bad. And I don't know about you, but after a day like today, I'm as hungry as a bear."

"After a day like today, I can really appreciate that remark," she answered pertly.

The meal Nat proceeded to fix over the campfire was surprisingly good, and Freddie spooned it up out of her tin bowl with gusto.

"Wandering around in the woods gives a person an appetite," she commented.

"Certainly does." He'd already consumed his food and was stretched out on his side, propped on one elbow and sipping coffee. His gaze as he spoke was on Freddie's mouth.

Self-consciously, she finished off the last of her stew.

"So you escaped the Parkers' valley and braved the dangers of the wild because you wanted to be with me," he drawled.

Freddie shifted uneasily. "Well, I also wanted to be closer to my plane," she replied.

"Don't go changing your line now. You said earlier that you'd missed me."

She had missed him. That part of her story was true. "Well, I did," she asserted stoutly.

"I'm curious. What was it about me that you couldn't live without?"

Freddie shot him a questioning look. "What do you mean by that?"

"Was it my sunny smile? My witty jokes? Or was it

something else that drew you through the trackless wilderness at the risk of life and limb?"

His tone made her study him nervously. "What are you getting at?"

"I'm getting at our sleeping arrangements," he answered. "After your recent narrow escape from my out-of-control lust, I would have thought you'd be glad to see the last of me. But here you are. So what am I to suppose?"

"Whatever you like." But she knew right away that that wasn't the best answer.

"All right." Calmly, he downed the last of his coffee. "Then I'll suppose that tonight I won't have to be noble and give up my sleeping bag because you'll be happy to share it with me."

"What?"

"Don't look so shocked. If you thought that the two of us rolling around on that cot was fun, wait till you try making it in a one-person sleeping bag. I can't wait."

Freddie's eyes sparkled with anger and hurt. Her memories of their last night together were beautiful, and she hated for him to trample on them. "For some reason you're being deliberately crude. Of course I don't intend to share your sleeping bag."

"Then why are you here?" he demanded.

"I told you."

"Because you missed me?" he asked. "Well, if it wasn't my lovemaking that you missed, it must have been something else. I wonder what." His gray eyes challenged her, and Freddie looked back down at the tin bowl still clutched between her hands. She knew she was going to have to give him some sort of answer.

"Nat, the other night when I said I wasn't ready to make love with you, you were very understanding. When I woke up and found you gone, I did miss you. And I do want to be with you. But—" She paused.

"But you're still playing hard to get?"

She gazed back at him mutely.

After a moment he sighed. "All right, you get the sleeping bag again. But the next time you decide you miss me, bring your own camping gear, will you?"

When they settled into his tent a short while later, neither of them was happy. As Nat rolled over with his back to Freddie and punched his pack trying to find a soft place to lay his head, his discontent was plain.

"Nat, I'm sorry," she whispered. "Are you very uncomfortable?"

"No, I'm hunky dory. The only improvement I can think of would be a bed of nails."

She rolled her eyes and turned away. It was going to be a long night. And tomorrow, she suspected, was going to be an even longer day. In fact, she'd gone from the proverbial frying pan into the fire and was once again in an impossible situation. Miserably, she lay awake listening to Nat's breathing. Had he gone to sleep? She couldn't tell, but sleep was certainly eluding her. She couldn't wait any longer for some convenient moment to get to that radio, she thought. She had to use it tonight.

An hour later, she sat up, crawled cautiously out of the sleeping bag, and inched toward the tent opening.

"Where are you going?" Nat's hard voice demanded.

Didn't the man *ever* shut down? Freddie rocked

back on her knees. "I have to answer the call of nature."

"All right, but take Pinky with you. I don't want you tangling with any more wildlife."

Almost sighing with relief, Freddie slipped outside. Pinky, who'd been dead to the world in the grass, raised his head.

"Come on," she whispered to him. None too happily, he got up stiffly and followed after her.

She thought she had a clear memory of the tree where Nat's radio was hidden, but she had trouble finding it now. The night when she'd spied him using the radio had been dark and rainy, and she'd been frightened. In this night's silvery moonlight, things looked different. And it didn't help that she was still nervous and frightened.

"Damn," she whispered after checking out the third wrong oak. "I know it was around here someplace." Pinky watched her curiously. "Do you know where it is?" she asked him. As he cocked his thick head, she put her hands on her hips and looked around. A worried frown was on her face. If she didn't find it pretty soon, she'd have to go back. Nat was bound to wonder what was keeping her so long.

She took a few more paces and then spotted another tree that seemed about the right size. When she knelt at its base, her breathing quickened. It had a hollow, and something was stowed inside. Carefully, she lifted the square object out and began to unwrap the plastic sheeting that protected it. She had just finished when she froze, caught in the sudden beam of a powerful flashlight. Gasping, she turned toward the light.

"Now I know why you came back here," Nat said

in a flat voice. "It wasn't me you missed. It was my radio."

Blinded by the glare, Freddie put her hand up before her eyes. Then suddenly the light snapped off, and she was plunged into darkness once more.

"Just what were you planning to do?" Nat asked conversationally. She could hear him walking toward her through the underbrush.

While her heart beat crazily, Freddie shrugged in defeat. "I was going to call for help."

"Sorry. I'm afraid I can't let you do that." Nat was now a dark shadow looming over her. He picked up the radio, rewrapped it, and stowed it back in the tree.

"Need a hand up?" he asked.

"No." Freddie pushed herself off the ground and got to her feet, stumbling a little since she was still half-blinded by his flashlight. "This is ridiculous, you know." To mask her distress, she straightened her skirt and brushed grass and leaves from her sweater. "You can't keep me here forever."

"I know I can't, and I don't intend to."

Although his words were uttered in a conversational tone, they made Freddie stop and lift her head. She'd never really believed that Nat meant to harm her, but what did he have in mind? What was going on here, really?

When she spoke, her voice had a slightly hysterical edge. "I'm not going anywhere until you tell me what you intend to do."

"Freddie, come on back to camp."

"No."

He reached out toward her, and she slapped at his hand. Ignoring that, he seized her wrist.

"Get your hands off me!"

"Willingly. Just come back to the campsite."

"Never!" she hissed. "You'll have to drag me back by force!"

His voice was harsh. "I aim to please." With one swift motion, he tossed her over his shoulder and headed back through the underbrush.

When she was able to catch her breath enough to utter a sound, she sputtered in outrage. But Nat's next gruff words silenced her.

"Just relax and enjoy the ride. When we get back, I'm going to tell you the whole story."

"The whole story?"

"I'm going to tell you what's really going on here."

In what seemed like no time, he strode through the circle of trees and into the clearing, where his tent was a triangular shadow in the moonlight. With a grunt, he bent his knee and put his hands on Freddie's waist. "Ride's over."

"Thank God," she gasped as she slid to the ground and struggled for balance. "What do you mean, you're going to tell me the whole story?"

"Exactly that. I couldn't before, but now I really have no choice, do I?"

She stared at him, trying to make out the expression on his face. But in the darkness it was impossible. All she could see was the pale glint of his eyes. At that moment she felt a sharp twinge of remorse for the way she'd tried to deceive him.

"Nat, I came back here because I wanted to use your radio," she said. "But it was true what I said about missing you. I really did."

"Did you?" He sounded skeptical. "Well, I hope you're telling the truth now, because you're going to get plenty of my company in the next couple of days."

"Nat, for God's sake! What's this all about? Please tell me."

He turned toward the tent. "Just let me get my matches. I feel a powerful need for a cigarette."

While Freddie waited impatiently, he disappeared to rummage around in his gear. Pinky appeared to be no longer surprised by the peculiar misadventures that seemed to occur whenever his master and this young woman got together, and he composed himself for sleep. Besides his heavy breathing and the rhythmic drone of the crickets, the woods were silent and still. Not even a wayward breeze ruffled the leaves, and the moon's radiant face shone down from a cloudless night sky.

"First off, about those marijuana fields," Nat said as he emerged from the tent. Pausing, he clamped a cigarette between his teeth and struck a match. As he continued to walk toward her, Freddie held her breath and stared anxiously at his handsome features, which were briefly lit in the flame's ruddy glow.

"What about the marijuana fields?" she whispered.

He doused the light and flicked the dead match into the grass. "They're not mine. I'm not growing marijuana."

In her heart she had known this. But to hear it from Nat's own lips was a heavenly confirmation. Freddie sighed with relief and unconsciously crossed her right hand up to her chest in the vicinity of her heart. "Whose are they, then? The Parkers'?"

"No."

"No? Do you mean that the Parkers aren't really marijuana farmers?" Next to learning that Nat was not growing the stuff, it would please her most to hear that the Parker family had no involvement either. During her brief stay in their valley, she had grown amazingly fond of those people. But Nat quickly dashed this hope.

"Oh, the Parkers are growing the stuff, all right. You must have seen it in their gardens."

"Yes." It shocked Freddie to realize how eager she had been to dismiss even the evidence of her own eyes. Was she being equally blind in taking Nat's word? Fixing her gaze on the glowing end of his cigarette, she asked, "If the Parkers are growing marijuana, and you're not, just what are you doing here? And what's your connection with them?"

The small fiery glow brightened as Nat took a drag and then slowly blew the smoke out. He was standing next to her, looking up at the moon. "I've known the Parker family for a long time," he said. "I first met them years ago when I hiked into these mountains to buy an instrument from Jim. Since then, I've come back on several occasions."

"For the old-time music?"

"That, and to collect songs and buy more of Jim's handiwork. As far as I'm concerned, Jim Parker makes the best guitars, fiddles, and banjos on the East Coast."

"You still haven't explained anything," Freddie pointed out.

"I know, I know. Okay." He turned toward her. "Freddie, I'm a special agent for Drug Enforcement. I'm here on assignment."

"You're a DEA agent?" Freddie felt her knees go weak with relief. Now *that* made some sense. But a moment later, she began to frown. "Why didn't you tell me this before? Why did you go on letting me think that you were a criminal?"

Nat flicked his cigarette into the embers of the campfire, then took her hand and led her to the edge of the stream. Several large rocks lined its bank. He settled her on one of them and propped his foot up on its edge.

"I couldn't tell you who I am because this is an undercover operation," he explained. "A couple of years ago, Lou and Marshall and Hap convinced Granny to grow some marijuana as a cash drop. It was strictly small-time—just what they could plant in their gardens."

"Yes, I know about that. Vandy told me."

"Did she tell you that last year things started going wrong? Through Hap's connections, the Parkers were able to deliver a prime but extremely limited crop. Drugs in Atlanta are controlled by a large and ruthless organization. When they got wind of the ideal growing conditions up here, they decided to take advantage of it."

"What do you mean?"

"They sent their people around and threatened the Parkers to keep them quiet and get their cooperation. Then they planted a dozen illegal fields and ringed them with antipersonnel devices."

Freddie's eyes widened. "Is that—"

"Yes," Nat said grimly. "You nearly got your back broken by one of them the afternoon you landed here."

Freddie was silent while she contemplated this information. "What exactly are you doing here now?"

Nat began to pace back and forth. "I happened to drop in on the Parkers shortly after these crops were planted. At the time, Granny didn't know that I worked for the government. She just thought I liked to play folk songs." He pushed a lock of hair back off his forehead. "She was very worried about the situation and confided in me. I told her I was an agent and persuaded her to accept a deal. The agency has been trying to get the goods on some of the drug kingpins in Atlanta. If I can snag their harvesting operation red-handed, it would give us a good chance to do that. In exchange for amnesty for her family, Granny agreed to let me stay up here as her guest during the month before harvest. She knows I'm an undercover agent and that when the harvesters come they'll be intercepted by the law."

"Do the other Parkers know, too?" Freddie asked.

Nat shook his head. "No. She wasn't worried about Jim's family or about Vandy. But she didn't want to tell the boys for fear they'd pass the information on to the wrong people."

"The day before I snuck away, they took their dogs and went hunting."

"That means they're wandering around in the woods someplace. I just hope they're not anywhere near here." Nat frowned. "Even though Marshall and Lou are Granny's kinfolk, she's not sure where their loyalties lie at this point. And frankly, neither am I."

Freddie nodded. "I think I understand."

"Does that mean you understand why I couldn't tell you and why I had to get rid of that plane of yours?"

"I'm not too sure about that."

Nat squatted down beside her and said earnestly, "I couldn't be completely certain you were who you claimed. You have to admit that your story was pretty bizarre."

Freddie's silence was his acknowledgment.

"Then," he continued, "there was my promise to Granny. If you'd inadvertently revealed any of this to Hap or the boys and they'd leaked the information to the wrong ears, it might have jeopardized this operation. It might also have put innocent people in a dangerous situation. It was far better that you not know. And if you'd just done what I asked and stayed put with Granny, you would have been all right."

"But I didn't," Freddie pointed out. "I'm here with you."

"That's true," Nat agreed. "Which means that when those harvesters arrive, there will be two of us here to greet them."

"Two of us?"

"You and me, Freddie. You and me."

CHAPTER ELEVEN

It was amazing how quickly and completely things had changed, Freddie thought. Nat was no longer her enemy; suddenly, they were allies.

"What will you do when the harvesters come?" she asked. As they talked, their low voices were a counterpoint to the water gurgling quietly in the creek nearby. Freddie was still perched on her rock, but Nat now stood a few feet away, one arm propped against a tree trunk.

"I'll use that radio you found and call in reinforcements."

"Who?"

"The state police. They'll come in on local military helicopters."

"A lot could happen before they arrive."

"Not if I pick myself out a safe observation post and lie low—which is what I intend to do."

"How can I help?"

He gave her a stern look. "Freddie, you can't. First thing tomorrow, I'm going to find you a safe place to hide. And that's what you'll do when they come—hide. Do you understand me?"

She couldn't help but feel offended by his tone. "Of

course I understand you. I'm not a fool, and I don't want to interfere with your plans."

Nat snorted. "Coming from you, that's pretty funny."

"If you'd just been honest with me from the beginning, I wouldn't have made so much trouble," she defended herself.

"You wouldn't have interfered when I dismantled your plane?"

"No. I'd have understood that it was necessary."

He straightened and then walked over and sat down next to her. "Actually, I have a pretty good idea how tough this has been on you, and I'm sorry. Believe me, there were a lot of times when I wanted to tell you what was really going on."

"When?"

He turned to her in surprise. "When? Can't you guess?"

She swallowed. "Did you want to tell me the truth that night when we . . ."

"When we almost made love?" His voice deepened. "Of course I did. I knew you had good reason not to trust me. When you were sleeping beside me, I wanted to wake you up and tell you everything."

She gazed up at him, mesmerized by the way the moonlight silvered his hair and carved his strong features into mysterious shadows. "I wish you had."

"Would it have made so much difference?"

"All the difference in the world."

At that moment Freddie admitted to herself just how deep her feelings for Nat really were. She'd been afraid that she'd never get over Carter, but since she'd met Nat, her painful memories of Carter had faded like wraiths in the clear light of day. She was falling in love with Nat in a way that made what she'd felt for Carter seem paltry. It still didn't make sense, her brain told her. Even though Nat Steele wasn't a criminal, he still wasn't the kind of man it was wise to give your heart to. But Freddie couldn't seem to listen to the warnings of wisdom. For days now she'd been fighting her feelings for Nat, and she was worn out from the struggle.

"You'd better get some sleep," he told her. "There's no telling what kind of a day we'll have tomorrow."

"I suppose you're right." Obediently, she slipped off the rock and followed him back toward the tent. "I've never seen the stars so bright," she remarked as they paused just outside it.

He tipped his head back and gazed up at the sky. "Yep, for stars there's nothing like these mountains on a clear night."

"Do you recognize any constellations?"

"A few. There's the Big Dipper and the Pleiades," he said, pointing at a small but brilliant cluster.

"You know," she answered, following the direction he indicated and staring up at the sparkling points of light, "I should have guessed you weren't really a marijuana farmer. You're far too well educated."

Nat laughed. "What's that got to do with it? And how could you tell, anyway? I don't recall writing you any history papers."

"Is that what you were, a history major?"

"Yes, as a matter of fact," he admitted, holding the tent flap back for her. "How about you?"

"Communications. I always wanted to work in radio or television."

"Behind the scenes or as a star?"

"Oh, definitely on the technical end. I never wanted to be on camera or anything like that."

"I don't know why not. You're pretty enough for it."

"Thank you." Pleased by the compliment, Freddie sank down on her hands and knees and crawled back in. When Nat joined her, she had already slipped back into his sleeping bag. The inside of the tent was small, and Nat's lanky body took up a great deal of space. Her heart fluttered slightly at his proximity. But he made no attempt to take advantage of the new trust and friendship developing between them. Instead, he jabbed at his pack. Finally, with a dissatisfied sigh, he propped his head against it.

"What's wrong?" she asked when he groaned for the third time and shifted position.

"This pack is full of hard-edged lumps. My harmonica was poking into the back of my head. I think I'll take it out."

She watched as he sat up and undid one of the pouches. "Do you always carry a harmonica when you camp?"

"Always. A guitar is too bulky, but something like this"—he withdrew the small silvery instrument and hefted its light weight—"is easy to stow and keeps me company. Lots of nights when I've been restless I've used it to put myself to sleep."

"You mean by playing songs?"

"Right. Works almost every time."

"Why don't you do that now?"

He shot her an inquiring look that she felt rather than saw in the darkness. "Won't it bother you?"

"No, I like your music. How about playing that

song about the dawn breaking?" She had a thought. "Did you ever learn any more verses?"

"I did, as a matter of fact." He lifted the harmonica to his lips and blew a tentative chord. "Old Bill gave me one."

"I'd love to hear it."

Obligingly, he began to produce the notes of the plaintive ballad. As she listened to the melody threading through the darkness, Freddie folded her arms behind her head and closed her eyes. Unconsciously, her lips curled in a smile. She didn't analyze the feeling, but she knew that for the moment she was happy and strangely content, perhaps more than she had ever been before in her life. It wasn't just that she'd finally learned the truth about Nat and could now feel safe with him. There was a lot more to it. The intimacy of this starry mountain night, of lying next to him and listening to him make music for her and her alone—it was all very special.

Softly, he sang the verses she'd already heard. She listened intently, but when he began a third verse, she turned her head toward him and opened her eyes.

> Beneath a pine tree I lay me down,
> And dreamed you there along my side.
> Your smile was sweet, your hair was long,
> You'll ne'er be another man's bride.

"Things are getting serious," she commented when the last notes faded away. "What do you suppose will happen next?"

"It's not hard to guess. Betrayal and death are common themes in love songs. I suppose it will be one or the other—or both."

"You sound cynical."

"No, realistic." He put the mouth organ down and leaned back against his pack. "In the songs love consists of wanting something you can't or shouldn't have."

"Not always."

"Not always, but usually." He reached out and touched her hand. "Like I want you."

Freddie drew a sharp breath. "Do you?"

"Yes. Fighting off bears, giving up my sleeping bag, worrying about your safety—those aren't the only reasons why I wish you'd stayed safe with Granny Parker. Trying to sleep next to you like this doesn't do a lot for my peace of mind, Frederica Davenport." He started to release her hand, but Freddie's fingers clung to his wrist.

"Nat, it's getting chilly. Why don't you share the sleeping bag with me?"

"We tried that," he answered in a gruff voice. "Don't you remember what it led to?"

"I remember." She paused, searching for a graceful way of wording what she wanted to say. None came to mind. "Maybe we should try again," she finally said.

Nat inhaled harshly. "My God, woman!" he exclaimed, rolling toward her across the few inches that separated them. "I've been hanging by a very fine thread, and whether you meant to or not, you just cut it away from me."

"I meant it," she whispered just before his mouth came down on hers.

Actually, Freddie wasn't sure of the reason for her sudden, bold invitation. It was certainly not in character for her. But when Nat's lips took possession of hers, all her doubts vanished. His mouth was hard and hungry, and she could feel that hunger underlined in the taut length of him. It matched the equally consuming hunger in her, and it wasn't long before he recognized that. Finally, he lifted his head and cradled her cheeks between his two leathery palms.

"I wish it weren't so dark. I'd like to see your face."

"Why? What's there to see?" she whispered.

"Your eyes. Those blue eyes of yours are beautiful, you know. I'd like to read their expression. Maybe it would tell me what you're thinking."

"What do you care?" she asked. "I've just offered myself to you. Isn't that enough?"

"It should be. I don't know why I should want more, but I do. You make me want a million things, Freddie." As he spoke, his mouth once more came down on hers. This time his kiss was surprisingly sweet. The desire and longing still flamed, but they were overlaid with a tenderness that was new and meltingly persuasive.

"Kissing you is different from kissing any other woman I've ever met," he whispered as his lips finally left hers and began to caress her face lightly.

"Why?" Her hands tightened on his forearms.

"I keep seeing pictures of you doing crazy things, crashing your airplane, climbing trees, laughing down at me, looking at me through the rain with those amazing eyes of yours. You're not just a warm body, Frederica Davenport, you're a set of memorable experiences."

"You're not just a warm body, either," she whispered back. Nevertheless, she reveled in the feel of him, drinking in his taste, touch, and masculine aroma as if she had been longing for them all her life. While he dropped light kisses along her hairline and behind her ears, she put her arms around his shoulders. With sensitive fingertips she mapped the territory of his solid rib cage and strong back. Touching him with this new freedom gave her all the pleasure an explorer about to stake a claim on unmined gold has. She particularly liked the scent of his hair and skin. Out here in the woods he wore no aftershave, so the fragrance she inhaled was his own and that of the pine bark and mossy grass that clung to him. It far outdid any of the high-priced aftershaves she'd ever smelled.

He hadn't shaved in over a day, so his jaw was scratchy against hers. She even liked that, and she found herself rubbing her cheek along the lower part of his face in sensual appreciation.

Meanwhile, he mapped his own delights. His hands cupped her breasts, obviously enjoying the feel of their weight and fullness. At last, his mouth moved down to nuzzle the warm hollow of her throat. "You taste so good," he murmured, "like ice cream and honey."

"A strange combination."

"A delicious combination, healthy and sweet and so very good."

Freddie closed her eyes, gasping with pleasure as he took the tip of first one breast and then the other into his mouth and loved them. When she had invited him to join her in the sleeping bag, she hadn't been completely sure of her response. Now there was no question. Her body answered his with rushing urgency. His touch kindled rare and wonderful fires in her—fires she hadn't even begun to feel in a long, long time.

Deftly, Nat slipped her ragged dress up over her head. Her bra he had already opened. She helped him unbutton his shirt and wriggle free of his blue jeans. Soon his hard, bare length was pressed intimately to hers.

It felt absolutely right, as if it had been meant. Freddie was no longer even capable of entertaining doubts about it. Her body ached for his, and Nat clearly felt the same. His excitement was evident—in the tautness of his sinewy length, in the scorching urgency of his kisses, in the rigid pressure of his manhood against the quivering softness of Freddie's stomach.

His hands slipped down to her waist and then to her rounded hips. His thumbs kneaded the silky skin that covered the cradle of her femininity. She was deliciously different from him, he thought. Yet his compact loins fit into her curving softness as if they were matching pieces of the same glorious design. And for a moment, as he arched his back and reveled in the sheer throbbing pleasure of this satisfying moment, he felt as if he were about to become something that was more than either he or the beautiful woman beneath him. All that was masculine in him wanted and needed her pliancy, her gentle curves, and the warmth of her rich body enclosing and taking all he had to give.

But then he had a thought that made him go still. "Freddie," he whispered, "I've just realized. You're not protected, are you?"

Freddie, who was now completely open to him and

aching for his possession, clutched at his narrow waist. "No," she admitted, "but it's all right."

Nat shuddered with the effort to control the extremity of his desire. If she were ready, so was he—more than ready. He felt as if all his very soul was pulsing with a need that was painful in its intensity. "I can't let you take that risk," he groaned.

Her hands went down to his buttocks, as hard and smooth as marble beneath her urging fingers. "It's okay, the timing is safe." She was telling the truth. Was he going to make her beg? she wondered as she tilted her pelvis up and urged him toward her.

Nat was only human. With another explosive groan, his exigency toppled his caution. The heat of his passion filled her, and she moaned with satisfaction. They both paused, savoring the union, but in the next moment they both wanted more. Nat began to move. Despite the urgency stampeding through every cell in his body, his thrusts were slow and controlled at first. He wanted to give Freddie pleasure. It seemed as if during so much of their time together he'd been forced to treat her harshly. Now he wanted it to be different. He wanted this drowning, aching sweetness to be mutual.

But there was more than sweetness in their union. Soon the flame of their shared passion melted the bounds of his control. In his desire to meld with her, to impart to her the essence of himself, his hips churned feverishly. Freddie wanted all he had to give. She wrapped her legs around his waist and lost herself in the sensual rhythm of his onslaught. Nat drove himself into her frantically and felt her body tighten and clasp him as he exploded within her. Colored lights flashed behind her eyelids. Enormous, richly hued flowers of purple, gold, and fiery red seemed to snap open against the black velvet of her and Nat's shared ecstasy, and for a long moment all consciousness fled.

When it was over, he lay cushioned on her body, his face buried in the hollow of her neck. For a long time Nat rested there, breathing in the fresh scent of her and savoring the pleasure their union had brought him.

Lifting his head, he stared down into her face, wishing again that he could see her more clearly in the darkness. "I know I shouldn't ask," he said, "but I have to know. Was it all right for you?"

"Yes," she told him simply. Her hands went up to clasp the back of his head. "Oh, yes."

"I should have stopped when I realized you weren't protected. But I couldn't."

"I didn't want you to. I think I made that plain."

He put his arms around her and rolled to one side, taking her with him so that they lay together still. Then he kissed her long and deeply. For Freddie his kiss said more than any words could. It was gentle, tender, loving. When finally he drew his mouth away, she sighed contentedly and buried her face against his shoulder. If only this moment could be captured and held like a talisman against the future, she thought wistfully.

For a long time they lay in silence, breathing in the scents of the night around them and of their lovemaking. When Nat spoke again, his deep voice was hesitant.

"Freddie, I'm glad this happened. But I can't help wondering—why?"

"Why do these things happen between men and women?"

"No. That I think I understand," he retorted dryly.

"Why did I invite you into my sleeping bag? Or rather"—she laughed—"your sleeping bag?"

"Yes." He nuzzled the top of her head. "Was it just because I told you what I'm really doing here?"

Freddie's fingers toyed with the hair on Nat's chest. "I guess it was partly that. And I suddenly realized that it's almost over."

"What do you mean?"

"Our time together in the mountains." She struggled to keep her voice dispassionate. "It's been like something out of a story, hasn't it?"

"Yes, it has," he allowed, drawing her even closer. "You've been a heroine."

She tipped her head up, trying to see his face. She didn't feel like a heroine. Those lucky women always walked away into the sunset with the hero. Freddie knew that that wasn't going to be how things happened for her. Real adventurers didn't want to commit themselves to boring rose-covered cottages. Even during the heat of their lovemaking, Nat hadn't made any promises or declarations. When his job was over here, he would go his own way and leave her behind.

That, she acknowledged inwardly, was why she'd been so brazen with him. She was falling in love, and she hadn't wanted to lose him without knowing what it was like to be his lover at least once. But now that she did know, it would be harder than ever to say good-bye.

"By rights," he said, "I should be snoring in your ear now. Neither of us has had any sleep, and it's almost dawn. But I'm wide awake. I think I'll go down to the stream and take a bath. Want to join me?"

"Won't it be awfully cold?" Actually, Freddie liked the way they were snuggled next to each other. She was almost ready to close her eyes and drift off in his arms.

"Freezing. I can tell from the tone of your voice that you're not enthusiastic about this project." He kissed her ear. "Stay here where it's warm and go to sleep. I won't be long."

But after he left and Freddie was alone in the sleeping bag, she sat up and peered wistfully out through the crack in the tent flap. The moon-washed night looked magical. The stars seemed so big and bright that she almost felt she could reach out and pluck them out of the sky. Now she regretted not accepting Nat's invitation. But it wasn't too late.

Quickly, she slipped on her dress and, not bothering with her mangled boots, went outside. The dewy grass felt delightful against the bottoms of her bare feet, but the chill in the air made her wrap her arms across her chest. A moment or two later, she spied Nat. He was standing in a waist-high section of the creek, splashing water across his bare chest and shoulders. She could see him clearly as moonlight spilled over his muscular torso, silvering it so that he looked almost unreal. Around him, the surface of the creek sparkled as if it were gilded with precious white gold and inlaid with tiny brilliants.

Nat turned and saw her on the edge of the bank. "Come on in. Once you take the plunge, it's invigorating."

Freddie dipped a cautious toe and then yanked it back. "It's icy!"

Playfully, Nat brushed the surface of the water and sent a shower skittering toward her. "Try it, you'll like it!"

Just then, Pinky ambled up. He yawned noisily and then plopped himself down a couple of yards away.

"Your dog's not going in," Freddie pointed out.

"That's because he has some sense. But who needs sense on a beautiful night like this?"

Freddie couldn't resist any longer. Feeling shy and reckless all at the same time, she tugged off her dress and stepped gingerly into the water. The shock of the cold made her gasp. For a moment she teetered on the rocks and pebbles underfoot. But Nat was already striding toward her. He grasped her hand and waited until she steadied. Then he led her through the flowing water to the deeper pool where he had been standing.

"There's almost enough water here to swim," he told her.

At the center of the pool, her feet were cushioned by its silky mud bottom. Strangely, the liquid that now eddied around her waist felt warmer. Or perhaps, she admitted to herself, being close to Nat like this made any accompanying discomfort seem negligible.

He stopped and turned toward her so that mere inches separated their bodies. No longer feeling cold at all, she ran her hands over the living sculpture of his chest and shoulders. He'd lured her in here with talk of the beautiful night. But the night was fast fading. Somewhere in the branches arching above them a bird twittered. A thin, pearly translucence overlaid the heavens. Into it the stars had begun to recede, and soon dawn would break.

Nat's body was no longer that of a silvery god's; his flesh was warm and real beneath Freddie's fingertips. He put his hands up to clasp her shoulders, and drops scattered like jewels from his fingers, bedewing her naked breasts.

"I'll never forget this night," he murmured just before he bent his head and kissed her lingeringly.

Freddie clasped his waist and returned the kiss, knowing that this was another precious moment she would treasure always. When he finally lifted his mouth from hers, it was only to bend her back slightly so that he could kiss away the beads of water that sparkled on her breasts. Freddie felt the heat of his renewed passion. She no longer had any thought of being cold. Fiery excitement raced through her veins.

Groaning at the intensity of his own mounting ardor, Nat reached down to stroke her gently. A moment later he put her arms around his neck, lifted her, and, holding her buttocks, joined their bodies. As his palms cupped her rounded flesh and pressed her toward him, he thrust deeply, murmuring as he did so a hoarse, satisfied "Ahhh."

While Freddie clung to him, he filled her with his driving, churning desire. As he lifted her with him in showers of piercingly beautiful feeling, she closed her eyes and laid her parted lips against the taut line of his throat.

Clinging together, they slowly descended from the heights. Then Nat regretfully withdrew from her and ran a loving hand down the graceful curve of her back. "What a night this has been," he murmured.

"It's almost day."

And so it was. The sky was now a milky color marbled by faint rays of pink.

Nat put his arm around Freddie's shoulder. "A mountain sunrise is the perfect way to cap the experience we've just had. Let's watch it together."

As much as Freddie agreed in principle, now that the heat of their mutual passion had subsided, she was beginning to shiver.

"I'll bring the towel and the sleeping bag," he told her, "so we can lie on the grass and keep warm."

He helped her out onto the bank and kissed her forehead. Then he strode toward the tent. Really shivering now, Freddie wrapped her dress around her torso and hopped slowly from foot to foot. Her gaze fell on Pinky, who was inspecting her curiously. "Well, you got an eyeful tonight," she said.

His pink tongue rolled out and he panted a luxurious acknowledgment, drooling slightly.

"I guess so," Freddie agreed with a laugh. Then she wondered if what Pinky had seen was actually a novelty. Had his master made love to other women on other mountains? It was not a comfortable thought, so she pushed it aside as Nat returned toting a large bundle. He had put on his jeans and shirt and had draped her sweater over his shoulder.

Briskly, he toweled her dry and then, while she laughed at his teasing remarks, dressed her. He spread the sleeping bag on a flat spot near the creek, and they had an unobstructed view of the sky. When they had slipped into the bag together, he took her in his arms and rested her curly head on his shoulder.

"In a minute we'll be warm and comfortable again."

Freddie already felt wonderful. Her skin was radiant from the combination of their lovemaking, the crisp air, and Nat's brisk toweling. Now, as she snuggled against him, she glowed with an encompassing sense of well-being. What more could she ask of life than this, she wondered—lying with her lover, breathing in pure, pine-scented air, and watching as the rising sun painted the sky with glorious colors?

"Heaven must be like this," Nat said, echoing her thoughts. His hand stroked through her curls.

Freddie fixed her gaze on the streaks of gold and lavender overhead. "Do you get to see many sunrises?"

"Yes. It's one of the benefits of my line of work, I guess. But usually I watch them alone."

Usually, but not always, Freddie thought. Aloud, she said, "As a special agent you must do quite a bit of this sort of thing."

"I run a lot of surveillance, and I've been in on a few sting operations."

Freddie's voice trembled slightly. "Your work is dangerous, isn't it?"

"Not if I'm careful and keep my wits about me—just like everything else in life."

Although Freddie's gaze was still fixed on the glory unfolding above them, her fingers stroked the length of Nat's arm, memorizing the texture of his skin and the smooth play of muscle and sinew beneath.

"How did you ever become a DEA agent? You said you were a history major. Did you go into police work after that?"

"No. That's how some guys get into it, but I was recruited straight from college."

Her next question came from left field. "Did you ever smoke pot yourself?"

"No," he answered after a moment. "Bret, my older brother, got heavily into drugs when he was in high school. It ruined his life, so I grew up with some pretty strong feelings on the subject. It didn't take much persuading to get me into this line of work. And I guess I must be an adventurer at heart. I like the excitement." He propped himself up on his elbow and leaned over her. "This is quite a cross-examination you're giving me. What more do you want to know?"

She smiled up into his eyes, which were dilated and almost black in the pink-and-gold-tinged light. "Just all the pertinent facts."

"As you may have noticed, there's one very pertinent fact between us right now, but that's probably not what you want to hear about." His head swooped so that he could briefly kiss her lips. "I was born in Atlanta, ran track and played basketball in high school, and graduated with a B average from the University of Virginia."

"A gentleman's school," Freddie murmured.

"Maybe, but I'm not feeling very gentlemanly right now." He pulled her to him, kissing her insistently. His hands slipped beneath her skirt to knead and stroke the rounded flesh of her bottom. "Who needs to smoke pot?" he whispered against her quivering mouth. "I'm higher than a kite on you."

That was how she felt, too. Already her flesh had warmed to him again, and she quivered with renewed desire. Her hands wandered down to the waistband of his jeans and then below where she could feel his hard arousal straining against the sturdy fabric.

Nat closed his eyes. "Oh Freddie, my God but I want you."

"I want you, too," she answered simply, her hand moving back up to unsnap his pants.

Just then, the sound of Pinky growling low in his throat interrupted them.

Nat lifted his head. Over his shoulder, Freddie saw that the dog was poised a few feet away, sniffing the wind. His menacing growls grew louder.

"What is it, boy?" Nat asked softly. "What do you smell?"

For a crazy instant, Freddie wondered if the mother bear was lurking nearby. But she instantly dismissed that possibility. It was something else.

Swiftly, Nat climbed out of the sleeping bag and stood. Freddie sat up and watched him. "What do you think it is?" she asked. Pinky was displaying all the signs of a dog scenting trouble.

"One of the fields isn't that far from here," Nat said curtly. "At this distance we wouldn't be able to hear or smell anything. But Pinky could. I think there's a good possibility that the harvesters have finally arrived."

CHAPTER TWELVE

Grim-faced, Nat retrieved his gun from the tent. "Stay put," he instructed Freddie. "I won't be long."

"Can't I come with you?"

"Not on your life."

She was tempted to argue, but Freddie knew from his expression that she'd better not. After he'd left to investigate, she brushed grass from the bottom of the sleeping bag and rolled it up. Then she quickly finished dressing and began to forage for breakfast. Crisis or no, she was hungry.

Freddie fixed fresh coffee and nibbled on a couple of the biscuits she'd discovered in Nat's pack. She tried hard not to give into anxiety about him as she sat hunched over on a fallen log. The sunrise was over, but the dewy morning was beautiful, too. There was a chill in the air, though, and something about the way the tops of the trees rustled made her suspect that later on it would be windy.

She was just finishing her second cup of coffee when Nat reappeared. His expression was even grimmer than before.

"What's wrong?" she asked. "Have they come?"

"Yes." He set down his rifle. "They used an old

logging road about a mile from here. I meant to watch it, but I was otherwise occupied this morning."

Freddie stiffened. "Does it matter? It's going to take awhile to clear those fields. The people you want to catch will be here all day."

"Yes," he answered curtly, "but I intended to call headquarters the minute they appeared. It shouldn't take long to muster those choppers, but I don't want to take any chances." This last was tossed over his shoulder as he crossed the clearing toward the spot where he'd hidden his radio.

While Nat was radioing for help, Freddie brooded over her empty coffee cup. She knew Nat was under strain, but she couldn't help feeling hurt by what he'd said. Was he accusing her of keeping him from his duty? He hadn't exactly spent the night making love to her unwillingly. In fact, watching the sunrise together had been his idea. For her it had been so beautiful. Now she felt as if she'd merely dreamt it all. Freddie shivered. Then, taking herself in hand, she set down her coffee cup and pushed her curls back off her forehead. She was being childish, she told herself. This was hardly the moment to expect loverlike behavior from Nat. A lot depended on the next few hours.

When he came back, she asked, "Would you like some coffee?"

"No time for that." He knelt in front of the tent opening and started pulling things out of it. "Put out that Sterno, will you? I want to break camp now."

While he rapidly took down the tent, Freddie crammed all the loose objects on the grass into his backpack. "You need to eat something," she told him. "You can't go all day on an empty stomach."

He reached down, scooped up the handful of biscuits she was proffering, and jammed them into his mouth. "There's some dried meat in the lower left-hand pouch," he said after he swallowed. "I'll take that, too."

Freddie found the meat and watched while he methodically devoured it. He never stopped working all the while he chewed. Fifteen minutes later, the tent and pack were hidden among the trees. Nat brushed over the clearing with some pine boughs until it looked as if it had never been disturbed.

"What now?" Freddie asked when he finished and turned toward her.

"Nothing complicated. I have to station myself someplace where I can see what's going on. When the time is right, I'll use this." He picked up a flare gun that he'd left out of his pack.

"Is that for signaling the helicopters?"

"Yes." Nat eyed her. "But before I can do any of that, I have to figure out what to do with you. I'd planned to take you to a cave I know about, but it's an hour's hike from here, and now I can't spare the time."

"There really isn't any need to put me in a cave all day."

"Freddie, I want you safe and out of the way."

"You radioed your people, and they'll be sending help soon," she pointed out. "You told me that you're not going to be doing anything terribly dangerous—just hiding and watching. Why can't I hide and watch with you?"

Nat frowned. "It shouldn't be dangerous, but there's always the chance that something could go wrong. I'd rather you stayed here."

"But those people could be all over the woods," she argued. "What if one of them found me alone? I'm safer with you."

Nat regarded her for a moment, then sighed and scratched his head. "All right. But you have to keep quiet and do what I say."

She promised, and they set off. Nat melted into the woods, and Freddie did her best to follow in his footsteps. As Pinky trotted along beside them, she cast the dog a worried look. "Are you sure he won't start barking and give us away?"

"Pinky knows how to behave. It's you I'm worried about."

Again, Freddie felt hurt. "You don't have to be concerned about me," she returned a trifle waspishly. "But maybe you should fill me in on the situation. Just how many of these people are there, and what exactly are they doing?"

Concisely, Nat described what he'd seen. "There are two crews of what look like a half-dozen laborers each. One is harvesting and the other brings the stuff down to the logging road. They're being overseen by four bosses, each carrying a submachine gun."

"Machine guns!" Freddie gasped.

"Yes." Nat turned and eyed her grimly. "That's why I wish you were safely back at Granny's. This isn't some kind of game. These people are ruthless."

"I know it's not a game. I promise I won't do anything to ruin your setup."

Catching sight of the angry sparkle in her eyes, he reached over and gave her an affectionate hug. "Sorry for the way that sounded. I know you won't get us in trouble deliberately. I'm just worried about you, that's all."

Warmed by his reassurance, all her resentment melted away and she smiled. "Where are we headed?"

"There are a dozen fields roughly scattered in a circle. Right now, going clockwise, they're clearing field number one. I want to see which field they go to next."

"If it's a circle, they'll either go clockwise or counterclockwise."

"Right. And once I've determined that, it'll be easy to keep a safe distance ahead of them."

The harvesters weren't exercising any particular caution about noise. Freddie could hear their voices long before she and Nat got close enough to see where they were working.

"They're speaking Spanish," she whispered.

"Right. The workers are probably illegal aliens who are so desperate to stay in the country they'll do anything. The men with the guns are the ones we're after. They can lead us to the big bosses."

When he finished speaking, he put a hand up to his mouth, signaling for silence, and then crept forward. Freddie held her breath while she watched him settle himself behind a fallen tree. After a moment he motioned for her to follow, and she quickly joined him. Once at his side, she squinted through the leaves and saw why he'd chosen the spot. Although it was well screened, it offered a good vantage point from which to view the entire field.

Freddie could also see the submachine guns Nat had mentioned. They were being carried by two tough-looking men who stood at opposite ends of the open area watching the workers. The one farthest away wore a pith helmet, while the closer of the two had dark hair growing low over his collar and a scraggly beard. He stood with his feet planted at least two feet apart and glanced suspiciously around at the screen of trees from time to time. He and his helmeted cohort looked mean and ruthless, Freddie thought with a little shiver.

It wasn't long before the field was bare of its crop. The marijuana had been baled and stacked and was ready to be carried away by the other team of workers, who seemed to be making much slower progress. The team doing the harvesting, led by the men with guns, began to move south. Nat watched their departure with a look of concern. "They're going clockwise."

"Is that bad?"

"Maybe not. But I had hoped they would go the other way."

When Freddie looked at him questioningly, he explained, "The spot where you landed is field number four, and this means they'll hit it sooner. If they see that sprung deadfall and the bushes that were damaged by your plane, they're bound to be suspicious. But," he added on a lighter note, "we probably don't have anything to worry about. It's not likely they'll get that far."

As the last of the harvesters disappeared, Nat stood up. Freddie did the same. "Do you want to follow them?"

He shook his head. "I calculate that it took about an hour and a half to clear that field. I think we can certainly look for those choppers by noon. That means we might as well go to field number three and find a good hiding spot. If things go according to plan, that's where we'll get some action."

Anxiously, Freddie glanced up at the tops of the trees and noted that the leaves were dancing. The sun shone brightly, but the air was crisp and the wind she'd predicted earlier that morning was beginning to rise.

"Nat, if it gets any windier, the choppers may have trouble getting here. They could be late." Indeed, if it got really bad, they might not be able to make it at all, she thought worriedly.

From the expression on Nat's face, she guessed he'd had the same thought. Like her, however, he didn't put it into words. Neither of them wanted to discuss such a possibility. Without comment, he motioned for her to follow him. She did so, slipping through the woods as silently as possible with Pinky just behind.

When they arrived at their destination, they searched for a hiding spot. Finally, they settled on a little rise overlooking the cleared area where the marijuana had been planted.

"It's well screened and gives us a good view," Nat said as he stretched out next to Freddie.

"How long do you think we have to wait?"

"Not more than an hour. And I hope it won't be long after that before we hear the sound of those choppers."

But what if they didn't hear them? Freddie thought. What if they never made it?

A stiff wind whistled overhead. She didn't know if it was strong enough to keep rotary aircraft out of the mountains. The temperature was also dropping. Freddie wrapped her arms around her chest.

"Cold?" Nat asked.

"A little."

"Front's going through." He took off his jacket and handed it to her.

"Won't you be cold without it?"

"Yes, but I can take it." He draped the garment around her shoulders. She smiled at him gratefully as she poked her arms into the sleeves. "There is something you can do to keep me comfortable."

"What's that?"

He drew her close and kissed her lightly on the lips. "You can let me hold on to your nice warm body."

He kissed her again. This time when they both came up for air, she managed to say, "You want me to be your hot-water bottle?"

"That's it."

"What about Pinky? He's probably warmer than I am."

"He doesn't smell as good."

While she batted at him in mock reproach, he gathered her tighter. Cuddled in each other's arms, they settled down to wait.

Nat had calculated the time very closely. Almost exactly an hour later, the band of harvesters with their gun-toting overseers straggled into view. After the gunmen issued a few sharp orders, the laborers set to work.

"They have this down to a science," Nat commented. "At this rate they can do all twelve fields and be out of here by tomorrow morning."

"The team carrying the stuff down to the logging road isn't working so fast."

"No," Nat agreed. "That's heavy work, and it's a long haul through rough terrain." He looked up at the empty sky. "I'd like to know where those helicopters are."

During the next hour Nat's concerned gaze frequently went to the sky. He'd been praying that help would arrive before the harvesting crew pressed on to field number four. Now that looked unlikely.

"They're almost finished. Maybe we should head for the next field and find ourselves a spot," he whispered in Freddie's ear. She nodded, and they silently got to their feet and slipped down the other side of the incline.

When they arrived at field number four, Freddie felt as if she were returning to a familiar stomping ground. So much had happened here. Her eyes went to the place where she'd landed her plane. The spot was marked by a patch of withered plants.

Nat's gaze followed hers. "Conspicuous, isn't it?"

"Maybe they'll think it's natural causes," Freddie offered.

"Natural causes don't usually uproot plants the size of those."

"Anyway, they'll never guess what really happened," she said, trying to make the best of things.

"No one in their right mind could guess what really happened here," Nat agreed dryly. "Now, we'd better get ourselves hidden."

Not long after they'd found cover among the trees, the harvesters and their armed overseers arrived. To Freddie's chagrin, the bosses, particularly the one with the beard, appeared to be very disturbed by the dead bushes. They stalked the perimeter of the field and scanned the surrounding woods with their guns raised at menacing angles. There was a shout as the one with the pith helmet discovered the deadfall that had been sprung. For several minutes they milled around it, talking in low, angry tones.

"I wish I could hear what they're saying," Nat muttered. "The bearded guy looks as if he's getting ready to spray the woods with bullets."

Freddie was almost glad that she couldn't hear any words. The men's body language was bad enough.

At that moment there was another loud exclamation, and the bosses huddled closer.

"Damn!" Nat exclaimed.

"What's wrong?"

"I think they must have found something. Maybe a bit of torn material from your blouse."

"So what if they have?" Freddie argued. "That won't really tell them much."

"No, but it will put them more on their guard. We'll have to be even more careful from here on out." He cast another anxious look at the sky. "Dammit, I thought the situation would be under control by this time."

Far from being under control, the situation suddenly took a severe turn for the worse. Three newcomers and a pack of dogs emerged from the trees at the far end of the field.

"It's Hap and the Parker boys," Freddie hissed.

"Damn!" Nat stared intently through the leaves. "What are they doing here?"

"Either they've been coerced into helping with the harvest or they've been stupid enough to agree willingly. I know they must be the ones who showed these thugs the logging road. It's been out of use so long, no one but a native would remember it's here." Nat put a hand on Pinky, who was showing signs of restlessness now that the other dogs were in view.

221

"Will the Parkers be arrested when your people come?" Freddie asked.

"They will if they're on this site. But I'll honor my deal with Granny and have them released afterward. That's not what has me worried."

She glanced up at his profile. "What is it?"

"The dogs," he said.

Freddie glanced back at the field and saw what he meant. At first the hounds had been too busy sniffing around the guns and the Mexican workers to look elsewhere. Now, however, they were trotting down the field toward the place where Nat and Freddie lay hidden.

"Do you think they can smell us?" she asked.

"Of course they can! They're downwind, which is my fault. I should have thought of this!"

"They're not barking," Freddie pointed out hopefully.

"No. Our scents are familiar to them. They're just going to pay us a little social call."

Freddie looked back at the field and saw, to her horror, that Nat was right. The hounds, their tongues lolling out and their ears flapping, were heading straight for their hiding place. And what was worse, they were being watched closely by the armed foremen.

Suddenly, Nat thrust his rifle, the flare gun and several flares at her. "Take these and get out of here!"

"But—"

"Listen to me for a change! You know how to fire a flare, don't you?"

She nodded. It was something that every glider pilot knew. In fact, there was a flare gun in the cockpit of her plane for use in case of emergencies.

"Find yourself a safer hiding place, and when you hear those copters, use it to signal them. Now get out of here!"

Freddie couldn't mistake the command in Nat's voice. She gave him one last frightened look and then jumped to her feet. She darted through the underbrush, deeper into the woods. She glanced back in time to see that Nat had covered her escape by getting up and strolling out from behind the trees, accompanied by Pinky. After silencing the Parker hounds with a curt word, he walked straight toward the foremen, who were watching his approach with their submachine guns ready.

"Hello there, you all," he called out cheerfully, affecting a twang that made him sound like a local. "Just thought I'd come out and offer to lend you a hand."

"Oh, my God!" Freddie moaned. She closed her eyes tight, expecting at any moment to hear the rattle of bullets. But instead, only the sound of angry voices assaulted her ears.

What was going on? She was sorely tempted to turn back and find out, but she knew she couldn't. She'd promised to do what Nat asked, and he'd told her to find a safe hiding place. Now, nothing on the ground seemed safe. Frantically, she looked around for a tree to climb and spotted one a few yards off. It was a spreading oak with good-size branches growing close enough to the ground so that if she took a running jump, she could swing herself up.

Casting one last frightened glance over her shoulder, she trotted to the oak, reached up to the limit of her height, and managed to balance Nat's rifle, flare gun and flares in the nook where the branches separated. Then she backed off and sprinted toward a large, low hanging branch. A moment later she was sprawled on top of it. She caught her breath and looked ruefully down at a fresh scrape on the inside of her thigh. "If I ever get out of this, I'm going to need a week in a hospital," she muttered as she inched back to retrieve Nat's weapons.

Burdened as she was by his rifle and flare gun, climbing wasn't easy. But ignoring the pain of her new scrapes, she managed to hoist herself up high enough that she could look down on the field.

Nat studied the expression on the foreman's thick features. It was a mixture of suspicion and astonishment—and suspicion had the upper hand.

Pinky, seeing the gun pointed at his master, began to growl. Keeping a smile firmly pasted across the lower half of his face, Nat silenced the dog with a gesture. Then he focused all his attention on the party waiting to greet him. At one side of the bearded overseer, Hap and the Parker boys stared in openmouthed surprise. Behind them, the other armed boss was crossing the field. A couple of the Mexican laborers had paused in their work to stare curiously. But the majority stolidly continued harvesting.

"And just who the hell might you be?" the nearest gunman demanded.

"Nat's the name." He waved a hand at Lou and Marshall. "These boys know me. They're friends of mine."

Without taking his eyes off Nat or lowering his weapon, the man growled, "Is that so? Do you clowns know this guy?"

Lou, his expression a study in consternation, hurried forward. "He's a friend of our Granny's."

"What's he doing here? Did you tell anyone we were coming today?"

"N-no sir, Mr. Butler, we never told nobody nothin'." Lou turned back to Nat. "What are you doin' here? We thought you was gone."

"No, just doing a little hunting nearby. I heard the noise and thought I'd investigate." Nat squinted out over the field and did his best to look dim-witted. "This is quite a project you got going."

Just then the gunman with the pith helmet joined Butler and demanded, "Who is this clodhopper? Is he the one who ripped up those plants?"

Both turned accusing eyes on Nat, who quickly denied all knowledge. "Hey, I just happened to be passing by. No harm intended, and if you don't need me, I'll be on my way," he drawled.

"You aren't going anywhere, mister." Stepping forward, Butler leveled his gun as if he meant to use it.

Looking horrified, Marshall tried to wedge himself between them. "He didn't mean no harm. You ain't going to tell anybody about this, are you Nat?"

"He's not going to get the chance," Butler threatened. "And maybe neither are you three," he added with a sneer. "You've been nothing but trouble lately." Roughly, he pushed Marshall aside. Then his gun swept not only Nat but the two Parkers and their friend Hap as well.

All three young men went white, and Nat wasn't feeling too good himself. He cast about in his mind for a way of defusing the situation. But just then Pinky made things even worse. Despite Nat's quieting hand, the dog had been growing more and more

225

restive. He obviously didn't like these men with guns, and when they leveled them at his master, he bared his teeth and flattened his ears menacingly.

"Look at that brute!" Butler exclaimed to the boss wearing the helmet. "Damned if that isn't the ugliest thing I've ever seen."

"Looks mean, too. Maybe you better shoot him."

Obligingly, Butler aimed his gun at Pinky. Nat prepared to spring. Perhaps he could wrestle the gun away, he told himself. And maybe the Parkers would follow his lead and overpower the other gunman. Someone was bound to get hurt, but the situation had gotten desperate enough to make it worth the effort.

At that moment a burst of fiery color against the sky distracted everyone. All six men stared up as a parachute flare slowly descended toward the middle of the field.

Butler was the first to speak. "Dammit! Someone else is out there!" He turned toward his helmeted cohort. "We've got to find them." Then, apparently forgetting that he'd been about to shoot Pinky, he motioned Nat, Hap, and the Parkers to start walking toward the trees. "You can come along, too. I intend to find out what the hell is going on."

The men fanned out—the thug with the helmet pushed Lou, Hap, and Marshall in front of him, and Butler concentrated on Nat. "Just who is your friend out there?" the bearded gunman demanded.

"No one I know," Nat lied, trying not to let his face give anything away. But behind his bland expression, he was desperately worried. There was no sign of the helicopters. For all he knew, it would be hours before they showed up. Why had Freddie shot that flare off? And where was she?

CHAPTER THIRTEEN

It never even occurred to Freddie not to try to save Pinky when she saw him being threatened. She had lifted the flare gun and aimed it so that the wind would carry it over the field. Then she'd watched in satisfaction as everyone stared up at the spectacular display the orange flare made. It had distracted them, just the way she'd hoped. And it had bought some time. Clutching her rifle, she saw the two gunmen push their captives in front of them and head toward the woods.

If only the helicopters would come, she thought. But the only sound to be heard overhead was the wind. She was well hidden, so it would be a while before anyone found her, she told herself. And she had Nat's rifle. If necessary, she would use it. Thank God the other two gun-carrying bosses were busy on the logging road. If they showed up, she and Nat would have no chance at all.

Tensely, she peered down as the men and dogs passed through the line of trees. Fortunately, they were not coming in her direction but were heading off to the left, toward the spot where her plane had been hidden. Pressing herself against the tree bark, she waited. Fifteen minutes later, she heard a shout, and her heart leaped into her throat. She couldn't see what had happened, but she knew. They had found the Schweizer.

How was Nat handling that? she wondered. She guessed that he was still feigning ignorance. But it wouldn't do any good. No matter what he said, they would never give up the search now. And when they thought to start using the hounds, they would be successful. She took a firm grip on the rifle, knowing that there was no alternative. She would soon have to use it.

It was then that she heard the sound—a hum, just a tone lower than the beat of the wind. If she hadn't been listening for it, she might not have noticed. Hopefully, no one else but she *had* noticed it.

With trembling fingers, Freddie reloaded the flare gun and peered up at the sky through the leaves while she aimed it. Along with the distant hum, she could hear voices and the barking of dogs nearby. How far away were the helicopters? If she sent the flare up now, would their pilots see it? And what would happen after she'd fired the thing for the second time? The men below were so close now that if she released the colorful signal, they were bound to find her. After the helicopter pilots spotted the flare, how long would it take them to close in? And what would she have to deal with in the meantime?

The whirring sound rose in volume. Soon the people below would notice it, too. Closing her eyes, Freddie squeezed the trigger and fired the second flare. Then, with her rifle at the ready, she looked down at the ground to see what would happen next.

The Parker boys and the man with the pith helmet appeared. They were headed toward the trees where she was hidden. A few feet away, prodding Nat from behind with the barrel of his machine gun, was the man with the beard.

"Here," the first gunman shouted, pulling out a scrap of material from his pocket and addressing Lou, "you tell your dogs to take a whiff of this and go find whoever it belongs to."

Freddie squinted. The faded scrap of cloth was practically unrecognizable. Yet she knew what it was. Nat had been right. They'd found some material that had been torn from her blouse when she'd tangled with that deadfall. But it had been out in the rain for several days. Surely none of her scent still clung to it, she told herself as she watched Lou kneel and show it to the dogs, who milled around him in a state of excited confusion.

"Those hounds are dumber than their owners," the man with the beard snapped in disgust. "Show it to this ugly brute over here." He gestured at Pinky.

Holding the bit of cloth between his thumb and forefinger, Lou got to his feet and took a tentative step toward Nat's dog.

"What's wrong with you? Are you afraid of him?" the bearded gunman sneered.

Lou flushed at the insult. "Mr. Butler, that's a real mean breed of dog, and he don't like to be fooled with."

Butler guffawed nastily and delivered another sharp poke to Nat's back. "Then give it to the clodhopper who owns him." He turned toward Nat. "You tell your dog to find whoever belongs to that, you hear, Bozo?"

Lou had dropped the material in Nat's hand and then quickly stepped to one side.

"Well, tell him!" the gunman snarled when Nat hesitated.

Nat continued to stand motionless. Freddie could guess what he must be thinking. If he told Pinky to find her, the animal would obey. On the other hand, the sound of the helicopters was getting louder. Nat must have noticed it by now and was stalling for time. She raised his rifle and squinted through the sight. She zeroed in on a spot just below the cocking handle on Butler's submachine gun.

"Do as I say, or your body will be so full of holes it won't even be worth a dog biscuit." As he issued his threat, Butler stepped toward Nat in a way that made Freddie abruptly take action. She squeezed the trigger. There was a sharp crack, and the submachine gun was knocked out of Butler's hand.

"What the hell!" he howled.

"If anybody moves, I'll shoot them," Freddie shouted.

But the second gunman paid no attention to her warning. "Choppers!" he yelled to his stunned compatriot. Running forward, he aimed his weapon up into the tree and sprayed bullets. As one of the shots sent bark flying inches from her head, Freddie heard Nat snap an attack command at Pinky.

She didn't see what happened next, but she heard first the sound of Pinky's snarl and then an anguished howl from the man who had been trying to kill her seconds earlier.

Parting the leaves, she stared down at an incredible scene. The man with the pith helmet rolled in a deadly battle with Pinky. His machine gun lay useless on the ground.

Taking advantage of the confusion, Nat leaped at

the momentarily disconcerted Butler. They, too, struggled on the ground, exchanging vicious punches and kicks. The hounds raced around barking hysterically just behind them. Hap and the Parker boys looked on in openmouthed astonishment.

"Help him, for God's sake!" Freddie shouted down at Lou and Marshall.

Then she wondered if that had been a wise request. Just who would the boys choose to help, Nat or Butler? Not even Granny had been sure where their loyalty would lie in a pinch. What if they turned on Nat? She glanced down at the abandoned submachine gun and then started to scramble from her position in the tree.

Her descent was almost as precipitous as the mother bear's had been the day before. When she jumped to the ground, she fell in a heap and wondered for a second if she'd broken something. Nevertheless, she struggled to her feet, thankful that her legs still seemed to work, even though they felt like jelly. Pivoting sharply, she dived at the submachine gun, peripherally aware as she did so that the noise from the helicopters was now a dull roar. She could hear the shouts from the workers as they escaped into the woods.

When Freddie raised the automatic weapon, she found to her relief that it wasn't needed. The Parker boys had come to Nat's aid and were holding the dazed and badly beaten Butler while Nat tried to pull Pinky off his partner.

That was a daunting task. The animal was in a frenzy and had locked his jaws around his terrified victim's leg. The man was whimpering, his face was bloodless, and his eyes were glazed with pain and fear as he tried vainly to free himself.

"You better not touch that dog," Lou warned Nat. "Them kind of bulldogs go crazy when they're in a fight. He could turn on you."

Ignoring the warning, Nat circled around Pinky, talking to him in a persuasive voice. "That's enough now, boy. Let go, let go. You don't have to fight him anymore."

At first Pinky seemed not to hear. The growls rumbling in his throat were fearsome. He'd pulled back his thick muzzle in a fixed snarl, and his tiny, lashless eyes glinted. But finally he did let go. Reluctantly, he released his victim's leg and backed off, looking up at Nat and whining.

"Good boy. You're a good dog," his master praised. After he'd patted Pinky's head, Nat picked up the other machine gun, swept Freddie with a glance that left her wondering what was in his mind, and then turned toward Lou, Marshall, and Hap. "Thanks for your help," he told them. "You'd better get out of here." He hooked a thumb in the direction of the field, where three helicopters were preparing to land.

"You know what this is about?" Hap asked.

"Yes, I do. Now skedaddle!"

The boys took the hint at once and melted into the woods with their dogs at their heels.

After that the confusion grew. The helicopters landed and armed policemen dressed for combat spilled out of them. They scattered, some giving chase to the fleeing pickers, others heading toward the spot where the second team had been loading the bales of harvested marijuana. It was only a matter of minutes before they found Freddie, Nat, and their prisoners.

Nat immediately identified himself. "It's about time you got here," he complained mildly.

"Sorry," a young blond policeman who introduced himself as Sergeant Brelsford apologized. "The wind slowed things up. We were worried about you. But it looks as if you took care of yourself okay." His gaze surveyed the area, pausing for a moment on Freddie, who was still sitting on the ground clutching the submachine gun she'd rescued.

"These are a couple of the men you want," Nat said. He gestured at the two bosses. Both looked utterly beaten. Butler sat slumped against a tree, and his partner, now minus his pith helmet and with his pants in shreds, was still lying moaning on the ground where Pinky had abandoned him.

"And this," Nat continued, "is Ms. Frederica Davenport." Briefly, he explained who Freddie was. "She's been through a lot the past few days and needs to be taken where she can get a hot meal and some rest."

"I think that can be arranged," Brelsford said. "One of the choppers can take her and these two men back now. We'll be here the rest of the day combing the woods, so there's plenty of time." He crossed over to Freddie and helped her to her feet. "Don't worry, Ms. Davenport. You'll be safe and sound before you know it."

During the past few hours Freddie had been functioning mainly on fear-induced adrenaline. As Sergeant Brelsford escorted her to one of the helicopters, that, too, deserted her, and she found that she could barely walk. After a backward look at Nat, who was already conferring with another policeman, a gray mantle of exhaustion settled over her, muting everything she saw and felt.

Butler and his cohort were put into a helicopter with armed guards. Brelsford issued some instructions and then settled Freddie into the seat next to the pilot. Nat, deep in conversation with yet another officer, only looked up once. Just before the aircraft started up its engine, he came forward to say goodbye.

"Can't you come with me?" she asked.

He shook his head. "I have to stay until things are cleaned up around here. Which could take awhile." He waved a hand at the confusion swirling around them. Men with squawkers shouted orders, and uniformed policemen disappeared into and emerged from the line of trees in a kind of frenetic ballet.

Dazedly, Freddie stared at the scene. The mountain's tranquillity had been completely shattered. Since she associated Nat with a wilderness that was unspoiled, it was jarring to imagine him fitting in with all this. Yet he did.

"You're quite a lady," he told her, reaching up to give her a light kiss on the cheek. "I guess I'm glad you dropped by, after all."

She looked back at him searchingly, waiting for him to say more. Of course, the situation didn't permit a tender parting. Nat could hardly declare his love with half a dozen policemen looking on. But surely he could say something about wanting to see her again. There was nothing like that, though, just a friendly squeeze of her hand and a smiling "Take care" before he turned away to resume his duties. Shouting questions at Brelsford, he strode off.

As the pilot started up the rotors and their noise drowned everything else out, Freddie leaned back and closed her eyes. Right now she was too tired to think or feel, but she knew that tomorrow her numbness would be gone. What would she feel then? she wondered.

When the helicopter touched down again, the two sullen criminals were taken away by guards and Freddie was driven to an emergency room. There she was thoroughly checked over, and her wounds, all of them superficial scratches, were dressed. After that she signed a statement and was fed some hot soup. Then she was driven to her brother's house.

"You don't have to worry about your plane," the driver told her when she asked about the fate of the Schweizer. "It will be back in Pritchard's gliderport by tomorrow afternoon."

Freddie thanked him and then allowed the polite young man to escort her to the door. Night had fallen, and the steps were dark.

"You sure you don't need any more help?"

"No," she said wearily. She took the spare key out of its hiding place in the front garden and twisted it in the lock. When the door was open, she reached in and switched on the porch light. "I'll be just fine. All I need now is some sleep."

"Well, if you're sure, then I'll say good-bye."

"Good-bye, and thanks again."

Inside, the house had a deserted feel. Of course—it had been empty for six days. Was it only that long? she asked herself. Sore from all she'd been through, Freddie limped into the kitchen and peered at the calendar next to the refrigerator. Yes, even though it seemed like a lifetime, she'd been gone for less than a week. Her brother wasn't due back for another two days. Wearily, Freddie opened the refrigerator. Nothing looked very good. The milk had probably gone sour by now, and much of the other food would need to be thrown out.

She closed the door with a sigh and looked around blearily. It was too much for her to handle. She couldn't deal with all the things that had happened—and that included Nat Steele. Oblivion was what she craved. Later, she'd try to pick up the pieces.

On that thought, Freddie headed for the guest bedroom, where she'd been staying before the start of her adventure. She stripped off her clothes and dropped them onto the floor. Then she climbed between the sheets. With another deep sigh, she closed her eyes.

When she next opened them, the sun was high overhead and the phone was ringing. Wrapping herself in the quilt, she stumbled out of bed and picked up the receiver.

"Hello?"

"Hello yourself, you little devil. Where have you been all this time?" It was Hank.

Freddie rubbed her forehead and perched on the edge of a rose-colored club chair. "You wouldn't believe me if I told you."

"After seeing the shape your brother's Schweizer is in, I'd believe just about anything. Some official types in uniforms delivered it here this morning. It looks like you flew it through a combat zone."

"You might say that I did," Freddie agreed dryly. "How bad is it? Can it be fixed?"

"Yes, but the repairs won't be cheap. The finish is mighty scratched."

"Fix it then, and send me the bill."

"All right, but I sure would like to hear what you've been up to," Hank wheedled.

Freddie closed her eyes. "Someday I'll tell you. But not now."

A few minutes later, she replaced the receiver. The clock on the table told her that it was past noon. She'd slept for more than twelve hours. Her gaze fell on the pile of clothing scattered on the floor at the foot of the bed. Granny's old dress, filthy and torn, was now hardly more than a rag. In Bert and Gracie's elegantly appointed guest room, it seemed ridiculously out of place. Jeremy's shredded army boots looked even more impossible. Had she actually worn those things for almost a week? Had she really fought off a bear with those shoes?

Shaking her head, Freddie gathered the flowered quilt around her and wandered over to the antique dressing table. There she peered into the mirror. The face of the young woman looking back at her was slightly thinner and more tanned than she remembered. Her hair was tangled and badly in need of a shampoo, and behind their thick screen of lashes her blue eyes were wide and faintly shadowed. This was the face Nat had looked into the last time she'd seen him. She touched a finger to her mouth. These were the lips he'd kissed so passionately the night before.

Slowly, Freddie dropped her hand. She opened the quilt that swathed her and then released it. As it slithered to the floor, she stood staring at herself, at the body to which Nat had made such ardent love. It looked much the same, but it was different—everything was different. She just wasn't sure yet how deep those differences were and what effect they were going to have on her.

On a more pragmatic note, she glanced down at her knees. Superficially, she hadn't emerged unscathed from the experience, either. Her body was stiff and sore, and she had scratches and bruises that wouldn't disappear completely for another week or two. The one above her breast caught her attention. Nat had been dressing that when she'd first lain eyes on him. Would she ever see him again?

Flinching as she remembered his impersonal goodbye, she turned away and crossed the room to the closet. After taking out her terry-cloth robe and slipping it on, she headed for the bathroom and a long hot shower. She had just emerged from the spray and was toweling her hair dry when the phone rang again.

"Ms. Davenport?"

"Yes."

"This is Sergeant Brelsford. Mr. Steele asked me to call and check on you and to tell you that your plane has been returned to Pritchard's gliderport."

"Yes, I've already spoken to Mr. Pritchard." Why hadn't Nat called her himself?

"I thought you might like to know," Brelsford went on, "that we're very pleased with the results of this raid. We must have burned enough marijuana to keep the city of Atlanta high for six months. And all four of the gunmen are under arrest. I think they'll soon be telling us what we need to know so that we'll be able to catch some much bigger fish in our net."

"That's good. Will you need me for anything more?"

"No. Your statement should be enough."

Freddie cleared her throat. "Is Mr. Steele all right?"

"He's fine. I suspect the department will give him a commendation for yesterday's work. It takes a special kind of person to do the jobs he takes on."

"Yes, I'm sure it does."

After thanking the man, Freddie hung up the phone. She sat staring off into space for several minutes. That Nat hadn't bothered to call her himself she interpreted as another rejection. And that bit about "it takes a special kind of person to do the jobs he takes on" wasn't exactly good news, either. Brelsford was right—it did take a special kind of man to risk his life the way Nat had, and her brain told her it wasn't the marrying kind, either. Like a child gingerly probing a recent injury, she tried to examine her reaction.

To her relief, she wasn't feeling much of anything yet. Her emotions were still numb. While it lasted, that was a good thing, she thought. It allowed her to think about the situation objectively and make some decisions.

As the noontime sun lit up the pretty pink and cream guest room, Freddie sat very still and cast her mind back over the last few days. Although it had been clear from the first that Nat wanted her, it had been at her invitation that he had become her lover. Had he ever said he cared for her? Or even that he wanted to go on seeing her when this was all over?

No, there had been nothing like that, she realized. Nat had whispered many sweet things into her eager ears, but he'd never indicated that he wanted a lasting relationship or even that theirs was anything more than a brief idyll.

"And that's all it was," Freddie said aloud, ignoring the tears gathering in the corners of her eyes. "It was just one of those crazy things." The words of the old song took on new meaning, and she almost laughed as she remembered the line about flying to the moon on gossamer wings. "It was just one of those crazy things," she repeated as she let the irony sink in.

Abruptly, she stood up and belted her robe more tightly. Then she strode to the closet and hauled out her suitcase. She realized that she couldn't stay there any longer. She had to get home, back to her normal life and her normal routine. And she had to do that before the numbness left and the misery she knew was in store for her really set in.

The shrill sound of the phone roused Nat from sleep. Unwillingly, he reached for the receiver and brought it to his ear.

"Did I wake you?" a familiar voice asked without sounding the least bit apologetic.

"Yes." Nat opened his eyes.

"Sorry. But it's been twenty-four hours. You must have had enough sleep by now."

"Not according to my body."

The man chuckled. "Maybe you're getting too old for this line of work."

"I was having the same thought myself," Nat replied. He reached for his cigarettes.

"Well, before you decide to retire, I thought I'd tell you that the Everett thing is about to come to a head.

Some very heavy weight is going to be moved, and we could use another man."

Nat knew that "weight" referred to cocaine. "Give me a break, Chuck."

"Why? I know you had a rough couple of days up in those mountains, but before that you were just lying around strumming your guitar and flirting with that pretty glider pilot. Time you did some real work."

"Sure." Nat lit a cigarette and inhaled deeply. "Give me a few hours to think on it, will you? I'll call you back."

Chuck sounded reluctant, but he agreed. "Okay—just don't let me down. I need you. Sorry I disturbed your beauty sleep."

After Nat hung up the phone, he lay back on his pillow and put his free hand behind his head. He'd finally gotten back to the one-room apartment he was subletting in Atlanta late in the afternoon of the day after the bust. And now it was the following morning. He glanced at the clock on the bedside table. Eight thirty. He'd been dead to the world for more than half a day. His gaze swept the place where he was sleeping. It wasn't much—just a kitchenette and a living room furnished with a table, a few mismatched chairs, and a sofabed.

Suddenly, he found himself trying to picture Freddie here beside him, but he couldn't. She didn't belong in a grungy little bachelor apartment. She deserved a nicer setting than this, a real home with curtains and rugs that weren't Salvation Army rejects. She deserved that rose-covered cottage she'd once admitted she wanted.

Struck by the oddness of his thinking, he sat up

and rubbed one of his temples. The irregular nature of his work would make keeping a nice apartment a waste of money. He'd never cared to before. The efficiency apartment for which he was now paying a minimum of rent was just a place to flop between cases. If he got serious about a woman, that would have to change. A lot of things would have to change, including the freewheeling life-style that he cherished.

Nat stubbed out his cigarette and lit another. It was unusual for him to chain smoke, but he was feeling restless. He knew why, too—Frederica Davenport. There was no point in trying to fool himself. He was crazy about her, crazy enough to want to see her again. Maybe even crazy enough to put that freewheeling life-style in jeopardy.

Frowning, he thought back on their parting. There had been a sense of dislocation about it, and he'd known from the dazed look in Freddie's beautiful blue eyes that she'd felt the same way. When they'd said good-bye, he'd been a law enforcement agent again, and the demands of that job had taken the upper hand by necessity. Had she understood? Now that their time alone together in the mountains was over, what was she feeling?

For him, what had started off as an improbable attraction had blossomed into something much more. Frederica Davenport was a woman in a thousand, he thought as he pictured her sitting on the ground clutching the submachine gun. But what about her? Now that she was back to reality, how was she dealing with all that had happened?

He'd laughed when she'd talked to him about prisoner syndrome. But as Nat reflected on that now, he wasn't even smiling. She had been his prisoner, and in a way he'd forced himself on her. What had seemed romantic to her in the mountains might, when reality set in, begin to seem like something quite different. In truth, he was almost afraid to see her again. He was afraid that the look of love that had been in her blue eyes might have changed to one of embarrassment or even distaste.

That was it, Nat thought stubbing out his second cigarette and reaching for a third. She had him running scared. This was a decision point. In the mountains they'd been thrown together—they could both pretend there was nothing more to it than that. But now there could be no further pretending. When they saw each other again, it would be because they chose to, and they'd both have to tell the truth. But what *was* the truth?

Nat raked a hand through his thick fair hair. Leaning over, he picked up the piece of paper on which Brelsford had jotted Freddie's number. Then he dialed and waited. But as it rang, some sixth sense told him that no one would answer. Regardless, he let it drone on a dozen times before giving up. Then he checked his watch again. It was almost nine. Where could she be? he wondered.

After opening a can of food for Pinky, Nat fixed himself a cup of coffee and scrounged a toaster waffle from the meager supply of food in the freezer. Then he tried the phone again—with the same result. Temporarily abandoning the effort, he dressed and put in a call to his parents. Although Pinky was his, the dog lived on their farm when Nat couldn't take him on an assignment.

"Come on, boy. Time to go home," he told Pinky.

As the old dog ambled out into the hall after Nat and then down the stairs to the parking lot, he cast his master a regretful look. It was almost as if he knew their time together was over for a spell.

"We'll work with each other again," Nat assured him. "This'll just give you a rest."

Nat stayed for dinner with his folks, so he didn't get back to his place until that evening. The first thing he did after sticking the six-pack of beer he'd bought into the almost empty refrigerator was to head for the telephone. This time when he dialed Freddie's number, there was an answer. But the deep voice on the other end of the line belonged to her brother.

"We got home a little early and found a note from her on the kitchen table," Bert Davenport told Nat. "She's gone back to Nashville."

After he replaced the receiver, Nat stood for a long moment. There was a thoughtful expression on his strongly cut features. "She's gone back to Nashville!" he muttered under his breath. So what now?

Hunching his shoulders, he leaned over and dialed Chuck's number at home. "How long will this Everett thing take?" he demanded when Chuck answered.

"A week."

"All right, I'm in."

Chuck sounded truly grateful. "Thanks, buddy. I knew I could count on you."

"Sure."

A few minutes later, Nat popped the tab on one of his beers and sat down at a window where he could look out at the skyline. Lit as it was by a flashing neon parking lot sign, it seemed a world away from the natural beauty that he and Freddie had admired together on their last night in the wilderness. Nat remembered that star-strewn night, and his mouth felt dry. Had he made the right decision just now? If Freddie had gone back to Nashville early, maybe that meant she was trying to avoid him. Or maybe it meant that they both needed some time to sort out their feelings. A week on the Everett case would give her that time. When they saw each other again, they'd both have a better idea about the truth.

But it wouldn't be easy to stay away from her that long, he realized as he took a sip of beer. Because while he wasn't sure he was the rose-covered cottage type, he already knew he missed her like hell.

CHAPTER FOURTEEN

Freddie tapped on the glass barrier, and Jimmy Moonshine turned his head. Removing his earphones, he sauntered out and closed the door behind him.

"What's up, babe?"

For a split second her gaze was distracted by the earring dangling from his right lobe. "I have a favor to ask."

"Anything, sweeetheart—you know that."

"How good are your connections over at Music Row?" she asked, referring to the square-mile area in Nashville that was the hub of the country music business.

"Good enough. Why do you want to know?"

Freddie fixed her gaze on Jimmy's sharp-featured face. When Carter had left for New York, Jimmy had replaced him, and he was now the top deejay at the station. His rowdy style was totally different from Carter's elegant cynicism, but he'd created his own following, and it was a large one.

From the beginning Jimmy had tried to be friendly to her, and he'd even asked her out. But she'd refused. Maybe it was because he occupied Carter's old chair, or maybe it was the long braid of hair that hung down his back. She'd never really taken to him. That wasn't making it any easier to ask his help now. But she had no choice. She'd promised Vandy.

Freddie cleared her throat. "There's a singer I'd like someone over there to hear."

"Well, have her leave a demo."

"Jimmy, you know that won't work. She needs someone to run interference for her."

He narrowed his eyes. "Who is this singer?"

As succinctly as she could, Freddie told him about Vandy. When she finished, he tugged on his scraggly beard and studied her speculatively. "Why I'm interested in a female who looks like a Madison Avenue shampoo ad is beyond me, but I'd like to take you out, Freddie girl. If I do something for this Vandy, will you go with me to the Tax Deferred concert this Friday?"

The request surprised her—especially since Jimmy specialized in rockabilly, and Tax Deferred was a punk rock group. Yet after a moment's reflection she agreed. "All right, but you'd better tell me how to dress. If I go to a show like that looking normal, the audience will probably beat me to death."

Jimmy laughed. "Time you loosened up and got dirty. Squeaky-clean went out years ago. Hadn't you heard?"

"Working in a place like this, I hear everything. I just don't want to listen to most of it," she retorted.

After Jimmy went back into the sound studio, Freddie breathed a sigh of relief and walked down the corridor to her office. She'd been back on the job for just over a week now. The past few days hadn't been easy, and she'd needed time to deal with her own tumultuous emotions before turning her attention to

Vandy. But now that she'd finally found the courage to approach Jimmy, she felt better. Her promise to the mountain girl had been weighing on her conscience.

After slipping into her tweed jacket, Freddie collected her things and went out to the parking lot. It was strange how everything was the same as it had been before and yet totally different, she mused as she pulled her Chevette from its space and headed toward her apartment. She was going through all the old familiar motions, but her mind was on Nat. Even though she'd told herself not to expect his call, some part of her had still hoped for it. During the past week she'd stayed close to her phone, willing it to ring with him on the other end of the line. But it hadn't, and now she'd resigned herself that it wouldn't. The only thing left was to keep her promise to Vandy and then do her best to forget everything else. But she knew she never would. The pain of loss would go away eventually, but the bittersweet memory would linger.

To try to keep herself from brooding, Freddie went to her closet after dinner and forced herself to think about the Tax Deferred concert. There was really nothing in her conservative wardrobe that was appropriate for it. Maybe Jimmy was right. Maybe it was time she kicked up her heels.

The next day, Freddie used her lunch hour to stop in at a trendy boutique and buy a leather miniskirt and jacket, a pair of rhinestone-encrusted spike heels, and a silver Lurex halter top. She had to spend an outrageous amount of money for what was in her mind a kind of Halloween costume, but she was in an outrageous mood, and it did her good.

Friday night, she completed the outfit with fake diamond earrings that dangled to her shoulders and a bottle of mousse that allowed her to stiffen her curls into spikes. She was just applying the last heavy stroke of deep red lipstick when the doorbell rang.

Jimmy couldn't accuse her of being too clean-cut tonight, she thought as she teetered across the living room. Grinning, she struck a sexy pose and threw open the front door.

The man who stood on the other side of the threshold gazing at her in amazement was Nat. In the first instant she almost didn't recognize him. He'd shaved off his moustache, and his blond hair had been razor cut. He was wearing a conservatively tailored gray suit, and he was carrying flowers and what looked like a box of candy.

Freddie's jaw sagged and her magenta shadowed eyelids opened wide. "Hi," she managed.

"Hi, yourself." From the top of her spiked head to her rhinestone-encrusted stiletto heels, he surveyed her. "Is that you? Have I got the wrong address?"

"No, it's me. Sort of." She stepped aside and gestured him in. "Are you here on business?"

Still eyeing her, he walked past. "No. I just got off a case, and I've taken a few weeks' leave. I came here to see you."

"Really?" Her heart was already beating as if she were in the middle of an aerobic workout. Closing the door, she faced him.

"I was hoping you'd let me take you out to dinner," he said.

Freddie felt like screaming with frustration. "Well, I'd love to. But I'm dressed this way because I'm supposed to go to a punk concert. I have a date."

"Date?"

Nat frowned, and suddenly, in a sharp mood shift, Freddie was glad this wasn't one of her customary nights home alone. Why hadn't he contacted her earlier? Did he imagine she was so hopelessly smitten that she would pine for him until he got around to finding time for her in his busy schedule? Of course, she *had* been pining, but she told herself that she was glad he wouldn't know it. Behind the thick layers of mascara she'd applied, her blue eyes brightened with defiance.

Just then, there was another knock on the door, and Freddie turned to open it. Her emotions took another swing when she saw Jimmy. He too had gone all out and was a vision of sartorial splendor in a red satin kimono embroidered with dragons. His feet were encased in motorcycle boots, and enormous hoop earrings supporting tiny plastic parrots weighed down his earlobes. Above them he wore shades, and his hair was neatly braided in pigtails. His left cheek sported a beauty patch.

"Well, if it isn't Prince Charming," she muttered.

"Awwlll right!" he approved when he took in Freddie's outfit. "We're going to howl tonight, baby!" Then his gaze slid to Nat. "Who's the dude?"

"This is Nat Steele, a—a friend of mine. And Nat, this is Jimmy Moonshine, a professional associate."

"I see." Nat set the candy and flowers down on a table. Then he took a step toward Jimmy and held out his hand. "Pleased to meet you, Mr. Moonshine." Turning, he gazed expressionlessly at Freddie, who stood with her arms crossed over her chest. Her fingers plucked at the hem of her Lurex top. "I'm sorry if I interrupted your plans. Have a good time tonight. I'll call you tomorrow."

There was a lump in Freddie's throat as she watched him walk out the door and disappear down the hall.

"Somebody special?" Jimmy asked. "Do you want to forget about the concert and go after him?"

Gathering up her jacket, Freddie pasted on a smile. "And lose the chance of finally going out with a guy who really knows how to dress? Are you kidding?" She took Jimmy's arm. "Now, tell me where you got those earrings."

He smiled and escorted her out the door with a flourish. "I had them custom made."

"Aw, gee, I wanted a pair just like them."

"No problem, baby. If you treat me right tonight, I'll give you my jeweler's name."

For some strange reason, Freddie did have a good time at the concert. After her return from the mountains, her life had seemed gray. The color and excitement of the Tax Deferred performance was a welcome relief. Many questions about the significance of Nat's unexpected appearance swirled in her head. But feeling defiant, she pushed them far enough to the back of her mind that she could enjoy the bizarre sights at the concert and Jimmy's wacky running commentary.

"See the blonde with the tire chain wrapped around her boot?"

"Yes." Freddie craned her head.

"She's a secretary at the station."

"You're kidding!" Freddie squinted at the freakishly dressed young woman. "It's Susie!"

"Right. Tomorrow she'll turn back into a pumpkin and be wearing a pageboy, pearls, and a silk blouse."

"You're amazingly observant, do you know that?"

"Sure I do." He tweaked one of Freddie's now somewhat wilted spikes. "I have all the cute chicks at the station picked out. I liked you the minute I saw you. But you didn't like me, did you?"

She shot him a look of surprise. "That's not true."

"I figured it was because I'd replaced your boyfriend," he continued, ignoring her protest. "But then I asked around and found out that you'd broken up with Carter. I thought maybe you were nursing a broken heart over the lout and I should give it time. Looks like I gave it too much time."

"What do you mean?"

"I mean the guy in your apartment, the one carrying the flowers and wearing the boring suit." He sighed. "Well, there's no accounting for tastes."

Freddie laughed and changed the subject. But she knew that Jimmy wasn't fooled.

Later, when he brought her home, Jimmy said, "Well, you've kept your part of the bargain. Guess it's time for me to keep mine. I gave Martin Pearle a call yesterday."

Freddie's eyes widened. Pearle was one of Music Row's most prestigious talent agents. "You spoke to him about Vandy?"

"Uh huh." Jimmy scratched behind his ear. "It wasn't easy, but I persuaded him to take a look at her."

"He has to do more than that. He has to hear her."

"That, too. When can you get this canary off her mountain and into town?"

"I'm not sure." Freddie frowned. That was something she'd have to talk to Nat about.

"Well, let me know, and I'll set up an appointment."

"Oh Jimmy, thank you!" Impulsively, Freddie leaned over and gave his thin cheek a kiss.

He grinned. "I wish I thought you meant that."

"I did."

"Not the way I wish you meant it. But that's okay, kid," he added good-humoredly. "Like I already said, there's no accounting for tastes."

A few minutes later, Jimmy saw her to her door. When he was gone, Freddie switched on the light in her living room and stared around. Her gaze lit on the flowers and candy box that Nat had left behind. She'd been so ruffled by his appearance that she hadn't even thought to put his gift in water. Now she scooped the flowers into her arms and rushed to the kitchen, where she dug out a glass pitcher and filled it from the tap.

When the dozen red rosebuds were arranged in it, she went back out to investigate the candy box he'd left. It was full of tiny Italian chocolates, an expensive brand that was one of her favorites. She'd never before had a suitor bring her flowers and candy at the same time. What a sweet, old-fashioned thing for Nat to do, she thought, placing one of the chocolates on her tongue and savoring the rich, dark taste while it slowly melted in her mouth. And how unlike the tough-guy image she had of him. In fact, in his gray suit it had been difficult to connect him with the man she'd known in the woods. Why hadn't he contacted her before? she asked herself again. And why had he come now?

* * *

At nine the next morning the phone on Freddie's desk rang. "I'm sorry to call you at the station, but when I tried you at home nobody answered," Nat said when she picked up the receiver. "Obviously, you have to work today."

There was a slight pause before Freddie answered, "I do have to work in the morning."

"Does that mean you can get the afternoon off?"

She glanced out the Plexiglas divider, where Susie with the pageboy was typing a letter—Jimmy had been right on the button there—and then studied her calendar, even though she already had it memorized. "Yes."

"Would you meet me for lunch?"

"Of course I would. Where?"

"You tell me."

"Okay." Freddie thought for a moment. "How about the Satsuma Tea Room on Union Street? It has southern cooking and fresh flowers on the tables, and it's not expensive."

"Sounds terrific. Twelve o'clock okay?"

"Make it twelve fifteen."

"Fine."

Freddie had dressed carefully in a tailored plum-colored suit over a dusty pink blouse to counteract the outrageous look she'd been sporting the night before, hoping that Nat would figure out how to call her at work. When she pushed open the door of Satsuma's, her heart fluttered. But in her gray leather pumps, with her makeup flawless and her hair neatly brushed, she appeared cool and collected. Certainly, no one who'd seen her at Jimmy's concert would recognize her now.

Nat had already taken a table and was waiting for her. He'd gone in the opposite direction and had relaxed the formality of his dress. Instead of a suit he wore a soft tan leather jacket that emphasized his golden looks and a tieless white silk shirt open at the throat. The effect was casually elegant. As he watched her approach, his expression was alert and slightly wary. Freddie was feeling equally wary, and again she experienced a sense of dislocation. It was so odd to see him in a restaurant. Was this impeccably groomed man the same Nat Steele she'd given her heart to in the wilderness, or was it someone she really didn't know?

"You look terrific," he said when she sat down opposite him.

"Thanks, so do you." It was the honest truth. He might not look the same, but his understated expensive clothes suited him. "What happened to your moustache?"

"I was working undercover last week and had to shave it off."

The waitress came, and they asked for drinks and put in their lunch orders. When she was gone, they studied each other, each taking in the details of the other's appearance.

"Did you have a good time at the concert last night?" Nat finally asked.

Freddie cleared her throat. "Let me explain about that." Quickly she outlined the whys and wherefores of her date with Jimmy. When she finished, Nat had relaxed visibly.

"Then this Jimmy Moonshine isn't anybody serious in your life?"

"No. He's just a friend." She smiled. "What did you think he was?"

"I didn't know what to think. It was hard to imagine that you were attracted to a guy who wears kimonos and hoop earrings, but there's no accounting for tastes."

Since those had been Jimmy's exact words, Freddie couldn't help chuckling. "No, there isn't," she allowed. "But I'll be honest with you. Earrings on men have never turned me on."

As she said the words, she felt her cheeks heat slightly. For an awkward instant, they stared across the table again, both remembering what *had* turned her on. Then Freddie looked away and lifted her wineglass. She wasn't ready to remember all that with this new Nat Steele. She had to get to know him again, find out if he was real and why exactly he was here.

"What do you think about getting Vandy down to Nashville?" she asked.

"You truly believe this friend of Jimmy's can do something for her?"

"I'm sure of it. Martin Pearle has got some of country music's biggest stars under contract. If he likes Vandy, he can get her in to see all the right people."

Nat reflected on that for a moment. "It's hard for me to imagine that child in this setting," he finally said, glancing out the restaurant window at the busy street. "It will be like uprooting a wildflower. I wonder if she'll survive?"

Freddie knew what he meant. Sometimes you couldn't transplant things. But she thought Vandy was a lot tougher and basically less childlike than

Nat realized. She told him so and then added, "She deserves a chance. Isolated the way she is up there, her talent will wither."

He took a swig of his beer and then nodded. "All right, I'll bring her down here."

"You'll bring her down personally?" Freddie's blue eyes widened in surprise. "You mean you'll go back into the mountains yourself?"

"It's the only way to get her out. She can't come by herself."

"But won't that be chancy? After what happened, the Parker boys may be angry with you. They might try to hurt you."

Nat shrugged. "They might, but I don't think so. Anyway, let's not talk about that now."

"All right. What shall we talk about?"

The waitress came with their food, so it was a minute or two before he could answer. When they were alone again, Nat leaned across the table and adjusted the single rosebud that was centered on it in a cut glass bud vase.

It reminded Freddie of his gifts. "Thanks for the flowers and candy," she said.

"After what I put you through, you deserve a lot more."

"Do I?" Nervously, she moistened her lips.

Nat's eyes sparkled, and at that moment, despite his slick appearance, he was the man she remembered. "Yes, but dolt that I am, instead of doing something for you, I'm going to ask a favor. I was hoping after lunch you'd show this old country boy some of the sights in your big, wicked city."

Freddie dropped her gaze. "Of course I will," she said. "I'd be delighted to."

After they finished lunch, Freddie suggested that they use her car since she was the one playing tour guide. "Most people associate Nashville with the music business," she told Nat as they headed toward the parking garage. "But it's also known as 'the Athens of the South.'"

To prove her point, she drove him out toward Centennial Park, just off West End Avenue. There they walked around Nashville's concrete, marble, and limestone reproduction of the Parthenon. The building, an exact-size replica of the Athenian original, had been built in 1896 for the Tennessee Centennial.

"This is certainly a side of the city I hadn't known about," Nat admitted. He shaded his eyes from the bright afternoon sun and looked up at the imposing structure with its rows of columns gleaming in the light. "You're proud of it, aren't you?"

"Yes, I am," Freddie admitted, realizing just how much she had come to love her adopted home. "It's a fascinating place to live, and not just for the obvious reasons. Nashville has fifteen universities and a lot of old money, old families, and old traditions. Speaking of which, I thought after this you might like to visit The Hermitage."

"Okay," Nat agreed, "but on our way, how about telling me more about what your life is like here?"

"Such as?"

"Your friends, your job, the people you work with." He smiled mischievously down at her. "Are there many more like Jimmy Moonshine?"

Freddie laughed. "No, he's one of a kind."

"What was Carter like?"

Nat had slipped the question in smoothly, but it stopped her cold. She turned and eyed him warily, noting that his expression had become serious. "Why do you ask?"

"When we first met, it was obvious you were still hung up on him. Are you now?"

"No." She didn't elaborate. Freddie wasn't yet prepared to admit to Nat how easily he'd more than filled Carter's place in her heart.

Nevertheless, her simple denial seemed to satisfy Nat. Instead of asking her more questions about her old lover, he quizzed her about her hobbies. While they drove to The Hermitage, she described the aerobics class she attended three evenings a week and the ceramics group she belonged to. As she talked, she found herself thinking that the afternoon was turning out to be almost like a first date. They were doing the kind of tentative exploring they hadn't had time for in the mountains.

"I thought you'd tell me your hobby was trap or skeet shooting," Nat remarked. "You're quite a markswoman. I don't know if I told you, but you were really something during that set-to we had with those thugs."

Freddie considered the compliment rather late in coming. Nevertheless, she was warmed by the sincere admiration in his voice. "Thanks," she replied lightly, "but if it hadn't been for Pinky, I'd be riddled with submachine-gun bullets. Where is he, by the way? I've missed him."

While they made a leisurely circuit of The Hermitage and some of its extensive grounds, Nat described the farm his parents had retired to and talked about Pinky's life on it.

"He has a fancy doghouse my dad and I built. But

he spends most of his time stretched out on the front porch, asleep."

"Sounds like an excellent idea, but I bet he misses you."

"I don't know. Maybe."

They had paused on a garden path, and she was able to look at her handsome and somewhat mystifying companion. No maybes about it, she thought. Despite all his faults, Nat Steele had a way of leaving a hole in her life when he wasn't around. Her gaze traveled up the chiseled line of his profile, pausing to admire his precision-cut golden hair.

He turned and smiled into her eyes. "You're getting used to me, aren't you?"

"Yes," she admitted, not bothering to comment on the fact that he'd read her mind.

"Me, too."

That made her raise her eyebrows. "You've had trouble getting used to me?"

"In that fancy suit you don't look much like the ragamuffin I remember, the one wearing the shapeless dress and army boots."

"Well, I hope not." Freddie started to laugh, but then she sobered. "Maybe I don't look like her, but I am her."

"Are you?"

"Yes, I am. But what about you? Those are pretty spiffy duds you've got on." She reached over and fingered the collar of his silk shirt.

He captured her hand and held it. "I'll tell you a secret. Just before I came here I deviated from form and had my hair cut by the most expensive barber in Atlanta. Then I went out and bought myself some new clothes."

"Why did you do that?"

"I wanted to make a good impression."

She lowered her eyes. "You must have known that you'd already done that."

He didn't answer. Instead, still holding her hand, he guided her back toward the parking lot. "It's getting late. Where would you like to go for dinner?"

"Why don't we pick up some groceries and then go to my place?" she suggested on a crazy impulse.

His fingers laced themselves between hers. "You won't get any argument from me about that idea."

They stopped at a supermarket and spent almost an hour wandering up and down the aisles debating what they should have for dinner. Freddie had figured Nat for a steak and potatoes man, but she was wrong.

"I have nothing against steak, but I like Oriental food, too, and I love Italian."

"How about lasagna, then?" Freddie suggested.

"Sure."

Back at her apartment, Nat looked around while she unpacked the groceries and got a big pot of water boiling for the pasta.

"Your rooms are like you," he commented.

"What do you mean?"

He touched one of the copper pots hanging over the stove. "Bright and cheerful, a little bit aggressive, high quality, and highly feminine." He came forward and rested his hands on her shoulders. When she stiffened slightly, he asked, "How can I help?"

"You can go out in the living room and relax. You fixed me enough meals over your Sterno. Now I want to prepare one for you."

"Not exactly the same thing," Nat commented,

but he left the kitchen without any further argument. She was glad, because when he'd touched her she'd been overwhelmed by a flood of contradictory emotions, and she just wasn't ready to cope with them yet.

Freddie wasn't a gourmet cook, but she knew her way around lasagna. Their dinner was good—the main course tasty, and the salad was crisp and flavorful.

As they ate, they shared a bottle of Chianti and talked. Their conversation ranged over a gamut of topics from the weather to the national news. As they shared their thoughts, Nat had the sense that they were like two jigsaw puzzle players who'd already put together the important part of the picture and were now just filling in the borders. Suddenly he realized that he didn't care if some of the edges were still a little ragged. During this afternoon he'd found out all he needed to know, and all his doubts were gone. Reaching across the table, he took Freddie's hand. She stared through the candles at him. Her beautiful blue eyes were luminous and slightly guarded—why, he didn't know.

"I missed you," he said.

The superficial pleasantries they'd been exchanging fell away. "Then why didn't you call? Why did you leave me thinking that you didn't want to see me again?" she demanded.

"Oh, sweetheart, is that what you thought?" Rising from his chair, he walked around the table and pulled her to her feet. "Freddie, I didn't call because I thought we both needed some time, and because I was afraid."

"Afraid?"

With quiet intensity, his gaze never leaving hers, he tried to explain how he'd phoned her and found her gone, and how his doubts had led him to accept the Everett assignment.

"It was a touchy sting, so after that I couldn't break my cover even long enough to call. And I was confused about us, I guess," he admitted. "But, darling, there are no doubts in my mind now."

Darling? Sweetheart? Freddie felt her knees go weak. When he bent his head and claimed her lips, her legs seemed to collapse beneath her, and she grasped his shoulders for support. The expensive aftershave Nat wore was a far cry from the natural, piney scent of the forest that had seduced her senses before, but it was still very appealing. His arms went around her waist, supporting her weight so that her feet barely brushed the floor. And as he kissed her into near-insensibility, he maneuvered her back toward the couch.

"I've missed you so much," he whispered gruffly. His lips began to trace urgent kisses from her cheeks down her throat. His mouth moved lower, and then he buried his face in the warm, gentle slope where her neck joined her shoulder. There he inhaled her fragrance as if he were thirsty for it. His grasp tightened. "I've thought about you every night—and about this." His hands stroked down her sides, seeming to measure the feminine indentation of her waist and the flare of her hips. Then his palms found and cupped her pert bottom, pulling her toward him possessively.

Dizzied by his amorous assault, Freddie clung to him while she struggled to clear her head. In the mountains Nat's lovemaking had been restrained.

But now it was aggressive. She could feel desire vibrating through his taut body. Caught in its field, she hadn't even been aware that they were moving toward the couch until she suddenly found herself on it, her body stretched beneath Nat's.

Assertively, his hands went to her breasts. They molded the soft mounds while his thumbs found and teased her nipples, which began to jut beneath the silky material of her blouse with a life of their own. His tongue circled the outer whorl of her ear, and then he whispered, "Underneath this prim little suit, your body hasn't changed, has it?"

That helped her fight her way back to semiconsciousness. "Nat, Nat, please," she protested weakly.

Her words were drowned in his kiss, a kiss that deepened into full possession as his tongue claimed the interior of her mouth.

"Freddie, let me stay the night. Let me make love to you," he whispered urgently. "I want you so much."

Her hands curled on his shoulders, and her troubled blue eyes stared up into his glittering gray ones. "Nat, why are you here?"

"To be with you. I told you that." His voice was impatient.

"For how long?"

He tried to kiss her lips again, but she turned her face. "For how long?" she repeated.

"I have three weeks."

"And you want to spend them here with me?"

He searched her face, frowning slightly. "Yes, that's exactly what I want. I don't think I've ever wanted anything more in my life."

A variety of emotions that he couldn't quite interpret crossed her face. "Then what?"

"What does it matter? Then I go back to work." He placed his palms on either side of her head.

Ignoring the familiar, possessive gesture, she reached up and touched a lock of his hair. Part of her unconsciously admired the elegant shape of his head, the intelligence in his eyes. "You once admitted to me that your work is very dangerous, and I've seen for myself just how true that is."

"Mostly it's boring."

"But you do get yourself into risky situations."

"Sometimes. Why do you ask?"

Her tone was wry. "You know, when I first met you, I thought of you as Mr. Wrong."

He laughed. "That was when you believed I was a criminal. Now you know I'm as law-abiding as they come."

"Maybe." The expression in her eyes was closed.

"What have you got on your mind now?" Nat demanded.

"Father bears."

"Father bears?"

"You told me they don't make very good family men. That's probably true of DEA agents as well."

Nat's eyebrows snapped together. "What are you getting at?"

"I'm not sure." Her gaze was suddenly focused squarely on him. "Stalling for time, maybe. Nat, I'm not ready for this yet."

"Not ready to make love?" Frustration simmered beneath the surface of his tone. "Back in the mountains—"

"Back in the mountains was different. We even talked about it being like something out of a storybook. But this is real, isn't it? And I know that a brief affair isn't what I want."

"Who said anything about brief? As far as I'm concerned, this is just the beginning."

"You mean a long affair? I've already gone that route, and I don't intend to mess myself up with it again."

He was silent for a full minute. His skin was flushed and his expression was puzzled. "Are you trying to tell me to leave you alone?"

"No. I don't want you to go." She took a deep breath. "Nat, I've fallen in love with you!"

He looked even more disturbed. "Freddie, I can't propose marriage at this stage. That's a big decision, and I don't think either of us is ready to make it."

"You're right. But there are other ways to get to know each other." She gestured at their bodies, which were still intimately enmeshed.

"Are you saying you want me to court you before we make love again?"

"If by 'court' you mean take some time so that we can get to know each other better, then yes, I guess I do. Today just wasn't enough."

"I haven't got a lot of time, Freddie."

"You have three weeks."

"Less, if I go back to get Vandy."

Her gaze was steadfast. "Nat, I think we need to start fresh. But it's up to you."

He sighed. Then he stroked her cheek and gathered her into his arms. "Did you mean it when you said you'd fallen in love with me?"

"Yes, fool that I am."

"All right," he murmured, laying his forehead against her brow. "What do you want to do tomorrow?"

CHAPTER FIFTEEN

Freddie wasn't sure why Nat chose to go along with her. Perhaps it was because she'd admitted her true feelings for him and her vulnerability touched him. For whatever reason, the next week went by in a kind of romantic dream. Instead of pressing her to renew their physical relationship, Nat slept in his motel, not her bed. When she couldn't be with him during the day, he explored the city on his own. They always spent the evenings together.

For that week he was all any woman could ask in a suitor—charming, gallant, thoughtful. He consulted her every whim and indulged her in one way or another every day. Sometimes they went out to dinner and then dedicated the hours afterward to enjoying Nashville's colorful night life. Other times they ate at her place and then went for long walks in the crisp autumn air. But what they really did was talk.

They talked about everything, starting off with their childhoods and branching out to topics as far-flung as authority in the church and psychological testing.

"I took a personality test when I started working for the government," Nat explained one evening after dinner as they strolled in the small park near her apartment.

"What did it show about you?"

"That I'm the perfect type for the job I do. I need a certain amount of challenge and excitement in my life, and my work supplies that."

Freddie looked away, but not before he had caught the expression in her eyes. "Is that what's bothering you about us?" he asked, putting his hands on her shoulders and turning her toward him.

A few other people were on the path where they stood, but neither Freddie nor Nat were conscious of them. They only had eyes for each other.

"Maybe that's part of it. You really love your job, don't you?"

"I don't know if love is the right word, but it's important to me. It seems to me that what I do is worthwhile and that I'm good at it."

"Oh, Nat, it's so dangerous."

"Everyone takes chances."

"Not the way you do."

He smiled and then whispered as he bent to kiss her, "Despite everything you say, you're not exactly the conservative type yourself, Freddie."

Her mouth seemed to dissolve beneath his, and when he took her hand and turned her back toward home, she leaned her head on his shoulder. These past days, while Nat had been courting her as she'd asked him to, she'd felt his impatience. It hadn't been in anything he'd said or done. Nevertheless, it had simmered just beneath the surface of their developing relationship. Sometimes she'd felt as if she had a barely controlled tiger on a leash. But Nat wasn't the tiger, she realized. It was the emotion between them demanding physical expression that was all but impossible to manage.

When they were back in her apartment and he'd shut the door firmly on the world outside, he pulled her close.

"You know what I think?" he whispered.

"What?" Her face was buried in the soft wool of his sweater, which muffled her voice.

After bending to kiss the top of her head, he said, "That experience we had together in the mountains was a kind of crucible. It stripped us both of the nonessentials and showed us what really counts about each other. You once said that I was Mr. Wrong. But Freddie, I know you. If you ever find Mr. Right, you'll be bored out of your mind by the guy."

She started to laugh, but Nat stopped the sound with his lips. In a sudden burst of need, she reached up and clasped his neck. Then she closed her eyes and kissed him back with a fervor that surprised even her.

"You're not bored by me." His voice was husky as he finally lifted his head.

"No," she agreed. "I never have been."

He drew her even more intimately into his arms. His body shuddered against hers. "I'll see to it that you never are. Darling, don't send me away tonight. Please."

Freddie closed her eyes. She wanted more from him than this. She wanted him to tell her that he would never leave her, that he belonged to her the way she knew she belonged to him. But as her blood sang in her ears and she gave herself up to his kisses, she couldn't find the strength to ask for all the seemingly impossible things she wanted.

That night, for the first time since they had been together in the wilderness, they made love. It was different from how it had been in the mountains. In Freddie's small bedroom with the glow from a streetlamp streaming through the window and a comfortable bed beneath them, it was a lot more civilized. But in another way, it was wilder. Freddie reflected that each time she was with Nat, she discovered a new dimension of him. This one—the lover who caressed her body into a frenzy and then drove his strength so deeply into her that her world seemed to shatter and then remake itself around him—was a revelation.

"Oh, Nat," she whispered afterward as they lay entwined together, his long legs laced around hers, "I do love you." She couldn't hold the words back.

"I love you, too," he answered against her ear.

She drew in her breath sharply. Trembling, she waited for him to say more, but he didn't. His breathing grew regular, and she knew from the way his body relaxed against hers that he was asleep. Had he known what he was saying? Would he remember it in the morning? Finally, she closed her eyes and told herself not to ask for more than she'd just been given. Nat wasn't a liar. Surely, if he loved her, the rest would come. She prayed so.

The next morning, Nat left for the mountains. "Now is the time," he told her at breakfast. "I'm going to bring Vandy out for you."

Freddie almost dropped the coffee pot she'd just picked up. "Oh, but—" She set the container down and clasped her hands together. "Do you have to go now? I'll be so worried."

He stood and took her fingers in his. "Freddie,

trust me. It'll be all right. And when I get back, we'll talk."

Wordlessly, she stared back at him. Did he mean that they would talk about what he'd said to her last night just before they'd gone to sleep? She'd been almost afraid to think of it, afraid that it had been a dream or that he'd only said he loved her because he felt he had to and it wasn't really true. Even now she couldn't bring herself to ask the questions burning within her. Too much depended on the answers.

Instead, she helped Nat get ready to leave and then watched him drive away. When his car disappeared around the corner, she turned from the window and contemplated the days ahead. They weren't going to be easy, she thought. While he was gone, she was going to be worried about his safety, and she'd be on tenterhooks about what would happen between them when he returned. For she knew that, despite her love for Nat, she couldn't allow their affair to drift into a long, uncommitted relationship. If he loved her back, he would have to prove it by making a commitment to her. And if he wouldn't do that, then she would have to find the strength to break it off between them.

Four days later, Freddie eyed her watch and then opened the brown paper bag sitting in the middle of her desk at the radio station. The bag contained a carton of yogurt and an apple. Just then, a tap on the Plexiglas divider made her look up. It was Jimmy Moonshine.

"Your canary make the scene yet?" he asked, poking his head through the doorway.

She smiled as she took in his outfit. He had his hair tied behind his back, and he wore overalls and a T-shirt that read DIRTY YOUNG MAN.

"No," she replied, "but I'm expecting them soon. Nat called last night and said they'd be getting in around one."

"I bet you were relieved to hear from him." Jimmy fingered one of his gypsy hoop earrings.

"That's an understatement."

"Did he have any trouble bringing her out?"

Freddie shook her head. "I don't think so. But to tell you the truth, when I talked to him he really didn't say much." As Nat had explained to her and as she had discovered for herself, he was not a "phone person." When he had a receiver in his hand, his conversation was always terse and to the point. He'd sounded cheerful enough when he'd called her from Atlanta, but all he'd said was that he'd be in her office at the station early that afternoon with Vandy and a surprise. There had been no personal messages or whispered endearments for her ears alone. And taking her cue from him, her reply had been equally brisk. She would just have to wait and see what happened when they had some time alone together again.

An hour later, the surprise Nat had promised walked in the door.

"Granny!" Freddie exclaimed. Dropping the schedule she'd been working on, she jumped up from her chair and ran across the tiny office.

"My land, girl, don't squeeze the life outta me!" the old woman protested after Freddie had given her an enthusiastic hug.

"It's just so wonderful to see you!" Freddie exclaimed. "Nat didn't tell me you'd be here, too."

"You surely didn't think I'd allow an innocent lamb like my Vandy to come to the city by herself?

'Sides," she added with a twinkle, "I wanted to see where you worked."

Smiling, Freddie watched while Granny inspected her office. She was dressed in what must have been her best outfit, a robin's egg blue suit and matching hat, that Freddie guessed was straight from a vintage Sears catalog. She looked wonderful.

A moment later, Nat and Vandy came in. Although Freddie stared at him for only a split second, her eyes devoured him. She had missed him terribly. He was wearing his leather jacket, yet he looked more like his old self, she thought. His haircut was starting to be a bit less precise, and he was letting his moustache grow back in. Freddie wanted to fling her arms around him. Instead, she squeezed his hand and whispered, "I'm glad to see you."

"I'm glad you're glad to see me," he returned with a grin.

Turning to Vandy, Freddie held out her hand. "It's wonderful you're here."

The girl clasped Freddie's fingers, smiling with shy delight. Despite the unstylish yellow dress she wore, which must have come from the same catalog as Granny's outfit, she looked radiantly pretty.

Freddie was just running a thoughtful eye over her and deciding to buy her something more stylish to wear to her audition when Jimmy Moonshine tapped on the Plexiglas window again.

"I heard all the commotion and thought I'd have a look-see," he said when Freddie invited him in. While the two mountain women studied him curiously, he ran an interested eye up and down Vandy. "Is this the talent?"

"Yes, it is." Freddie brought Vandy forward.

After the introductions were made, Jimmy said, "Well, it's all set up with Pearle for ten o'clock tomorrow morning. I'll take her."

"That won't be necessary," Nat said.

But Jimmy insisted. "Pearle knows me. It's better if I'm the one who introduces her to him. Just tell me where to pick her up."

While Nat wrote down the address and telephone number of the motel where he'd already checked the Parkers in, Freddie whispered in Jimmy's ear, "I thought I'd buy her something a little more stylish to wear. What do you suggest?"

"I suggest leaving perfection alone," Jimmy retorted. "She should be wearing what she's got on when Pearle sees her. He'll feel like she's just stepped out of a time machine. It's perfect."

After Jimmy left, Vandy turned to Freddie. "I got to admit I wasn't sure you'd keep your promise. But you're as good as your word, and I'm grateful. I just hope I don't make a fool of myself with these city folks."

"You won't," Freddie assured her. "Just sing the way you did in the mountains."

Vandy looked nervous. "I hope I can."

"Of course you can!" Granny sniffed. "A Parker woman can do anything she puts her mind to, and don't you forget it. But you be careful around that Mr. Moonshine. I didn't like his T-shirt or his hairdo."

To help Vandy relax and to get both Parkers a bit more acclimated to their surroundings, Nat and Freddie decided to take them sightseeing.

They went to see the Ryman Auditorium, the old home of the Grand Ole Opry, and climbed onto its creaky wooden stage. There and later in the Country Music Hall of Fame they saw mementos of the stars of days gone by. Afterward, Nat drove them past the homes of some of those stars. Granny could only stare at their architectural splendor in openmouthed amazement.

"It don't seem right for people to have such big places," she said matter-of-factly.

"If this were Memphis, I'd take you to see Graceland," Nat answered with a laugh. "Now that really is something."

Granny and Vandy were adequately impressed with what they'd seen in Nashville. But there was more to come. The crowning touch was a performance of the city's biggest drawing card, the Grand Ole Opry. Freddie had gone out of her way to secure tickets for the two-and-a-half-hour extravaganza.

Up on stage in the very fancy new Grand Ole Opry House, guitarists in glittery, rhinestoned leisure suits played for female vocalists with curly manes and slinky dresses. Square dancers in a blizzard of ruffled white petticoats danced up a storm, and comedians in overalls and straw hats told jokes. For each performer the audience clapped, whistled, and jumped up and down. Flashbulbs popped continually. It was an exciting evening, but finally it came to an end.

"Well, that was somethin'," Granny said as Nat escorted her up the aisle and out toward the parking lot. "Now I've seen everything."

"Not quite everything," Freddie retorted. She winked at Vandy. "Tomorrow you'll be having a look at Music Row from the inside. Not many tourists get to do that."

Vandy shook her head. "No point in being nervy, I guess. All a person can do is their best."

Freddie put a reassuring arm around the girl's shoulder. "I have a feeling that tomorrow is your lucky day."

"Maybe," Granny agreed dryly. "But just to make sure her luck don't pass her by while she's lookin' the other way, I think we'd best both get to our beds. I'm so tired, I could sleep standing up in a corner."

Vandy agreed, and Freddie and Nat obliged by taking the two mountain women back to their motel. When they saw them to their door, Granny put a gnarled hand around Freddie's wrist and pulled her inside.

"You go wait in the car," she told Nat. "I want to have a word with this gal." She shut the door in Nat's face and hustled Freddie into a chair. "I should be mad with you for schemin' with Vandy and runnin' off the way you did," she began, putting her hands on her hips and gazing down accusingly.

Freddie started to apologize, but Granny cut her off. "Never mind, I know why you did it. What I want to know is if you thought on what I told you back in the valley."

"I don't know what you mean."

Granny rolled her eyes. "I told you that someday some smart gal is goin' to catch Nat Steele. Well, I've been with him the past three days, and that boy is ready to be caught. He didn't say much, but he was moonin' after you the whole time."

Freddie felt her heart beat a little faster. "How could you tell?"

"I haven't been alive for more than seventy years without learnin' a thing or two. I could tell."

Freddie cast a swift glance at Vandy, but the girl didn't seem in the least troubled by Granny's words. She was picking out a tune on her guitar and humming a harmony. Obviously, she was completely absorbed in thoughts of her morning audition. Satisfied that Vandy's crush on Nat was no longer an issue, Freddie cleared her throat and focused on Granny.

"Nat and I haven't known each other very long."

Impatiently, the old woman brushed that away. "I haven't seen much of the city, but I've seen a lot of life. There comes a time when fruit ripens and needs to be plucked if you're to taste its sweetness. That's true of love between a man and a woman. You have to know when to reach out for it. The time is right for you and Nat. I can feel it in my bones." She sat back on the bed. "Now that's all I'm going to say to you, Frederica Davenport. But if you're as smart as I think you are, you'll mark what I've told you and do something about it."

Freddie didn't quite know how to respond, but after she'd kissed Granny good-bye and wished Vandy luck, the old woman's words were very much on her mind.

"What was that all about?" Nat asked when she went back to the car.

"Oh, just woman talk. Do you think Vandy will do all right?" she asked to change the subject. Nat shot her a curious look and then started the engine.

"If this Martin Pearle has eyes and ears, I don't see how she can miss."

They were silent while Nat guided his Audi through traffic. "I gather you didn't have any problems up in the mountains," Freddie finally said.

"No. Hap was gone. But Lou and Marshall were

there, and they greeted me with open arms. They were very glad to be safe at home and not stuffed away in a jail in Atlanta. They had destroyed all their marijuana plants and have vowed to cultivate nothing but vegetables from here on out."

"That must make Granny happy."

"She's pretty pleased about the way things have turned out." He shot Freddie a sideways glance. "She gave me a lecture about you one night."

"She did?" Freddie was instantly alert. "What did she say?"

"I'll tell you about it when we get back to your place."

A few minutes later, they pulled up in front of Freddie's apartment building. When Nat escorted her to her door, she felt as nervous as Vandy was about her audition. A ridiculous amount of time passed while she rummaged through her purse in search of her keys. When she finally found them, her fingers were shaking so that she could hardly insert them in the lock. Without comment, Nat took them from her and unlocked the door.

When they were inside, he switched on the light and led her to the couch. While wings seemed to flutter inside her stomach, Freddie sat down and waited. Nat settled himself next to her and then took her shoulders in his strong hands and turned her toward him.

"Freddie, first let me kiss you. While I was gone I missed you like hell." He bent his head and drank thirstily from her willing lips. But to her surprise, a moment later he drew back. "It's time we talked about us," he said. Pausing, he looked straight into her eyes. "I love you."

She felt her heart squeeze with happiness. "I love you, too."

"But do you love me enough? That's what I have to know."

"Enough for what?"

Nat's gray eyes regarded her solemnly. "In some ways this trip resolved a lot of things for me, but I didn't need Granny's lecture on how wonderful you are and how I'd better not take any chances of losing you. I already knew all that." He paused. "You told me a few days back that you didn't want an affair." He shook his head. "Well, that's not for me either. I don't want to just see you now and then—to spend the rest of the time wondering what you're doing while I'm not there and who you're doing it with." He reached up to brush her cheek with a gentle finger. "Freddie, darling, it's a miracle that we found each other. Now that it's happened, I don't want to risk us drifting apart again."

So far, all he'd said fell on her ears like a beautiful melody. "I don't want that either," she told him.

"I want to marry you. I want to make you mine. I just don't know if we can work it out."

Alarmed, she reached out to him. "What do you mean?"

"I know you're not happy about my job. Do you think that you could live with it for a while?"

She hesitated, her blue eyes gazing at him worriedly. "Live with the danger?"

"It's not just that. There are times when I'd be away working undercover and you wouldn't even know where I was," he explained anxiously. "I know that would be tough on you, but it would only be for another couple of years while I'm still useful in the department. After that, there are a lot of options. I could go into administration. Or I could go back to school and get a degree in ethnomusicology. That's something I've thought about from time to time." He clasped her hand tightly. "But I can't change everything all at once. Would you be willing to take me the way I am for another two years?"

Freddie didn't hesitate. She'd already figured out that if she wanted Nat Steele, she'd have to accept all of him—including the risky way he made his living. Throwing herself at the man, she wrapped her arms around him as if she never intended to let go—which she didn't. "Nat Steele, I love you. I'll take you any way I can get you!"

Laughing, he hugged her back, and for a long time that's all there was—just the two of them enfolded in each other's embrace, kissing and murmuring sweet words of love and longing.

"I was lost from the moment I saw you," Nat admitted as he dropped little kisses onto her cheeks and throat. "You were an adorable little dragon lady who bewitched me from the first."

"You were so stern and so cool," she complained.

"I was never cool when you were around. The effect you had on me was downright painful, and not cooling in the least." He shook his head in remembrance.

She gazed at him wide-eyed. "I wouldn't have known it."

"Well, you know it now." His questing fingers had opened her blouse, and he was busily undoing the snaps on her bra. "When we're married, I won't allow you to wear one of these things at home."

"What? I can see you're going to be a very bossy husband."

"You can stand up for yourself," he murmured thickly. "I think our marriage is going to be very interesting."

"I'm sure of it."

But there was no answer from Nat. His lips were on her breasts, caressing them with his mouth and tongue until they were stiff peaks of desire. For a moment, her head cushioned on the couch pillows, Freddie abandoned herself to the waves of excitement tingling through her body.

Nat made love the way he did everything else— thoroughly and expertly. When she felt his hands slip beneath her skirt to caress her thighs, her own fingers busied themselves on the buttons of his shirt. "Don't you want to go into the bedroom?" she collected herself to whisper.

"I don't think I can make it to the bedroom," he groaned as he fumbled at his belt. "Oh, Freddie, touching your beautiful body like this gets me so excited, I can't even think. How I ever managed to sleep next to you two nights in a row on that cot is beyond me."

She laughed, realizing with a thrill of pleasure how true his words were. The cool, collected Nat Steele was so aroused that he couldn't get his buckle undone. Reaching down, she helped him—none too expertly, as she was almost as eager as he. Somehow, they both managed to remove their clothes, and when they came together again, it was with a passionate, unrestrained exuberance that left them both completely satisfied and spent.

"Sweetheart, I can't even imagine living without

you now," Nat whispered, kissing her with fierce tenderness. "You're more important to me than anything else. If you want me to quit my job, I will."

"No," she answered. She didn't want a concession like that from him now, because she knew that later he would regret it. She stroked his hair and rubbed her cheek against his. Then she settled herself into his arms more comfortably and pulled the afghan down from the back of the couch where it had been draped. When it was arranged around them, she said, "I just wish I could go along with you on all your assignments and make sure you don't get into any trouble."

He laughed. "You might have something there. You certainly made a mighty fine partner back in those fields. Maybe you should join the department."

"Maybe I should," she responded. There were tears in Freddie's eyes. While Nat hugged her to him, she buried her face against his chest and let the tears spill down her cheeks. Eventually they dampened his skin as well.

"Why are you crying, sweetheart?" he asked. "There's nothing to cry about."

"I'm just so happy. Oh, Nat, I wanted you to love me, and I was so afraid that you didn't."

"I do love you," he whispered fiercely. "I don't think any woman has ever been more loved by a man. And I'll always love you."

"Always?"

"Always, my darling Freddie."

She pressed herself against him more tightly. For a long time they lay cuddled together. But finally Freddie pulled back. "It's getting late," she said a little shyly, "but I don't feel like going to sleep just yet. Can I get you something to drink? There's wine, and I have a couple cans of beer in the refrigerator."

"A beer would be good," he said.

Wrapping the afghan around her like a sarong, Freddie stood up and padded into the kitchen. When she came back with a glass of wine for herself and the beer for Nat, she found he'd put on his pants and was sitting on a chair tuning the old guitar she kept propped in one corner.

He looked up at her and smiled, his gray eyes alight with love. "I learned the fourth verse to that song."

"The one about the dawn breaking?"

"Yep." He struck a chord. "Would you like to hear it?"

"I'd love to hear it."

Placing the beer next to him on the table, she settled herself on the couch, tucking her feet comfortably beneath her while she took a sip of wine.

"Come nigh to me, the dawn is breaking," Nat began in his pleasant baritone. "My love come nigh. It's almost day." Skillfully playing the haunting melody, he sang the verses that Freddie had already heard. Then, while she took another sip of wine and listened closely, he began the last verse.

The moonlight swam upon her window.
Through the open door she went outside.
And on the grass she met her lover.
"John Haynes, I'll be yours or no man's bride."

Nat strummed the final chord and then looked up from the guitar, an expression of grave sweetness on his lips. "So you see, it ended happily after all."

As she gazed across at him, Freddie's eyes shone with joy. "Yes, it did."

Now you can reserve January's Candlelights *before* they're published!

- ♥ You'll have copies set aside for *you* the instant they come off press.
- ♥ You'll save yourself precious shopping time by arranging for *home delivery*.
- ♥ You'll feel proud and efficient about organizing a system that *guarantees* delivery.
- ♥ You'll avoid the disappointment of not finding *every* title you want and need.

ECSTASY SUPREMES $2.75 each

- ☐ 153 **JEWEL OF INDIA**, Sue Gross 14188-5
- ☐ 154 **BREATHLESS TEMPTATION**, Eleanor Woods . . 10837-3
- ☐ 155 **A MAN TO REMEMBER**, Tate McKenna 15190-2
- ☐ 156 **DANGER IN PARADISE**, Kit Daley 11714-3

ECSTASY ROMANCES $2.25 each

- ☐ 480 **WORTH HIS WEIGHT IN GOLD**, Molly Katz . . . 19792-9
- ☐ 481 **GARDEN OF ENCHANTMENT**, Christine King . . 12934-6
- ☐ 482 **A HANDFUL OF TROUBLE**, Cathie Linz 13839-6
- ☐ 483 **MYSTERIOUS STRANGER**, Madeline Garry . . . 15924-5
- ☐ 484 **ONCE MORE WITH PASSION**, Noelle B. McCue 16588-1
- ☐ 485 **UNDER THE NORTHERN LIGHTS**, Marilyn Cunningham 16427-3
- ☐ 31 *WEB OF DESIRE*, Jean Hager 19434-2
- ☐ 56 *DOUBLE OCCUPANCY*, Elaine Raco Chase . . . 11732-1

At your local bookstore or use this handy coupon for ordering:

Dell **DELL READERS SERVICE—DEPT. B1343A**
6 REGENT ST., LIVINGSTON, N.J. 07039

Please send me the above title(s) I am enclosing $ _____ (please add 75¢ per copy to cover postage and handling) Send check or money order—no cash or CODs Please allow 3-4 weeks for shipment

Ms./Mrs./Mr _____

Address _____

City/State _____ Zip _____

The perfect gift to give yourself <u>and</u> someone you love—

Motherhood The Second Oldest Profession

by ERMA BOMBECK

"The biggest on-the-job training program ever," is Erma Bombeck's description of motherhood, that ageless institution filled with all *kinds* of moms: the one who writes Christmas newsletters that rhyme; the mother who eats her children's Halloween candy after telling them the ants got it; and the shameless ones who have discovered that guilt works wonders in motivating kids.

Erma is a thing of beauty (thighs *don't* count) and a joy forever. MOTHERHOOD is her treasure trove of love and laughter, fun and old fashioned wisdom. Buy a copy for yourself and one for someone you love. You'll *both* laugh out loud!

15900-8-18 $3.95

At your local bookstore or use this handy coupon for ordering:

Dell DELL READERS SERVICE—DEPT. B1343B
6 REGENT ST., LIVINGSTON, N.J. 07039

Please send me the above title(s). I am enclosing $_____ (please add 75¢ per copy to cover postage and handling.) Send check or money order—no cash or CODs. Please allow 3-4 weeks for shipment.

Ms./Mrs./Mr._____

Address_____

City/State_____ Zip_____